The
Injured
Party

The
Injured
Party

Susan Fromberg Schaeffer

St. Martin's Press
New York

This is a work of fiction. Any resemblance to people, living or dead, is unintended, purely coincidental, and should not be inferred.

S.F.S.

THE INJURED PARTY. Copyright © 1986 by Susan Fromberg Schaeffer. All rights reserved. Printed in the United States of America. No part of this book may be used or reproduced in any manner whatsoever without written permission except in the case of brief quotations embodied in critical articles or reviews. For information, address St. Martin's Press, 175 Fifth Avenue, New York, N.Y. 10010.

Design by Doris Borowsky

Library of Congress Cataloging in Publication Data

Schaeffer, Susan Fromberg.
    The injured party.
    I. Title.
PS3569.C3515   1986   813'.54   86-13854
ISBN 0-312-41798-5

First Edition
10 9 8 7 6 5 4 3 2 1

For Neil
and
Edna Elizabeth Heatherington

Contents

The author wishes to thank the
John Simon Guggenheim Memorial Foundation
for their generous support while
this book was being written

PART ONE

The Room

1

HE STOOD IN the doorway to their bedroom, looked at his wife, and thought, I am married to a stone, a drift of snow. His wife, Iris, named for her great-aunt whom she was said to resemble, lay, as usual, on her side, one arm stretched out, so that her fingers touched the great oak headboard of the bed. The tips of her nails explored the edges of the carved rays of the sun that formed the headboard's central design. Was that accidental, or was she comforted by what she touched? Everything in the world held symbolic meaning for her.

Her head rested on her arm. Her back was to the room, to the family. He never knew, when he came in, whether she was awake or asleep. Sometimes she answered when he spoke to her; sometimes she didn't. He asked her how she felt. When she didn't answer, he picked up her notebook on the bedside table and opened it. He made as much noise as he could, ruffling the pages. His wife did not stir.

He was sure her eyes were open. What did she see as she stared out their bedroom window? The eternal sameness of that scene in winter! The boughs of the great elms moved gently and heavily up and down in a mild wind. Yesterday, the boughs had been lined with soft scarves of snow. Today, the wind had blown the snow off. He looked out the window and tried to imagine what she saw.

It changed. The branches were no longer branches but massed black crosses, swaying desperately in the wind as if to keep evil spirits back. Thick branches were crossed by thin bony ones, at right angles, at oblique angles, a mob of crazily drawn crosses, sketched hastily, as if there were only seconds in which to draw, to fill the window. A blue jay landed on one of the thinner branches, his weight lowering it so that the branch on which he sat became the second horizontal branch crossing a thicker vertical one. The crosses were massed against the terror of the season. He felt it suddenly, an unstoppable cold, which could not be alleviated by additional clothing, furnaces, electric heaters, the sun itself. Only the crosses could beat such cold back. Although he wanted to, he could not look away from the window. Finally, his eyes closed. When he opened them, the elms were elms only. The blue jay had flown out of the picture framed by the window.

Increasingly, he thought of this room, their bedroom, as her room. He looked at the bed again. She was under the covers. Where was her head? Where was the tangled mass of gold hair? How did she manage to make herself so flat against the mattress, so that the white swell of the blanket barely seemed to cover a body? There were days when he came in and thought that the mattress had swallowed her at last. How long had this been going on? Almost three weeks. He was a responsible man. He had called the internist who had watched over her in the hospital. No medical reason for it at all, the doctor said. Tell her to get up.

That was impossible. There was something supernatural in her need to remain undisturbed. Even their daughter, intrepid soul, had retreated when faced by that absolute determined stillness. He realized he no longer thought of the bed as a real bed but a small plot of earth, into which his wife was slowly sinking. The internist had recommended an analyst, but when he called, the

4

analyst said he only treated patients who were healthy enough to come to the office. So he had gone to the internist's office. Perhaps something had happened in the hospital? Something small, apparently insignificant, and no one had thought to mention it? As if something had erased their pupils, the internist's eyes went blank. No, nothing had happened, he said. She was there, on an intravenous, for six weeks. Nothing happened.

So something *had* happened. But no one would—or could—tell him what it was.

He had begun to find "notes," unmistakably in his wife's handwriting, exceedingly small, but very clear, so that if one held a magnifying glass to the page on which she wrote, the letters were perfectly formed, remarkably easy to read, round and clear, the kind of handwriting one would expect from a personality without convolutions or complexity. Clear as it was—under a magnifying glass—her handwriting was, to most people, indecipherable, so minute was her lettering. She didn't like other people looking at her notebooks. Her drafts were usually hidden in strange places, come upon occasionally by accident, and the next day, if one looked, she had changed her hiding place.

Whenever she thought of him, she saw an animal in the woods, a cat, with bright green eyes and great claws. It was always night and the moon lit his eyes like two huge moons. He was unearthly in his grace, even when still. Sometimes he lay along the arm of a tree.

When he thought of her, he thought of an animal caught in a trap, a pit so deep she could not climb out of it. But even trapped as she was, she knew she was better than anyone else. He wanted to help her, but she was wild, she had been trapped so long. Always, wild, lonely, and caught.

5

This was the first of the notes he found, a loose page lying on top of her notebook. The page was still there. The tiny letters were a kind of code, what they had to say hidden in plain sight. He looked from the page to his wife, as if what she had written might provide some kind of clue. Whom had she been writing about? Not him, surely. No one would describe him as unearthly in his grace. Was she the person in the trap? She had come home from the hospital, officially cured of a fever of unknown origin, and had taken to her bed. Was the bed the trap?

"It may be something simpler than you think," said a friend he had known from childhood, whom he called late at night. "Maybe it's a mild form of hospitalitis. She may need time to get over it. Hospitals are terrible places. I'll never forget my first year on the wards. Things happen. I thought internship would be the end of my marriage."

"What things?"

"Things."

"The children think she's spoiled."

"Is she?"

"No."

"Then leave her alone. She'll get out of bed. No one can stay in bed forever."

He began riffling the pages of the notebook again. This notebook contained only one entry. In the middle of the page, exactly in the center of the notebook, his wife had written, *Something to depend on. A missing piece.* He flipped backward and forward. Nothing more. He looked at the loose page he was holding in his hand. Perhaps she was losing her mind. It was possible.

She no longer seemed to know she had children. To get her attention, Evelyn and Nate would have to walk between the bed and the window and bend over her. "Mother?" they would say. "Mother?" She would smile at them or wiggle the fingers of her one visible hand. Nate had stopped coming in. He would sit on the couch in the room across the hall, apparently watching television, but when Mike came down, he would find his son looking into their bedroom, his eyes moving automatically from the television set to the doorway of his mother's room.

Evelyn was less peaceable. Once a day she would enter the room her mother had turned into a kind of hole in the fabric of things, a bizarre temple to silence, stand at the foot of the bed, and say, "Mother! This is ridiculous! Get up! We know you get up to go to the bathroom! Get up! The doctor says there's nothing wrong with you!"

"I will," Iris would say, without stirring. Evelyn would stand there, looking at her mother, or the strange shape her mother had become, turn on her heel, her face angry and set, her lips pursed, her eyes slit like a cat's, stamp out, and slam the door behind her. A few minutes later, Nate, who was watching television across the hall, would get up and open the door and sit down again on the couch.

"What does she *think* about?" Evelyn asked her brother.

"God knows," he said. "Maybe we don't want to know."

"I'd like to know if she can still *think* at all."

"Do you believe she'd be in there if she couldn't think?" he asked.

"What's that supposed to mean?"

Nate didn't answer her.

"Don't do that!" Evelyn shouted at him. "If one more person stops speaking, I'll lock myself in *my* room."

"Will you two keep quiet?" thundered their father from his study on the third floor.

They looked at one another and smiled. Some things didn't change.

2

IRIS STARED OUT the window and looked at the branches massed like crosses against the pale gray sky. The color of ice, the color of cold. It brought to mind Crusades, medieval times, suggestions of an era when people were sure of their faith. She heard her children discussing her in the television room across the hall. This is a poor state of affairs, she thought. I really should get up. No one needs this much peace and quiet. She knew that if there were an emergency, if she were to wake and smell smoke and the rest of them were asleep, she would get out of bed and awaken everyone. But there was no fire, no smoke.

It would be wonderful, she thought, if I could say to myself that for good and compelling reasons I am unable to leave this bed and talk to members of my own family. There were, she knew, good and compelling reasons, but she had no idea of what they were. A frightening state of affairs. She looked again at the black crosses swaying in the wind. They were more agitated now than they had been this morning. Perhaps it would snow. Later, when everyone was out of the house, she would get up and walk around the room. In the hospital, her doctor had repeatedly warned her about bed rest. "It saps your strength," he said. The diabetic woman with whom she roomed for three weeks said the same thing. "The bed drinks up all your strength," she said. "Get up out of it. What you want to make your bed strong for?"

Now, at home, she got up and walked around the room for the sake of her muscles. When there was no one to see her, she did not feel as if she was walking. It was as if she had left her body safely behind in the bed and was floating, spirit-free, through the room. Bodiless. How I want to be bodiless.

There was complete silence in the house. The children must have gone out. Later she would write in her notebook. She was not losing her mind. She would tell her husband that when he next came in. He was becoming accustomed to the cryptic utterances, the telegraphs, before the wire went dead, from his wife's bed.

If only she could move *back* into the time she had spent in the hospital. Because something had gone wrong there, she didn't know what, and she felt she had only narrowly escaped from the hospital before whatever was wrong had killed her. At night, when the floor quieted, when the only voice was the high mechanical voice of the hospital public address system, calling doctors to duty, she would stare at the dark wall opposite her bed, while light from cars in the streets, from the moon insecurely hung in the sky, drifted across the wall and finally formed into silhouettes of men. Men bareheaded, men wearing hats, featureless, each figure like a doorway made of light, each one hoping to be recognized, and she felt their disappointment when she could not summon them by name, call them forth from the wall. Outside, traffic would slow, the light on the wall would fade, the moon would slide behind a cloud, her eyes would begin to close, and the anonymous shapes would disappear, their disappointment in going without first being recognized washing over her; and, as she saw them go, her own grief pressed her deeper and deeper into the bed. Were there more than one, or were the shapes she saw all versions of the same man, as, in a photograph album, one finds hundreds of pictures of the same man, but at different stages in his life, in different places,

9

in different positions, seen from the side, from a distance, seen in a haze, seen in glare, seen clearly, barely seen at all, come upon suddenly, as one sometimes comes upon one's own face unexpectedly when walking into a mirrored room.

Whom had she lost? If she could have called out the right name, the shape, the shade would have turned to her. Instead, her energy, her will, flowed into shapes of light that were the silhouettes of a man or men she could not name, shapes of light that were also doors forever closed to her. If Mike had only come in when the light painted those shapes on the wall! If it was his shadow on the wall! But she knew it was not his shadow. Those doors of light were tears in the fabric of this life, into which this life was fast disappearing.

My life, she thought, looking out at the black crosses, is discontinuous now. She had always thought of living as a long, thin road which would wind this way and that through the landscape one called one's life. If there was a break in the road ahead, it was impossible to go on and the future was forever inaccessible. If there was a break in the road behind, you could not go back and examine your own past. Which break was worse, the break in the road behind you, which kept your past hidden from you, or the break ahead of you, which kept you from your future?

Outside, the branches swayed up and down. It was impossible to feel discontinuous and still live. It was necessary to believe that from the minute you drew breath until you stopped, your life would be continuous. What was personality if it was not memory over continuous time? But she could not think back to the hospital, could not let herself remember it. She understood, now, why amnesiacs were said to be so terrified, so frantic to recover their lost lives, why they could not resign themselves to what they had lost and say, All right, now I will start again. It was not so much their belief that they had nothing to start with, but their fear that their life could once again be erased. In the face of such terror, it was impossible to proceed.

What other things had she lost? There might be other things she had erased from her memory. Present, past, and the expectation of the future had to exist simultaneously in the mind. Before the time in the hospital, she remembered, or thought she remembered, everything that had happened to her since earliest childhood. But part of her past was gone, and her expectation of a future had gone along with it. What was left? Nothing. Nonexistence.

She awoke and felt her fingers against the carved wooden sun of the headboard. Although it was only a carved sun, it felt warm to the touch. Someone had believed enough in the sun to carve it at the head of this bed. Perhaps that was wrong; perhaps the woodworker had carved the sun (always above their heads, even on the darkest nights) because he was afraid that one day the sun would not return. Perhaps, Iris, she said to herself, he carved the sun because that was a popular design to carve at the time. She slid her fingers along the carved wooden rays.

No, the woodworker had carved it because he was afraid.

In the silent house, alone in her room, she talked to the carved sun, ignoring the real one, floating high and small, like a disk of ice above a sterile world of ice and snow.

My husband, she thought, had this dream: He was standing at the bottom of an enormous flight of marble steps, standing between his mother and his father, holding their hands. He looked up to the top of the steps where they blended with the line of the sky, and there stood a great many important people, all of them dressed in long white gowns. One was the President of the country, and another was the Pope, and another was the Supreme Rabbi of Brooklyn. His mother and father insisted that he go up and talk to the Supreme Rabbi of Brooklyn, but he didn't want to go. His mother and father started up the steps, pushing him before them. When they were near the top step, they told him to go to the Supreme Rabbi and speak to him. My husband walked slowly and unsteadily to this very important rabbi, and he and all the other great men bent down toward him, their faces kind. My husband, who was only a child of nine, looked up at their faces, looked down again, and threw up all over their shoes. He remembers their consternation and the commotion he caused, but after that he remembers nothing more about the dream.

My father tells this story. His mother had gone to Florida, leaving him alone with my grandfather. The two of them took up residence in a steam bath in Lower Manhattan. While my father was sitting on a bench near the swimming pool, the biggest of the big *rebbes* came in, surrounded by his faithful apprentices. He took off his glasses and gave them to one of the men walking behind him, and that man put the glasses in the pocket of his blue terry-cloth robe. Without his glasses, the rabbi could not see a thing. My father watched the great man walk to the shallow end of the pool, where he ostentatiously prepared to dive in.

"Rabbi," my father called, "you can't dive in there."

The rabbi looked up, insulted. Who had the effrontery to address him in such a way? His followers glared at my father. My father watched while the rabbi raised his hands over his head and dove into the pool. There was an enormous thump, and the rabbi stood up and wove out of the water, blood streaming from his gashed forehead.

"What good does it do you to be the greatest rabbi in the world," asked my father, "if you still don't have any brains?"

Iris stared out of the window and wondered why she should be thinking about rabbis. She soon decided rabbis were not what interested her, but men were. All her life she had been surrounded by men—her father, her brothers, her husband, her son—but she hadn't understood them. Why should she be trying to understand them now?

The two incidents, she concluded, led her to believe that men have a great deal of trouble with vanity and very much resent anyone who seems to be in a position of authority. She tried to retell the two stories, this time imagining very important women at the top of the stairs, and she could not imagine that fear of *any* woman would cause a nine-year-old boy to throw up. She tried to imagine a woman diving in at the shallow end of a pool against the advice of a bystander and found that equally impossible to imagine, although for different reasons. No woman would be stupid enough to do such a thing. A woman who wanted to dive into a pool and was told that the water was too shallow would either test out the water or pretend that she did not want to dive in in the first place. There was no woman alive who would believe so fully in the accuracy of her view of the world. Thus, a woman would be saved from cracking her skull and unnecessarily alarming small children.

Women did not believe they had magic powers. However, they often believed men had them. Women believed in magic protectors. Perhaps when the rabbi dived into the pool, it was the fault of the women who at other times surrounded him, women who needed to believe there was someone who could dive into shallow water without hurting himself, and their belief was so strong it eventually took possession of the rabbi. Women could entertain insane beliefs about men, yet remain sensible about their own limitations.

By the same token, Iris thought, most women would be too sensible to take to their beds and refuse to get out.

I want a magic protector, Iris thought, watching the crosses. I want my magic protector back.

I *am* losing my mind, she thought.

Iris listened carefully and heard nothing, the usual noises: the dog coming up the oak steps, his long nails, which should have been clipped, clicking against the wood; the cat skidding away from him on the third-floor landing; the muffled sound of the washing machine spinning in the basement where her housekeeper, Etheline, was ironing. She always irons, thought Iris, when she's upset. If I don't get up soon, she'll be ironing the carpets. The house was empty. The children spent more and more of their time at friends' houses. They couldn't stay home with a mother who was turning the house into a mausoleum. She listened again, heard nothing, and picked up her notebook, a large notebook, covered in red paisley fabric. "Why bother with such expensive things?" her mother had asked her. "Why spend hours staring at something ugly?" she'd answered.

She would not trouble to buy such a notebook now. If this notebook had not been lying on the table, she would have written on the back of an envelope, in the margins of a mail-order catalog, anything. She told herself she wouldn't write anything if her pen wasn't next to the notebook; it would be too much trouble to find it. However, her pen was lying next to it.

For a long time—they were lost in the woods. There were only two of them there beneath the moon, and the moon had no interest in them. There were animals lying along the limbs of trees, but the animals were black in the darkness and could not be seen, so they were not there, although they could be feared all the same. They soon learned to say that it was the moon who feared the animals and transmitted its fear to them so that they were not really afraid.

The smoothed-out faces of the saints.

Sometimes the lake is like that.

There was some argument about whether the traps had been there from the beginning. They were simple traps, usually pits that had been covered over by leaves and branches. They were very effective, and during the day the animals they found caught in them did not at all resemble the animals they knew slept in the branches at night. Later, the traps became more complicated, and they told themselves they had simply forgotten the nature of the traps they had originally set. They refused to believe that someone else might have entered the forest and that whoever it was might have plans of his own. If there was another person in the forest, he must be afraid of the moon and the dark in which it lived.

Iris sat on the edge of the bed and read what she had just written. The page before her seemed entirely alien, as if someone else had taken her hand and guided it from left to right. A story was trying to tell itself to her, and it was about something she didn't want to hear, which was why it was a story about forests and animals and traps. All symbols. *What* does it mean? She would just have to wait, she thought, until she wrote the end of the story.

It was so cold in the room. Hopeless, she swung her legs up on the bed and pulled the covers over her head.

"How are you?" her husband asked. She could always sense his presence, even before he spoke. She didn't answer him.

The sky behind the great elms had turned a brilliant purple, and as the sun dropped, a line of white showed above the sharp roof ridge of the house behind theirs. Slate-blue clouds were fattening as they climbed the sky. Soon it would be dark. She wondered if there would be a moon. The left corner of the window brightened to a brilliant rose. The light pulsed and faded and pulsed again as if a great heart beating in the sky were slowing, trying to start up, and stopping. The inky blue network of twigs veined her window. She wanted to answer her husband but could not. After a few minutes, she heard his steps receding.

She heard him stop in the hallway and knew he was looking back at her. Probably he was shaking his head.

He was not a man who believed in the world, who loved it indiscriminately. He loved her and he loved his children, and without them he was lost. What excuse did she have for this? If she could begin writing in her journals again—sensible things, accounts of the day, which showed her belief in the unique nature of each of them. If she could persuade herself to get up, go to her study, sit up and type.

She fell asleep.

She awoke in the middle of the night. She was alone in bed. Angry, her husband must have fallen asleep in his study chair. That was her fault. He would not get enough sleep; he would sicken and die. She would have no one to blame but herself. She ought to get up and wake him, but she had never been so conscious of how wonderfully the bed held her up. She reached out and pulled her notebook from the table next to the bed. It opened to the page on which she had last written.

My father tells this story.

During the war, he was manufacturing men's clothes, just as my grandfather was. He depended on my grandfather for much of his business. My grandfather made up the clothing which my father finished and sold. My grandfather sent my father a bill and overcharged him fifty dollars. My father believed my grandfather had made a mistake, so he subtracted the fifty dollars and sent him a check for the rest. My grandfather got the check and called him up and said if my father didn't send him the fifty dollars, he'd stop doing my father's work for him and he'd sue him.

My father was furious. He used to take the car and drive my grandfather to work and drive him home, but that night he didn't pick him up. He went home instead, and when he finished dinner, he went right over to his mother, my grandmother, and told her what had happened.

"So," my father told me, "she says to me—that shows how smart she is—she says, '*You need the work?*' " My father said he needed the work. And my grandmother said, "I tell you what to do. Pay the meshuggener his fifty dollars."

"You couldn't get anything made," my father told me.

So he gave her the fifty dollars to give to my grandfather.

That night, my grandmother and grandfather came over to sit on my father's front porch. My grandfather gave my mother a savings bond for a thousand dollars. My father told me that he said, " 'What kind of man are you? You say you're going to sue me, and you come here and throw money around like peanuts,' and your grandfather's answer, I'll never forget it, was '*One thing has nothing to do with the other.*' And you know what?" my father told me. "Your grandfather was right."

Iris had never been able to make sense of this story. *Why* didn't one thing have anything to do with the other? Did her grandfather mean to teach her father that family and business were separate? Did he mean to teach him that certain ties were unshakable, and no matter how badly one behaved, he had to be forgiven? Because most things one did counted for nothing? Because it was important to disregard most of life? Because most of what one did was trivial, had, in fact, no significance, was done by reflex, under pressure, had as little significance as a moment of monkey chatter? Did he want to say, Listen for the deep chord, not the random noise? Had my father mistaken the random noise for the text when, really, he had yet to find the note? Because he was like a scholar who read the footnotes and ignored the text?

I want to understand this story, thought Iris, because I am like my father. So many things have nothing to do with one another. But how do you know which things do and which things don't? How do you know when to drop a line that will twist and strangle you if you hold onto it? How do you know which line to hold because, if you drop it, the whole fabric will unravel? I have never, she thought, been able to let go of anything.

She could not separate one thing from another. Everything was equally important. She was forever trying to tie everything together. Apparently, she had succeeded. She had woven her life into a net and now she was caught in it. She had made some kind of mistake, and until she undid it, she was caught.

She put the notebook back and laid her head on her outstretched arm. She could see the thick elm boughs moving up and down. The moon would not come out from behind the clouds. If people were lucky, she thought, drifting into sleep, they were like fortune cookies. When they got to the end of their lives, they would find a message inside themselves. And what would the little piece of paper say, unscrolling from her lips like the little scroll floating up from the mouths of the dying in medieval paintings? *You should have done better.* That's what it would say.

In the morning, Mike came in, stood next to the bed, and inspected it. He looked out the window and saw the black branches heaving in the high wind. There was a draft. He could feel it where he stood. He would have to tape the seams where the windows met the walls. He looked at the bed with some envy. Men weren't allowed to get sick. They had their work to do. His own attitude toward illness left something to be desired. First there was illness; then there was death. Recovery was not in the

natural order of things. It was something miraculous. The sudden
stab of fear he felt was followed by a wave of anger. He felt the
flush first in his cheeks, then his stomach. As if it had suddenly
been switched on, he could hear his father's voice on the answering machine.

"Mike, your mother's in the hospital. Call this number.

"Mike, your mother's very sick. Call this number.

"Your mother's dying. Call this number.

"Your mother just died. Call me at your aunt's house."

Iris had come home and played back the messages, called him
at work, and told him what happened. When he came upstairs,
he saw her in their bedroom. She had her back to him and was
playing back the messages, then erasing them, one at a time. She
didn't want him to hear them. As she played back and erased,
played back and erased, she said to the empty room, "How can
you leave messages like that on an *answering machine?*"

She had always protected him. He was angry at her, her
absence. Listening to an answering machine that's been disconnected for months, that's what comes of sitting in a room with
a motionless woman. He had to stop thinking of her as dead and
buried. The day she came back from the hospital, cured, he had
been told, of her fever of unknown origin, he and Etheline, their
housekeeper, had brought her extra pillows, straightened the
covers, and propped her up so she could look out her beloved
window. "Stop treating me as if I'm dying," she said. "I'll get
over it. Give me some time." If it was time she wanted, she was
taking it with both hands.

He was a young man: forty-three. He felt old. He looked at
the backs of his hands. He had always seen them as good strong
hands, large, able to do the job. He opened all the jars the rest
of the household brought him. He loved the expressions on their
faces when he handed the jars back, open. Sometimes it took so
little to please them. Such thanks for opening a jar. They made

him feel needed, irreplaceable. "The car won't start?" Iris asked their son, Nate. "Call the Magician." That was how she thought of him. But now he was helpless. Her illness, whatever it was that kept her in bed, was stripping him of his powers. He was losing his sense of having a place in the world. He looked at the backs of his hands. The veins were blue and ropy. The hair that grew from his wrist to the base of his fingers was still black. *These are old man's hands.*

He considered sitting on the edge of the bed, but decided against it. During the day, the bed seemed forbidden to him, just as it had been in the hospital. He was a good man. At least he was not a bad one. He had a terrible temper. He knew his children called him the Troll. He knew, too, that his wife didn't try to stop them. In fact, she agreed with them. He had always considered that treacherous. But what was this, this endless lying in bed? He blamed himself for not insisting she go to a better hospital. Iris was, as she herself admitted, a sensitive plant.

He thought he knew his wife. He had gone to the hospital every day, and she told him everything that happened. At least in the beginning she had. Near the end of her six weeks there, she volunteered some information but quickly changed the subject and asked what was happening at home. She stopped answering the telephone, turned off the television set, and pulled the curtains around her bed. Finally she announced that she was leaving on her birthday whether or not the doctors were willing to release her. He had agreed. She was getting weaker and more remote every day. They decided if she came home and the fever returned they would see another doctor and consider admitting her to another hospital. They were surprised when their doctor agreed.

In the car, all the way home, she cried with relief.

When they got into the house, she sat in his study and watched him read. But she was so exhausted that climbing one flight of stairs left her damp and out of breath, and he insisted she get into bed. She got into bed and didn't get out.

He thought, watching the bed, that life can build up in the body like a toxin, a poison. The days burn up in you and leave their thick sediment in your blood. He had always thought that Iris was addicted to life; perhaps she wasn't. Perhaps no one was. Living was, according to him, like driving on the highway, the children screaming in the back, and if you took your eye from the road, the car crashed, and so you kept your eye on the road, limited your glances into the rearview mirror, did not change the tape in the tape deck if the road was slippery, drove in silence while your wife slept, your eyes on the road, and the next thing you knew, you were there, wherever that was, understanding nothing of the journey you'd just made, except that you had to make it no matter how perilous, thrilling, or heartrending it was. And then you might refuse to go any farther, and would it be any wonder? The wonder was that you'd come this far, without asking questions, carried along by a wind in the blood.

"Talk to her," said the internist when Mike went to his office. "Even when patients seem to be unconscious, we talk to them. You never know when you'll have an effect."

He'd try that some other time. Right now he'd feel like an imbecile addressing the sarcophagus that was his wife. He recalled a time about a month before she'd gone into the hospital when they'd been lying in bed. The children had fought their way out the front door and were on their way to school.

"You know," said Iris, "if I were single, if I were living alone, I'd never know there was anything the matter with me. Up here." She tapped her head.

He thought that was very funny, the notion that very possibly, all over Manhattan, single people were living in studio apartments, completely mad, convinced they were absolutely sane.

"Yesterday," Iris said, "Evelyn came in and took my boots,

21

and when I told her to put them back she said I was selfish and never wanted to share anything. I told her to put them back again, and she said I'd never really loved her. I asked her how she knew, and she said it was easy to know. Then she slammed the door on her way out. Then Nate came in and wanted to know if I'd mind staying home because the answering machine wasn't working and he was expecting a call and Etheline never takes messages right. I said no, I had to go to the office, and he said I was never home. By the time they made their lunches and got out of the house, I was completely mad. I mean, without them, how would I know I was demented? *Why* would I know?

"If I were single . . ." she said dreamily.

"You never wanted to be single," he said.

"If I'd only known," said his wife.

Perhaps tomorrow he would ask her if she'd been unhappy with him.

"Don't say anything to disturb her," the internist had told him. "Stick to neutral topics."

For Iris, there were no such things as neutral topics.

Outside, he heard the flapping of wings, a loud burbling. Something had disturbed the doves. He looked out the window and thought he saw a large bird circling high above the houses, just where the moon would be if it were visible. If they were in Vermont, where they had a country house, he would be sure he was watching a hawk. It was impossible, something so wild in such a domesticated place. And then he saw the bird as if it were his wife's mind, circling, looking for something. As he stared out the window, he saw the sky was not monochromatic, but subtly ribbed with bands that resembled eccentrically drawn bars.

Like a hawk in a cage, like that hallucination of a hawk—how could it be there?—she was flying in circles, coming lower and lower, until she found what she wanted. But if she never did? That, too, was possible. He had read somewhere that vultures, because they were so heavy and expended so much energy in lifting off from the ground, had one chance to come down and find something to prey upon. If they made a mistake, landed, and found nothing to eat, they might not be able to climb the stairways of air back to their safe place in the sky, and then they themselves were preyed upon by animals on the ground.

A vulture. There was something vulturous in her silence.

"Iris," he said, "I'm going. I have work to do."

She waited until he left, then turned and stared out the window. A sky full of clouds. Outside, the arms of the trees swayed, cut off from her by a wall of glass.

3

LATER THAT NIGHT, sitting in his office, he could hear Nate and Evelyn talking.

"The way they met was so romantic," Evelyn was saying. "He went to a party and heard her laughing and decided he wanted to marry her. They made up their minds *the first time.*"

"What's so romantic about that?" Nate asked. He was thirteen, his sister fifteen. He was the cynic. "They probably wore themselves out on other people."

"Oh, *God,*" said Evelyn.

"Besides," Nate said, "did you ever see pictures of her? She was gorgeous. She looked like a movie star. Probably other people wanted to marry her."

"People keep saying how beautiful she is now," Evelyn said.

"What people?" Nate asked. "Relatives? They tell *Grandma* she's beautiful."

"*He* looked like a movie star," Evelyn said.

"It's just the pictures," Nate said. "They had a great photographer."

"*I* look like her," Evelyn said.

"Did you ever think of plastic surgery?" said Nate.

"Remember how they used to fight?" Evelyn asked. "I always hated it when they fought."

"I wish they'd fight now," said Nate; "don't you?"

"God yes," said Evelyn. "Noise. Sound."

Mike sighed and looked around his study. The disorder had become chaos. He would love to fight with his wife, to demand an explanation of her behavior, to pick up a pillow and beat the footboard with it. Instead, he lost his temper with everyone at work.

Iris was a hermit. She could spend weeks in the house. When she was working, she wore the same thing every day. At night, she would get undressed in front of the washing machine, pour in some soap powder, and turn the dial. In the morning, she would take up yesterday's clothing, put it in the dryer when she got up, make breakfast, and take it out afterward. While she was writing her first novel, she had worn a shapeless pink-colored thing that came to her knees. He remembered it well. It had a square neck, and the sleeves were bordered by a white band. For her second novel, she had wrapped herself in a shapeless blue kimono she found in an antique shop. She asked him to guess how much it cost, this treasure, and he said he imagined they paid her three dollars to take it away. She disappeared into the basement to wash the magic garment.

In the beginning, her work habits worried him. Suppose she began an enormously long book? Would she stay in the house for two years? Would she never wear anything but the blue kimono? When she began her third novel, she turned the house upside down looking for the pink thing and eventually gave up and settled on an old maroon silk robe she'd inherited from her grandfather. He had never questioned Iris' strange creative habits, her need to lock herself in rooms for days on end. He had simply accustomed himself to her odd uniforms, her seasonal unavailability. Once they had children, he saw more of her. When she had to take their son to the doctor for his perpetual ear infections, she had to get dressed. Children were the balance wheel of the world.

She was a great thinker, his wife. There was nothing too small to attract her attention, nothing that escaped her glance, nothing she did not want to think about and talk about, for hours, weeks, months. Years! She didn't stop until she understood whatever it was. His wife understood cats, geraniums, stones, the motives of the nonsegmented worm when it surfaced after a rainstorm. She inspected good news as if its wrapping had been tampered with. Good news was like lightning. If it flashed, could thunder be far behind?

This, of course, had to do with her mother. Iris insisted that she'd had a happy childhood, but he didn't believe her. *No one* had a happy childhood. He'd listened for years to her telephone conversations. When his wife's first book first appeared on the best-seller list, she called her mother and put him on the extension.

"What number?" asked her mother.

"Seven," said his wife.

Her mother didn't say anything.

"Maybe it will climb," Iris said. She sounded hopeless. She had just realized that number seven was a dreadful number. He waited to hear what her mother would say next.

"Let's *hope* it climbs," said his mother-in-law.

Now there was a silence at his end of the phone.

"And how are the children?" his mother-in-law asked.

"Dead," said Iris, and hung up.

Did no one in her family ever finish a conversation? They began peacefully enough. Then the shouts and the insults started, followed by long, seemingly endless silences. Maybe it was easier to slam the phone down than to say goodbye. Iris hated to say goodbye. The first time Mike had to take a plane to a convention, she spent so much time telling him when to call her and when she would call him that he almost missed the plane.

If he sat up here long enough, he'd fall asleep.

* * *

In the morning, she heard a dove burbling to the right of the windowpane. They had such lovely voices. She heard two doves speaking, one to the other. And then a ripping sound, a hammering, and she knew they were tearing a cedar shingle from the outside wall of the house, and inside, amid the insulation, they were building their nest. I love birds, she thought. The sky was light blue, streaked with tenuous clouds, white lint that even now the polishing hand of the wind was removing bit by bit. There was so much she ought to be doing.

She looked nervously at her notebook. Last night, she heard Nate on the phone. "Mother's suffering from Total Body Breakdown. TBB." She picked up the notebook. It was easy to write lying on her side, now that she had learned to hold the ballpoint pen at the correct angle so it would keep on writing. She wanted to write another story her father had told her but found herself becoming sleepy, her hand leaden, and the pen, as if it were alive, began pulling her hand across the empty sheet of paper.

Many of the animals they used to see were gone, and so they came to believe the woods were getting larger. He wanted to find out what was at the end of the woods, whether or not it was true that if one got to the place where the trees stopped, the sun rested on the horizon like a great round door and anyone could walk into it as if into a forest of light. The sun was another forest of trees blazing, but they stood in place forever, never falling to the ground or turning to ash. She did not want him to go. If the woods were larger, it was possible to become lost and not to be able to return. The animals at night were dangerous, and if anything happened to him, she would not hear of it for a long time. She reminded him of the traps set in the woods, but he said

27

there had never been any traps. They had only imagined them. Although she did not want to go, she set off to look for the edge of the woods with him because she was afraid that if the legend were true and if the sun rested at the edge of the forest like a great door, he would not be able to stop himself but would walk through into that flaming world without her and then he would never want to come back. He had told her that the flaming forest was the most beautiful forest of all and was not happy to hear her talk of her love for this wood, dark, damp, moss-covered. She felt the shape of animals lying along the branches, and the cold metal of the traps was in the wind she felt on her skin. Out of the corner of her eye she saw someone else who was in the wood like a dark shadow among shadows, but when she saw he was determined to go whether or not she stayed, she said nothing about what she heard or felt. There is danger in this, she said to herself, but she did not say it aloud. In any case, he knew what she was thinking.

As she looked at the page, voices and images flew at her, like birds flying into the sky reflected in a window.

Where's my shoe? He sat in the back last time! The dog got out! I'm going after him on my bike. You said I could go! What's the matter with you two? You want a divorce? If you go blind, I'll cross you over. What do they do with the dead babies? Abbie said they eat them. Did you give the dead baby a name? You could get a job in the country if you really wanted to! Oh, Ma! Nobody gets pregnant anymore! Ma, are you really good at money? If you are, you could get a job. I know a job. You could be a cashier. Daddy's a good cooker. Then we would live in the country. I want Daddy to sleep with me in the hospital. Ma, Sam killed the cat! Are you old? Are you going to die? Stop saying you can't stand it! You can't stand anything!

She supposed the blue and violet veins were still there, delicate branches beneath their hair. She couldn't see them. The children were old too. Odd that she'd never understood what that meant before: old. *How old are you, Ma? Is Grandma older than you? Who's older than Grandma?* No one.

Old was the toaster beyond fixing. Old was the car when it could no longer start. Old was the pot in the yard, its bottom rusted away. Old was what happened to everything rusting in the stream of time. Was that what was wrong with her? That she had bitten into the apple of old age? But she had always felt old. When she was sixteen, two of her knuckles were already deformed by arthritis. She had spent hours as a teenager, sitting in the offices of specialists among old ladies who glared at her as if she were there to mock them.

Her husband came into the room and asked her what she wanted for lunch.

Anything.

"You have no objection to chicken salad?"

No answer.

"Do you want company for lunch?"

When did she eat? How did she eat? He never saw her.

"I'll be at the office this afternoon," he said. "Big tenure decisions coming up. Another budget crisis." When he got to work, everyone would ask him about Iris. What should he say? *Fine. Bearing up well. In the twenty-second day of her captivity.*

"Etheline," he said on the way out, "I'll be back at six."

"Soup?" she asked.

"Soup."

Slowly she was acquiring Iris' considerable culinary skills.

Poor man, Etheline thought.

He knew what she was thinking. That made it worse.

When he got home, Evelyn was waiting for him.

"For God's sake, Daddy, do something! *Find* a doctor that will come and see her!"

"It won't do any good," Mike said. "They say we have to wait. The only doctor she wanted to talk to won't come. Why should he? They call analysis the talking cure. She won't talk. What's he supposed to do?"

"He could give her something."

"Like what?"

"Elavil."

"What do you know about Elavil?"

"I read about it in the doctor's office."

"You're not taking pills, are you?"

"I never take pills."

Iris, who was listening, sighed with relief and closed her eyes.

"Look how she sleeps," Evelyn said. "The same position all day."

"I know," said Mike.

"She's setting a bad example for me!" Evelyn said. "I'm only fifteen! And what about Nate? He's only thirteen!"

"What do you want me to do?" Mike asked.

"*Talk* to her!" Evelyn said.

"You know she won't talk," Nate shouted from his room. "And don't talk outside her door."

Iris heard their footsteps, going downstairs.

After dinner, Mike came into their room and sat down in the peacock chair at the foot of their bed. In the royal blue and black light, his wife was invisible on the bed. He got up, picked up her notebook and took it out onto the hall landing, and began flipping through the pages. Nothing new today. Then he turned to the last page and found several loose sheets of paper and the note about the two people who had left the forest. After he read it, he turned the other loose pages over, and saw a clipping he had given Iris to read while she was still in the hospital. What meaning did it have for her now? Some, evidently, since she kept it.

He sat back down in the peacock chair and stared at the bed.

When he called the internist from the office that afternoon, the doctor said they would have to "do something" if this went on much longer. Three weeks had passed already and nothing changed. Twice a week, Iris lay across the bed, her head over the side, while Etheline washed her hair in a large basin. When it was over, Iris would say thank you and smile, but the smile, like the thank-you, seemed to be recorded messages left from some previous time.

The internist was becoming more definite about what he thought should be done. "Intervention," he said, was called for. He meant, Mike knew, hospitalization. That, however, was out of the question. The hospital, he believed, had caused his wife to take to her bed.

"I can't believe it," said an old friend he called regularly. "Iris is a fighter."

"Come look for yourself," said Mike. "What we need," he said, "is a wild card."

"I'll be over this weekend."

"She won't talk to you," Mike said.

"If she won't talk to me, you better do something. She always calls me when there's trouble."

"A wild card," Mike said again.

Outside, a car coughed and started its engine. People were going places. The light was falling on her notebook as if it intended to write the next few pages itself. The trees outside her window seemed less clear; perhaps it was foggy.

When I used to look out the window, thought Iris, the houses in back of us were solid. They cut their outline into the sky as if into gray metal. No more. Now they seem permeable, as if they were made up of dots moving farther and farther apart. They look, thought Iris, like houses in a pointillist painting.

31

Can the mind lose its solidity? Can its elements begin moving farther and farther apart, until the spaces between the elements become more important than the elements themselves? Then, thought Iris, this is like dying, a slow dispersing of the mind, a lifting away from the earth, like a mist the sun burns away in the morning.

Her own thoughts frightened her, and she picked up her notebook. She took out one of the loose sheets she kept in the back and began to write.

It is not known—she wrote—whether they found the sun at the edge of things. It is known that they left the forest. After many years, animals began living in the odd tree house they abandoned when they left the forest behind. Among themselves, the animals agreed to keep watch in the event they returned. The animals had never been vicious. They had always respected the boundaries of the two who had gone.

Eventually the two of them came back to live just at the edge of the forest. Every morning and every night, the animals came to the edge of the woods and watched them. They kept their backs to the forest; they never turned toward the forest. They seemed not to know it was there. They were often seen looking up at the moon, but when the moon rose over the forest, they never turned to look at it.

They told one another there had never been a forest, a wood. They complained bitterly about their life on the arid plain where the only shadows were ones they themselves cast and which afforded no relief from the hot staring eye of the sun. Someday, they told one another, we will find the wood we have dreamed of, and the animals in the wood behind them watched them and listened. At night, when the moon rose over the dark tree line, the animals howled, as if to draw their attention, but they would not turn toward them.

They sat on the arid plain, under the hungry sun, and burned to the blackness of burnt wood. After some time, they rarely moved unless they were hunting for food. Months would go by, and one of them would jump up, point down the arid plain, and ask, Was that it? Was that the shadow of the forest, the forest itself, coming closer? Then the mirage vanished, and they sat again on the plain, turning darker than the night sky, while behind them, the animals howled.

Outside the window, the branches were absolutely still. The sky behind them was iron gray. Hours passed and she did not notice. The last time she'd looked out the window it was one thirty. Now it was three o'clock.

4

IN THE MORNING, the room was filled with a light the color of white mist off the ocean. There was a radiance in the room. Unseen, an occasional car went slowly by: *Whoosh. Whoosh.* The windows were covered by cotton mats of snow, snow that a child, pasting bits of cotton to construction paper, would make.

The snow lay in thick lines across the closed glass louvers of the windows. Thick but fragile bars of snow, hinting that imprisonment did not last forever. A high, small sun, yellow-white, suggested itself above the falling snow. The small sun swam like a fish beneath a thickly iced-over lake.

A car horn blared, once, twice: *Mupp. Mupp.* Someone had come to pick someone up. Next door, the old station wagon roared to life, imposing its heartbeat on the world. Their neighbor still hadn't repaired its muffler: *Ta-ta-ta-ta. Ta-ta-ta-ta.*

Inside the room, the objects took on a new air of importance, even glory. The gingerbread pendulum clock, which had stopped the day they moved into the house, glowed as if it expected to resume functioning. Its grain strained to stand out from the wood. The furniture was coming alive in the light. *Look how warm we are.*

The flowered Victorian wallpaper was better than new. In fifteen years, it had not faded or been soiled. Instead, the background had turned color, cream to the rich gold of old vellum. The flowers on the oriental rugs lifted from the backgrounds. In the corners of the windowsill, the ten-year-old geraniums had, with careful feeding and the passage of time, grown into long if skinny vines. *Age falls from us,* they said. They took the strange light into themselves. The leaves were like odd-shaped hands, lovely scalloped shapes, holding their lifelines up to the light.

Through the snow, it was impossible to see the trees clearly. They were dark shadows, thick bars obscuring the light. A patch of snow began sliding down the window. When it fell from the glass, she could see the snow falling in thick, large flakes. As each flake hit the window, it left behind a tiny paw print. There was a slight tremor in the room, a shudder. A great mass of snow had detached itself from the roof. It fell onto the rosebushes, on top of the lily bulbs buried in front of them.

In the main bathroom, a transistor radio switched on to the weather report. The peculiar, artificial urgency of the announcer describing the weather crept into all corners of the house, as if trying to attack the peace in which everything floated. In a few minutes, Iris thought, Mike would change the station.

The familiar strains of the Second Brandenburg Concerto took over. The music, Iris thought, was too fast for the weather. The channel changed again. WNBC. *Imus in the Morning.* Nate must be in the bathroom. Strange music, like the theme from *Jaws.* Imus' Moby Worm was eating up a high school.

The sound of polite, if exasperated, quarreling. Mike was telling their son to get out of the bathroom and let Evelyn in. There were four bathrooms in the house. Everyone had to use the same one.

The schools would be closed; buses would not be running; Etheline would not get to work. When the children were smaller, Etheline would have walked two miles through the mounting snow, pushed the back door open, collapsed onto the kitchen chair, panting, the snow from her boots melting and pooling on the linoleum. Then she would go down into the basement and hang her dripping things on the clothesline where the heat from the furnace would dry them.

When she came back up, she would make herself a cup of herb tea: Celestial Seasonings. Heaven pleased her. She believed in it. There were Bibles all over her little apartment. Whenever they wanted to give Etheline a present and couldn't think of anything, Iris always told them to get her a Bible. New translations, new exegeses. Etheline had been pleased with each and every one of them. The enormous leather-bound concordance had been a landmark. She would sit at their round oak table, her knee resting against the mouth of one of the four gargoyles that formed the table's pedestal, and read from her Bible. Between the tea and the Bible, she warmed herself.

Outside Iris' door, an argument was in progress. Mike was informing the children that someone had to stay home with Mother. She couldn't be left alone. Suppose the house caught fire? Could they depend on their mother's common sense? Would she get up, put on a coat, and go out?

Evelyn's voice, sullen. Nate's voice, sullen. Evelyn's door, slamming. She had been elected to stand guard.

That is exactly, thought Iris, how *my* mother used to talk to me about my grandmother. Senile at seventy-eight, her grandmother would leave things burning on the stove, bend down holding a match to look at something on the carpet and set fire to the curtains.

The front door slammed shut. Much stomping in the front hall.

"It cold out there, man. That wind hurt my lungs, man."

Etheline was here after all. Now Evelyn could go out.

She heard Etheline outside her door.

"Them buses," she was saying. "They ought to pay you to take them, man."

Mike asked her something.

"Like walking through the deep hot sands of the desert," Etheline said.

Whenever she had been to church over the weekend, she arrived with new and peculiar expressions.

"Take off that clothing, miss," she was saying. "You ain't going nowhere today, miss."

An inaudible protest from Evelyn.

"Let him come fetch you," Etheline said. "Men's good for something."

Slam. And *slam* again.

"Why ain't you out there shoveling?" she asked Nate.

Iris waited.

Slam.

"How about eggs for Iris?" Etheline asked Mike.

Eggs, thought Iris. Please.

"You take off that coat, man," she was saying to Mike. "You ain't going nowhere yourself. Turn on the radio! They closed them schools. They fastened the gate with big black locks. You needs to catch the ammonia in this snow? You can't *walk* out there, man!"

The sound of Mike's feet going up the steps to his study. His chair was just above her head.

Her hand on the sheet. She wore too many rings. A large silver ring covered her wedding band. Her engagement ring was still in the cinnamon canister awaiting repair. It had been waiting there five years.

The doorbell rang, a loud horizontal noise. Everything on the windowsill seemed to jump, startled.

"Now who may be that be?" Etheline grumbled. "It sure ain't the mailman. Not in this here snow. Probably is one of them Jehoshaphat's Witnesses."

Probably United Parcel bringing oranges from Florida. Her

parents studied weather maps the way ancient prophets studied entrails. With the onset of cold weather came the arrival of cartons of oranges.

"*I'll* get it!" Evelyn called out. "It's for me. It's Justin."

Iris heard Etheline trudging back up from the landing.

"Say the word *Justin,* and that girl shoots like a bat out of hell," she said.

Outside, men and children were shoveling the sidewalks in front of their houses and then moving on to their alleyways. The day was brilliant and the snow, as it fell from their shovels, caught the light and fell again, sparkling like crystals. Naturally enough, the man who turned the corner and began walking down their street attracted their attention. He, however, seemed unaware of them. Every so often, he would stop, not as if he were tired, but because he seemed interested in the look of the buildings. He would stand still, not resting his suitcase, which was expensive, on the snowy ground, and study the houses as if he were memorizing the look of them.

A Victorian neighborhood, he thought. He'd always had a secret love for these ornate buildings. He came from northern Nebraska, just outside of Lincoln, and sod houses were still to be found there, built into the side of swells in the earth, windowless caves, although now they no longer had walls of earth, but cement. His father, an architect, thought the flatness of the land required vertical structures, landmarks, each building like a compass point. Without them, he said, the land was like the sea, directionless, endless.

A man stopped shoveling and moved aside to let him pass.

Finally, he saw the house he wanted, an enormous cream-colored house, its wood trim dark brown, three stories high, a wraparound enclosed porch running the full length of the first floor, an octagonal turret growing crazily above the third-floor roof. It was just what he expected.

He walked up the concrete steps, painted red, and took note of the peeling paint. He expected that, too. There were already prints in the snow, going up but not coming down. He was not the first visitor this morning. He nodded to himself and twisted the little knob of a bell beside the porch door. He waited but nothing happened. Then he saw the little electric button set into the door itself and pushed it.

He waited and heard footsteps running downstairs. He peered into the porch and saw the wicker couches and chairs and, beyond them, the carved oak door. He noticed the silver alarm tapes on all the windows. Apparently, the neighborhood was not completely safe.

The oak door opened, and there she was, wearing the same black Chinese robe he remembered. On its back was embroidered an enormous gold dragon, the threads real gold and thick. The embroidery rose almost half an inch from the surface of the fabric.

How was it possible that after all these years she had not aged a day? Her hair was still that shiny spun gold, tight curls in a huge halo around her head. She had not fattened or broadened with time.

As he saw her struggling with the lock of the porch door, the world around him became insubstantial. He felt as if he were standing inside a dome of light. So it was true, after all. There was such a thing as immortality. There were some people time did not touch. Or perhaps she had aged, even died in the middle of a night, and had come back again. Somehow, almost twenty-six years had been canceled out and the woman he met twenty-six years ago had been reincarnated, reborn, untouched by time. She was just as she was then.

The porch door opened and he found himself staring into those still-familiar, wide-set, slightly slanted green eyes.

"Iris!" he said.

Evelyn stared at him. He was a vision. Justin, whom she had

expected to see, fell over the edge of the earth and was forever lost. She had never seen such a handsome man, such a distinguished one. He was the man in the Marlboro ad, he was Mel Gibson and Robert Redford and everyone she had ever dreamed about. All the boys or men she knew were either thin or fat. This man was slender. She was staring at a remarkable face, one that might have been carved from rock. He did not come from New York. His existence was a miracle.

She was so confused she stood still, the door open, a frigid wind blowing in, staring at him while he stared back at her.

"I'm not Iris," she managed to say.

Apparently, he didn't hear her. He stared at her out of his own green eyes. The two of them looked as if they might stand there forever, looking at one another, when the oak door was suddenly yanked open and Etheline saw Evelyn, wearing nothing but a Chinese robe, staring into the eyes of a strange man.

"You taken leave of your senses, Lady Clare?" she shouted at her. "Get inside out of them drafts! And put some clothes on!"

Evelyn turned, looked through her, and went through the oak door into the hall, where she stood, looking out at the distinguished man in the gray flannel coat.

"I came to see Iris," he said.

"And who might you be?" Etheline asked.

"An old friend of hers," he said.

"How old a friend is that?" asked Etheline. "I been here sixteen years, and I don't know that face you got on."

"I was engaged to her almost twenty years ago," he said.

"What's that there in your hand?" Etheline demanded. She had suddenly noticed the suitcase.

"A suitcase," said the man.

"I know it's a suitcase. What you need it for?"

"Just tell her I'm here," the man said.

"You want me to go up there and tell that lady some bum she

once took up with is here with his goods in a bag? What you think they pay me for?"

She started to close the door.

"Don't close the door," he said.

Etheline, the dragon, the protector, hesitated. Something in the man's eyes. Something in the eyes, like her mother when she was dying.

Now Mike was at the top of the stairs, watching.

"Who is it, Etheline?" he asked.

"You come and see this for yourself," she said. "How'd you get here, man?" she asked through the crack between the door and the frame. "There ain't nothing in the city running."

"A cab brought me," he said.

"No damn cab can get down this street," Etheline said.

"He left me at the corner of Ocean and Foster," said the man.

"Yes?" said Mike, who was under the impression the man at the door had come to the wrong house.

"I'm here to see Iris Michaels," the man said. "I'm John Stone. She may have mentioned my name."

Oh, good God, thought Mike, the world is coming apart. Thread by thread, it is coming apart.

"She mentioned your name," said Mike. What was the man doing here? He was just as handsome as Iris said he'd been. Once, just once, he'd let himself be enticed into discussing John Stone.

"Just imagine the man in the cigarette ads, the one standing in front of a herd of horses. That's what he looked like," Iris said. "The cheekbones, the rugged look, the broad shoulders. The red flannel shirt, all of it."

"My wife," said Mike. "She's not . . ."

What should he say? That she wasn't well? That she wouldn't get out of bed? That she hadn't spoken, except in monosyllables, for over twenty-six days?

"Iris isn't well," he said.

41

"That's all right," said the tall, elegant man. "I'm dying. I'm not afraid of catching anything."

"Dying!" exclaimed Evelyn.

"Dying?" asked Mike.

"What she need with a dying person?" Etheline asked.

Mike was speechless. He was standing at the door to his own house, speaking, apparently, to a ghost from his wife's past, a ghost who, moreover, claimed to be dying.

"That's why I came," said the man.

"That's why you came?" asked Mike.

This was Iris' fault. She had driven them all crazy. Still, *someone* was standing there. Etheline could see him. No one could drive *her* crazy. Evelyn was mesmerized by him. He was incontestably *there*.

"Yes," said John.

"Iris isn't a medical doctor," Mike said. He felt like an idiot.

"Iris made me a promise," said the man.

"Promised you what?" asked Mike.

"She said that if I ever needed anything, I could come to her."

"You have some memory," said Mike. He was stalling for time.

"Ask her yourself," the man said. "She's standing right there."

"What?" Mike said.

"He's crazy, man," said Etheline.

"She's right there," said John annoyed. He pointed at Evelyn.

"I'm not my mother," said Evelyn, her voice shaking. "I mean, I'm not Iris. I'm her daughter."

"Her daughter," said John.

The light went out of his eyes. Before Mike's eyes, he aged ten years.

"Look," said Mike, "people don't just show up on the doorsteps of their ex-fiancées more than twenty years later. It isn't done."

Iris had been engaged to John for over seven years. It wasn't, she said, an engagement. Not really. It was a marriage. She'd met him when she was sixteen. Mike had refused to read his wife's first novel when a friend told him it was all about John, the man now standing in front of him.

Perhaps he should let him in. Was he really considering it? Allowing his wife's first love into the house? *She* was the one who insisted you never stopped loving anyone. You never got over your past.

He looked beyond the man—John—and up at the sky. The sun glowed small and white as if someone were searching from above with a flashlight, looking for something down below. Good luck to him.

"Look," said Mike, fortified by the sight of the real sun in the real sky, "this isn't a Kafka story. This is real life."

"I don't know much about literature," said the man. "Probably Iris told you that."

Mike stared at him. Evelyn had never taken her eyes from him.

"This is real life!" Mike said. He was having a great deal of trouble making that point. "My wife doesn't owe you anything. What about your family? What about your own wife?"

"Everyone but my sister is dead."

"What about your sister?"

"She lives in China."

"Then go to China," said Mike.

"Amen," said Etheline.

"She's in a mental hospital there. I can't go."

"Etheline," said Mike, "go back upstairs. Evelyn, go back upstairs. And get dressed."

"Send that loon back where he came from," said Etheline, pushing Evelyn in front of her.

"What do you really want from Iris?" asked Mike.

"I want her to take me in. At least for a while."

Mike heard Etheline snort behind him.

"If you'd tell her I was here," John said.

I'll be the laughingstock of the neighborhood, thought Mike.

Iris was, however, a rescuer. If John was who he said he was, perhaps he should let the man in. Stray cats, crazy people. His wife couldn't resist them. *Send these, the wretched, tempest tossed, to me. I lift my lamp beside the golden shore.*

"Iris has been very sick," he said finally. "She hasn't been talking. She won't get out of bed. I don't know if I should let you in to see her."

John said it was up to him. He remembered his friend's advice: they needed a wild card. Perhaps this man was what they needed.

"Let him in," he told Etheline. "I'll go up and tell Iris he's here."

He started upstairs, but Etheline grabbed him by the arm.

"Wait just where you is!" she said. "You knows what this man's dying from? You want to kill off the whole house? What you dying from?" she demanded.

"A degenerative disease," the man said to Etheline. "My muscles are going. The heart's a muscle. When it's weakened enough, it's going to stop. It isn't painful and it isn't catching."

"Degenerative!" exclaimed Etheline, peering at John and backing away.

"No," Mike said to her. "It's all right."

"How do you know he's telling the truth?"

"Are you telling the truth?" Mike asked.

"Yes," said John.

"You believe in Santa Claus, too?" Etheline demanded.

"He believed in the Tooth Fairy," said Nate from his place on the landing, "until it bit him."

"That's my son," said Mike, "waiting to see what will happen next. Nate," he said, turning around, "go to your room. Evelyn, go to your room."

Neither of the children moved.

44

"In your rooms!" Mike said. "And close your doors."

"Follow me," he said to John. "Etheline, take his suitcase."

"I'm taking it, all right," she said.

"Dry it off and leave it in the front hall," Mike told her.

"You gone crazy, man," she said, her hands on her hips, watching Mike go up the stairs followed by John.

"Here he is, Iris," Mike said.

What was he doing, bringing his ex-wife's lover into their bedroom? He ought to be locked up.

Iris was lying on her side, facing the door, propped up on her elbow. Her hair shone in the light. After Etheline washed it, she tucked Iris' hair into the plastic cap of the portable dryer, plugged the dryer in, and went about her work. She came back a half hour later, pulled out the plug, removed the hair dryer, and scolded Iris while she combed out her hair. If it weren't for Etheline, Iris would be infested with lice. And once Iris had been so vain.

Iris was staring, her eyes open so wide, her face so white, Mike thought he had made the wrong decision. She was in another kind of coma. *Now* she was catatonic. John was standing next to him, and since both of them could not pass through the doorway together, Mike stepped through first.

"Iris," he asked, "is this the man? The one you used to know?"

She nodded slowly, her mouth slightly open.

"Well, sit down," Mike said, pointing to the peacock chair.

He looked at Iris, who was propped up slightly, staring at the man now sitting in the chair.

"Do you have a place to stay?" Mike asked him.

"No," said John.

"There's a whole city of hotels out there at the other end of the train line," Etheline said from the doorway.

"You can't send him out in weather like this!" cried Evelyn, who was leaning around her and looking into the room.

45

"What you doing out here on the landing, still naked?" Etheline said. "Didn't I tell you to go get dressed?"

"Get dressed, Evelyn," Mike said. "Now."

"Do you want me to go?" Evelyn asked John, who was still staring at her.

Her father turned to her, astonished.

"Go to your room *now!*" he shouted. When she didn't move, he grabbed her by the arm and steered her down the hall and into her room, fastening the chain lock from the outside. He hadn't locked Evelyn in her room since she was eight years old.

Etheline was waiting for him in the hall.

"That man's here five minutes and the whole house is going straight to hell," she said.

He ignored her and went back to their bedroom. Iris and John were staring at one another like two wary cats.

He decided to wait in the doorway.

"You don't look much older," said John. "No gray hairs."

Iris sank back against the headboard, her head against the carved sun, and watched him. She would have known him anywhere. His face had not changed, although age had sharpened his cheekbones and his skin was crisscrossed by tiny wrinkles. The magnificent quilting on the faces of the elders, she thought, and then remembered that he was only four years older than she was. Her hand went to her own face. There were gray hairs in his beard and his eyebrows were half gray. He was thinner than she remembered.

Mike watched his wife, then looked at John. Five minutes had gone by and still Iris had not said a word. John did not seem unnerved by her silence.

"When I got out of the train station," John said to the room at large, "there was a man in a kangaroo suit handing out leaflets for a new Australian movie."

Iris stared at him.

"When the plane coming here took off," John went on, "we were flying right into the sun. It was a setting sun but it was impossible to tell. It was very bright all the same."

Mike turned around. Evelyn had crept up behind him.

"He talks beautifully, doesn't he?" Evelyn whispered to her father.

"How did you get out of your room?" he asked her, exasperated.

"The same way I always did," said Evelyn. "I put a pencil between the door and the frame and lifted up the chain."

"This is your last chance to get back in your room," Mike warned her.

"You're always trying to get rid of me." Evelyn went back.

"Iris," Mike said, "he says he's dying and he's got no place to stay."

Had his wife forgotten how to blink? He had no idea her eyes could open so wide.

"Do you want him to stay?"

They all—Etheline behind him, Evelyn leaning out of her doorway, Nate leaning out of his—held their breath.

Iris' eyes moved from Mike to John.

"Yes," she said. "It's all right."

"What do you think you doing, man?" Etheline whispered to Mike.

"At least she's talking," Mike said.

"Four words," said Nate, who had come out of his room.

"Come with me," Mike said to John, who followed him into the hall.

5

I WILL NOT believe John is here, Iris thought. He is not here. He left twenty years ago, and I haven't seen him for two decades. It's some kind of hallucination. She turned toward the window and watched the branches: the same trees, the same buildings, the same season, the cold preserving everything as it was. After staring at the familiar scene, she decided that she'd had a dream while she was awake. It could happen. It did not mean she was losing her mind. The thing to do was think about something else, something familiar. People in isolation, she knew, started to suffer from delusions, then hallucinations. That was all it was, a product of her unnatural confinement in her own room. No purple hues in the sky today, she thought: a slate-gray sky. Snow and more snow.

She thought about taking out the newspaper clipping her husband had cut out for her when she was in the hospital but decided against it. She had the short text committed to memory.

MURDERESS ARRESTED IN MANCHESTER

Myrna Loy Roberts, wife of Ed Roberts of Manchester, was arrested today on two charges of murder. Mrs. Roberts is believed to be the Oklahoma woman who two years ago poisoned her husband and daughter.

Mrs. Roberts, originally from Tulsa, Oklahoma, disappeared after administering arsenic to her husband and daughter. Her husband died immediately, her daughter several days later. Police had no idea of her whereabouts until last month, when Mrs. Roberts, who had returned to Tulsa, placed an obituary for herself in the paper. Vermont police noticed the obituary because of the unusual first names, Myrna Loy, which had been the name of Ed Roberts' wife. They decided to investigate, and discovered that Mrs. Roberts was the same Myrna Loy James the Oklahoma police were seeking.

The story is a bizarre one. After murdering her husband and child, Myrna Loy James fled to Vermont, where she worked at the Vermont Printing Press. She soon met Ed Roberts and married him.

Apparently afraid that the Oklahoma police might trace her to Vermont, she returned to Oklahoma where she placed an obituary for herself in the Tulsa newspaper.

Since she was now officially dead, she did not know how she could return to her husband in Vermont. After some time, she concocted an elaborate story. Pretending to be her own twin sister, she wrote her husband a letter telling him his wife had unexpectedly died and enclosing a copy of the obituary.

She waited two months, lost twenty pounds, dyed her hair blond and returned to Mr. Roberts' house, introducing herself as his "dead" wife's twin sister. Mr. Roberts, unaware that the blond, thinner woman was his wife, remarried her.

When the police came to investigate, hoping to find Myrna Loy James, they suspected the twin sister of being the woman they sought. She was fingerprinted and found to be Myrna Loy James.

She will be returned to Tulsa, Oklahoma, under extradition.

When Mr. Roberts was asked how he felt upon learning that his wife had not only been a murderess but had faked her own death and then reappeared as her own twin sister to remarry him, Mr. Roberts said, "I think it's damn strange." When asked if he would marry again, he said, "Why not? I'm the marrying kind."

Members of the community who had known and liked Mrs. Roberts, and welcomed her with open arms, professed great astonishment at such goings-on in their midst.

The house was silent. She turned over and faced into the room. An odd light, sun behind the fog, turning the oak parquet floor gold. How she loved the wax museum, which was what other people called her house. She felt something cool under her left hand and pulled a copy of *People* from beneath her hip. Her children had noticed that if they left simple things on the bed, things that were not beyond her, like *People* or *The Enquirer,* sometimes she read them. They knew that because, when they came to get the magazines, they were thumbed through.

She picked up *The Enquirer* and looked at the headline: RAQUEL SAYS YOU CAN HAVE IT ALL. Big block letters. In smaller, red letters, *The Enquirer* told you what *all* was: a career, marriage, and children. Iris didn't want to read it.

Outside the window, the black crosses of the elms were swaying up and down, slowly, rhythmically, as if mourning something invisible to see.

I would give a great deal, Iris thought, to know what the husband in Vermont really made of those events. He thought he had a wife, and he presumed, before he married her, he knew her well. Probably the first husband thought the same thing. Then the husband in Vermont was informed, by letter, that his wife was dead. He grieved and two months later was comforted by the arrival of his dead wife's twin sister. This woman, the one he married twice, once tried to kill everyone who was close to her. If she'd had enough time, she probably would have poisoned her husband in Vermont.

Masks living with masks. No one knew why the woman killed her husband and daughter. Perhaps she loved them so desperately she couldn't endure worrying about them. Or she might have thought she would die if she had to live with them one more day.

In that clipping, Iris thought, is a true image of family life. The Vermont husband's ignorance kept him safe. Until he died, the Oklahoma husband's ignorance kept him happy. Probably not even Myrna Loy James Roberts knew what passions were animating her. Ignorance was the secret of the family's high-wire act. House samplers should be embroidered *Don't Look Down*.

The husband in Vermont was, it turned out, an idiot, although no more an idiot than the first, murdered, husband in Oklahoma, and the wife was a maniac who needed to have a husband. She needed to have a husband and then she needed not to have one.

She could hear Etheline downstairs, vacuuming. She hoped the rest of the family would soon come back. She had to learn to think about the hospital. If anyone asked her what happened there, she could answer their questions. She didn't have amnesia. But she could not think about it, about what it meant. Instead she lay here, her mind floating this way and that, helpless, afraid to move.

Cars were going by more frequently now. It must be after five. No limousines, though. When she was a child, six or seven, her grandfather still had his big black limousine, and every Saturday after her brother was born, he would come pick her up and take her for a ride around Prospect Park. He was so proud of that car;

51

he had been so poor as a child. He wanted to give his family, and particularly his granddaughter, luxury, elegance, everything he'd never had. He kept red carnations in little glass vases attached to the car between the side windows. Because he'd never learned to drive, he hired a chauffeur and sat with Iris in the back. He always smelled of green cigars.

Two years later, driving with her grandfather after the limousine was gone, they passed a funeral home, and in front of it was a hearse, its back open, and in it a brown wood coffin, very shiny and surrounded by flowers. She turned to her grandfather and asked him, "Grandpa, why did we use to drive around with dead bodies?"

Her grandfather was horrified. He never knew his granddaughter thought the limousine was a hearse.

So much, thought Iris, for good intentions. So much for knowing what other people think.

When she next looked out the window, the elms were like wild-haired women.

Whenever she'd accused her father of not loving her, he'd tell her about the wild woman in the Catskills who one morning went mad and began tearing off her clothes and no one was strong enough to restrain her. She threw people through the air as if they were pillows. But when her daughter came toward her, she quieted and held her arms out to the child. Iris' father said that was what it was to be a parent. When the woman saw her child, she was a different person. There was, her father said, nothing like the tie between parent and child.

Then what about the woman in Oklahoma who poisoned her daughter? What about the husband in Vermont who didn't know his own wife?

The stories, Iris thought, keep telling themselves. They tell *themselves*. And each time, they change. Like the sky as the day goes on, they turn darker. They grow. They interbreed. Images painted on glass, sheet after sheet of glass, Myrna Loy James standing in front of the wild-haired woman, the chauffeur taking them for a ride in the big black hearse.

They turn darker.

When she looked out the window, the house behind theirs rose up above their garage so that its peak looked like the closed beak of a bird. There was a brownish tinge to the sky. Its color fascinated her. In Illinois, where she had once lived, brown skies meant tornadoes. They could sweep everything away.

When she awoke, it was dark. She heard her daughter entering the room. She knew who it was immediately. Evelyn, the terrible teenager, entered rooms as if she were breaking into a strange house. She felt her daughter standing over her.

"For God's sake, Mother," said her daughter.

Iris didn't answer.

"Daddy told me to ask you if you wanted anything."

"No," said Iris. Her voice was loud and frightened her.

She waited for her daughter to leave. When she heard the door click shut, she would know she was gone. The door clicked shut. What that noise meant was clear enough: If Mother's going to stay in there like a suitcase in a closet, we don't have to look at her.

She wanted to call her daughter back, she heard herself calling her back, but she hadn't made a sound.

Iris sank back against the pillows and stared at the pile of journals her husband had put on the bedside table last week, books that recorded the last fifteen years of her life. She knew why they were there. He hoped she would look into them and they would bring back small but necessary moments of happiness; the lines of writing would be like spider threads which would weave up from the page, wrap around her, and reconnect her to life. She knew, without reading more than a page, that there was nothing in the journals to help her. The journal on top of the pile lay open to the first of the pages she had written describing her stay in Cornwall, the only time isolation had ever made her unhappy. She knew those pages by heart. The first sentence read, *It was a mistake to have come here in the first place.*

Was it possible that John Stone was sitting in her bedroom? *Why* had he come? *Why* had she said he could stay? She turned to the window and looked out. The snow was still falling heavily. She heard a man's voice imitating the cooing of the doves. If she were to sit up, she would see the priest who lived in the house behind theirs scattering bread crumbs for the birds who stayed behind for the winter.

Something in her chest twinged painfully. At first she thought the sensation she felt was physical, but when she felt it again, she realized it was memory of previous pain. The veins that had been punctured for the needles of her intravenous began to ache and throb. She felt as if an electric current were running through her body, as if two wires, long severed, had somehow woven together. She felt immense relief, as if for months she had been watching a gold snake, cut in half, struggling to make itself whole, and now, before her eyes, it was. And whole, it was beautiful.

Who can really know which people are most important to them? That is the impossible question, thought Iris. It reminded her of the riddle of the Sphinx. The answer to the Sphinx's riddle was generic. "Man," said Oedipus, and so he was allowed to pass unharmed. Perhaps the Sphinx had wanted him to find the correct answer to the riddle. But if the Sphinx had *told* him the answer to the riddle and then had asked who—who in particular—goes on four legs, then on two, then on three, what then? Could Oedipus have guessed which person the Sphinx had in mind? What would Oedipus' chances have been? None. He would have been eaten immediately. And in light of what was to happen later, it might have been better if the riddle had gone unanswered and the Sphinx had instantly eaten him. If Oedipus had known what was coming, might he not have lied, given the wrong answer, in order to be eaten? If someone asked someone else which people he loved best, he would say his family, his wife, his children, his parents. He would give the generic answer, the sphinxes of his life would applaud him, and he would pass unharmed. But he might be wrong. You didn't always know.

The Sphinx, thought Iris, is life. It lets you go, only to eat you later, when you have fattened and care most about being eaten. It comes for you when you think you are safe, when you believe you know the world.

When you go beyond the general, Iris thought, when you ask who—which particular person, not which species, what kind of thing—you come to the specific questions. Those are the ones you can't answer. Or if you become aware of the answers, they are like ground glass in the throat, sure to kill you. No one, she thought, escapes the jaws of the Sphinx. Sooner or later, it gets you. Sooner might be better, when you have less to lose.

He matters to me, Iris thought, horrified.

Could he be lying?

No one lied about dying. Besides, he didn't know how to lie. A Baptist from Nebraska didn't know how to lie.

Outside her room, she heard Evelyn saying, "But this is *interesting*. Nothing interesting ever happens around here."

"Back," Etheline said, pushing Iris' door shut.

"You have nice children," said John.

My husband hates talking to someone who won't talk back, Iris thought. John, on the other hand, never knew whether the people around him were dead or alive. No wonder he didn't mind.

"When I first saw Evelyn," he said, "I thought I was looking at you. Of course it couldn't have been you. But I thought it was."

His voice sounded sad.

"What," asked Iris, without moving, "are you doing here?"

"I'm dying," he said.

"So I gathered," said Iris.

"I had nowhere else to go."

"What about that wife you were so anxious to leave me for?"

"I didn't exactly leave you," he said.

"The wife," said Iris. "What about the wife?"

"She divorced me. Ten years ago. We didn't have children, and she was tired of how much time I spent in the lab. She said she wanted to make a life for herself before it was too late."

"Did she?"

"She never remarried."

"Did you?"

"Yes."

"What about the second wife?"

"She died in a car accident."

"Oh," said Iris. "I'm sorry. What does this have to do with me?"

"You always said if I needed you, I could come back."

Iris sighed. Even criminals, she thought, aren't liable for their crimes forever. There are such things as statutes of limitation.

"Are you really dying?"

He nodded.

"Are you afraid?"

He shook his head.

"Why not?"

"I'm lonely. Not afraid."

"I thought," said Iris, "you never got lonely. Not as long as you had your lab."

"That was before my daughter died," he said. "After that, the experiments weren't working out. It would take longer than I've got to figure out what went wrong with them. So I left."

"You don't have any money. Is that it?"

"Actually," he said, "I have plenty of money."

"From working at the university?"

"From the land in Nebraska. My parents left it to me. I sold it."

"Your parents," said Iris, studying him. "What happened to them?"

"That's a long story," he said.

She wasn't sure she wanted to hear it. For the seven years of their engagement, his parents had been represented to her as the perfect parents, the most happily married couple on earth. He brought her home to meet them, and they immediately disapproved of her, her wild hair, her refusal to wear stockings, her determination to be a doctor, which in those days had been her ambition. Had they *both* disapproved of her? Probably only the mother, who resented the way she so monopolized their son. And if they were such wonderful parents, why did their son come down with a migraine headache at breakfast every morning they were there? No doubt the long story ended unhappily, as long stories about perfect people always do. She was sure she didn't want to hear it.

"You sold the sacred ground?" she asked.

"Yes," he said. "I did."

"You can't stay here," Iris said. "My husband's a wonderful man, but he's jealous."

"My first wife got along well with my second wife," he said.

Iris thought this over. She could imagine how well the two must have gotten along.

"What's wrong with you?" he asked.

"I was sick. I had a fever. They put me in the hospital, and when I came out I didn't want to talk to anyone. That's all. End of story."

"How did it come to this?" he asked. "You always had such a strong will."

"I got here riding an exercycle," Iris said, remembering the days before the fever began, when she rode the exercycle in her study, pedaling and crying, pedaling and crying, watching the sunsets come and go, thinking that this stationary bicycling which took you nowhere but gave you the illusion of movement had become a metaphor for her life.

"Come *on,* Iris," he said.

"Come on, Iris! You leave me alone in Chicago with a kidney infection and go off to England and send me a postcard three months later telling me it was all for the best because you didn't love me, and you show up here and tell me you're dying. Are you out of your mind?"

Had no time passed? They were snapping at one another as if they'd been living together for years.

"You're probably not dying at all!"

"I am."

"In the first place," she went on as if she hadn't heard him, "you never loved me. What kind of claim can you possibly have on me?"

"I loved you," he said. "For the first five years."

"You never loved me!"

He looked down. "I loved you. *You* didn't love me. I always knew that. You didn't have the slightest idea of what kind of person I was. I spent an entire vacation carving a wooden Eeyore for you, and you thought I did it because I was cheap."

"You *were* cheap," said Iris, who was hoping he would not turn around and look at her dresser. Eeyore grazed there, missing his four legs, just as he had grazed there for the last twenty years.

Why was she being subjected to this?

Little brown spots began floating before her eyes.

"My eyes," she said. "There's something wrong with them. I see spots."

He was a molecular biologist. Once he had studied eyes.

"What kind of spots?"

"Little brown ones."

"If you fix your eyes on a single point, do the spots stop moving?" he asked.

"No."

"They're floaters," he said. "Don't worry about it."

"Do you have floaters?" she asked suspiciously.

"I never had good eyes. You know that, Iris."

"How do I know what kind of bad eyes you had?" she asked.

Was this conversation never coming to an end? Was she never to lie back in bed, turn on her side, and look out the window?

"You have to go. Tomorrow. This is a household, a family. It has its own ways. Its own language. Its own *purposes*. There's no room for you. My husband won't like it. I'm not accustomed to changing husbands every ten years."

To her astonishment, his eyes filled. She had been engaged to John for over seven years. He had never cried.

"Are you crying?" she asked. "You never cry."

She was horrified at herself. She hadn't intended to bring up the past, as if she still cared, as if she still remembered it well. She pulled the comforter up under her chin.

"Of course it's hard to tell," he said, "but you look quite thin."

"Did you think I'd turn into a blimp?"

"You weren't always thin," he said.

"*You* thought anything wider than a matchstick was obese. Is your sister still so thin?"

"She's in a mental hospital in China," he said.

"I don't want to hear about it," said Iris.

Had he come to destroy all her illusions about people she'd once known? Everyone had agreed that his sister was completely perfect, so perfect she ought to be put in the Hall of Standards, the thing against which all other excellent things are measured. How she had gotten into a Chinese mental hospital was undoubtedly a long story too.

"Look," Iris said. "You say you have money. Go to a good hotel. Go to Switzerland. Go to a resort. Get a good nurse. You don't want to do this. It won't do either of us any good."

"Have you been out of the country yet?" he asked her.

"Yes. Stick to the topic. Why come here?"

"You know why."

Her cheeks burned. So it was true. She still loved him. He still loved her.

"I thought we never loved each other," she said.

She loved the pigeons outside her window, but she wouldn't let them in.

"It isn't that," he said. "It's to finish things."

She was frightened. She'd been in this room for so long, barely moving. Now when she got up, she was dizzy. Perhaps he was really the angel of death. Death surrounded him. His child had died, his second wife had died. Death surrounded the people in his family. His brother's girlfriend had tried to shoot herself, and the family discussed why the kind of gun she'd chosen had been unfortunate for her purposes. His sister married a man fifteen years older than she was and, in the weeks following her marriage, involved them in discussions of what hobbies would comfort her in her widowhood. She had already bought three aquariums full of tropical fish and was investigating weaving. A loom, ready to be assembled, was prominently displayed among her wedding gifts.

"You're staring at me," said John.

She said nothing.

"Your parents must have been happy," he said, "when you decided to marry a Jewish man."

Her skin turned to ice. He *was* death. He was trying to make life flash before her eyes.

"Stop that," she said. "Stop referring to ties between us."

"I always thought," he said, "you'd marry Ed. Sooner or later."

"You knew I never wanted to marry Ed. Not after I met you. Stop changing the subject. A nurse. A resort. Switzerland."

"I want to be with someone," he said. His voice was soft.

Was he or wasn't he death? He didn't sound like death. But death was said to be tricky.

"With me?" Iris asked. "I can't take care of myself." She picked at a thread on the blue comforter. "If you stayed," she asked, "what would you want from us?"

"Just to stay. To be part of things."

"I don't know," Iris said. "You're already part of things." She was utterly confused.

"And when it came to it, I'd want you to let me die peacefully. No more hospitals."

"You want to move in here and let us kill you?"

"No," he said. "I just want you to let me alone. At the end."

Oh, God, thought Iris.

"Did Ed send you?" she asked him.

"I don't want Ed to know I'm here," John said. "He'll feel sorry for me."

"And you think we won't? You think we're monsters?"

"You're different," he said.

"How do you know?"

"From reading your books."

"My books," said Iris weakly.

The door opened and Mike stuck his head in.

"Oh," he said. "You're talking. Should I come in?"

"No," said his wife.

No.

He closed the door, turned around, and found himself pressed into Etheline.

"What do you think?" he asked her.

"Kill me if I know," she said.

"They're talking," he said. "She's propped herself up."

"Well," said Etheline, "I see the writing on the wall. I see I

61

got my work cut out for me. The spare room gets cleaned out and the poor man's suitcase gets unpacked."

Poor man!

"Dying is something we all come to sooner or later," she said. "It is the end of us all."

"I better talk to the children about it," he said.

"They running the house now?"

"They live here," he said.

"*Really?*" said Evelyn. "She was engaged to him once? Twenty-two years ago? And he's come back here because he's dying?"

"That," said Mike, "is the long and short of it."

"It's so romantic!" said Evelyn. "A mad passion! My mother!"

"Twenty-six years ago," Mike reminded her; "he met her *twenty-six* years ago."

"I think it's silly," said Nate.

"Is it all right with you?" Mike asked.

"As long as I don't have to take care of him," Nate said.

"*I'd* love to help out," said Evelyn.

Mike went back into the hall. "It's all set," he told Etheline. "You have your cross to bear."

"Doesn't do to make fun of God," she said, picking up the suitcase and carrying it down the hall to the guest room.

"Maybe he'd rather stay in Mother's room," said Evelyn.

"You keep that mouth shut," said Etheline.

"Amen," said Mike.

He looked into their room. His wife was talking. Her cheeks were flushed.

On her way out of the guest room, Etheline was giving orders to both children. "Clean your rooms, man. We have a guest staying here. He ain't used to your ways. And turn that record *down*. I got me a headache already." She went by Mike and down the stairs saying something about lunch trays. It must be, he thought, her religious training. Give her a sick person, he thought, and she smiled as if she'd found a diamond necklace.

"How did you find me?" Iris asked. She had an unlisted number, unlisted under her maiden name.

He must have called her publishing house and used his title: Dr. Stone. "When in doubt, when you want something," her mother used to say, "use your title. Doctor." She wondered what kind of life he'd had. From what little he'd said, it had been one disaster after another. She was surprised to hear he'd had a child. She hadn't though him capable of emotions that lasted for long periods of time.

She stared out the window. The snow was never going to stop. They would all be buried in here together like the mummies in the pyramids. When archaeologists dug them out and found the bones, they would think, naturally, that John was part of the family.

On the other hand, in another sense, his bones had always been here. *He* was what she had been looking for. *He* was the one she had been writing the stories about. He and she were the two people in the woods.

"It's a dream," she said aloud.

"A dream," he said, moving his hand impatiently.

She had sunk back again, silent, on the pillows.

"Are you going to stop talking again?" he asked her.

"I really don't know. It was never a conscious decision."

He pushed his glasses back and rested his head on his hand.

"Are you tired?" she asked him.

"It was a long walk here," he said.

"Why can't you just say you're tired?" she asked. He never could admit to fatigue, any weakness of the body. How did he expect to go about dying?

"Say you're tired," she said.

"All right," he said. "I am."

"Etheline!" she called.

She heard her footsteps, running up the steps.

"What's the matter, the room on fire?"

"He's tired," Iris said.

"His room ready," Etheline said.

His room, thought Iris. She turned on her side and looked out the window. "Well, take him to it. Please."

After a while, Mike came in and asked her if she approved of the arrangements. She nodded. He asked her what she made of it. Was she only, he wondered, going to talk to John?

"For a minute," she said, "I thought he was Death come to get me."

"I hope you didn't tell him that."

"*What* is he going to do all day?" Iris asked. "You don't know him. He has that midwestern conscience. If he wastes more than fifteen minutes, he feels guilty. Get him all the *Time* magazines you can find. When it stops snowing, send Nate out for magazines on foreign affairs. Ones that are about catastrophes and famines in Ethiopia. He likes to suffer over the problems of distant people."

"Right now he's busy talking to Evelyn. She wants to know the story of his life. She's taking notes on the back of a manila envelope, and when she gets through, she's going to the library to look up the disease he has. *So she can be prepared.*"

"He's bringing out the Florence Nightingale streak in everyone," said Iris. "Remember when Evelyn refused to go see your mother because she was so afraid of sick people? She wouldn't go to the funeral either. Notes?"

"Notes," said Mike, sitting down on the edge of the bed. His wife rested her open hand against the flat of his back.

"I'm not better yet," she said.

"I know," he said. "But you're back."

"Partway back."

"What *are* we going to do with him?"

"We'll wait," said Iris. "Until we see Evelyn's notes."

"Do you still love him?" he asked her.

"I never knew what went wrong," Iris said. "Between him and me."

"Why do you have to know?"

"Who knows? But I do. Now I'll have a chance to find out."

"I'd like to know," he said, losing his temper, "what went wrong *here*. When are we going to have a chance to find that out?" He got up and walked to the door. "How do you think it feels to see you talking to a total stranger when you wouldn't talk to me? How do you think it feels, Iris?"

"Don't be angry," she said softly.

"Angry!" he said. "I'm not angry! I'm enraged! Iris, I'm going out. *I* have to shovel the walk. *Nate* has to move a television into the guest room. *You* have to stay in bed."

"I'm sorry," Iris said.

He went out and slammed the door.

6

IN THE SILENCE, Iris automatically turned back to the window. The snow fell in thick slanting lines, forcing a wedding between earth, air, and sky. Why had he had only one child, and then not until he remarried? When she met him, she had not wanted children. She had been convinced she would not be a good mother. He'd had no doubts about his ability to father children and raise them well.

John came back in, found Iris asleep, sat down in the peacock chair, and looked around the room. So many things! There was a whole world on her windowsill. When he first met her, she was the only undergraduate who had her own furniture in her dormitory room.

The windowsill was wide and long, evidently part of a window put in long after the house had been built. A Victorian fringed runner ran the length of it, tannish-brown macramé, a red ribbon threading its way through the upper section. That's a beautiful thing, he thought. That must have taken hundreds of hours to make. She prized things like that. She said she had so little patience. In the middle of the sill was an empty house which had once been a clock casing, and through its round window he saw the eyes of an antique doll watching him. On each side of it were two miniature couches upholstered in red velvet, both covered with gray cat fur. Scale models. He had seen things like that in his father's office. His father would like them, would put them inside one of his model buildings. He used to complain how hard it was for prospective builders to imagine how beautiful the spaces would appear until they were filled with the right objects.

The black walnut house had necklaces hanging from its tower, and one, a long gold snake, trailed onto the sill. There were several woven boxes, and on the post that divided the window in two was a picture he recognized: an embroidered picture of a little doe in a gilt frame. He remembered going into an antique store on Fifty-third Street in Chicago with her and watching her pick up a torn, embroidered evening bag. "How much?" she asked the man. "Oh, two dollars." Two dollars for a torn bag, stiff with age. Then she took it home, cut out the good side of the bag, and took it to be framed.

"No wonder you've never got any money," he'd said.

It was exquisite. It reminded him of his family lake house in Wisconsin. Who had it now? Did they love it, or had they bought it as an investment?

He looked at her ornately carved oak dresser. On it was a forest of cut-glass perfume bottles, jewelry boxes made of pink marble, of Chinese cloisonné, three necklace stands, acrylic stems surmounted by antique doll heads. How did she find anything in such clutter? A gingerbread clock, its pendulum stopped, was hung with more necklaces. Why didn't she fix it? Underneath everything, an elaborate lace runner patterned with what? He pulled his glasses farther down on his nose. Angels. Little pillows, covered with string lace, were laden down by ornate rhinestone jewelry. Not a practical thing in sight.

He got up to look at the dresser. It was worse than he imagined. There were little silver trays filled with earrings. He looked back at the bed. When he had been engaged to her, she never wore jewelry. She went through one winter in Bermuda shorts, knee socks, and university sweatshirts. One of their friends said he wouldn't sit at the same table in the dining hall with them if she didn't wear something else on Thanksgiving. He looked down at the collection of jewelry and remembered that she'd never liked the engagement ring he'd designed for her, a single piece of platinum, twisted at each end, a tiny ruby held up in an arch made by the metal.

"Here," she said when she knew he was leaving her. "Take it back. It looks like the Brooklyn Bridge." When he refused to take it, she said she'd throw it in the lake. Had she? Probably. Women were vindictive. After he left, she took the stereo system he built, each speaker made up of thirty-five smaller speakers, and gave it to the first man she'd had an affair with. She'd been angry. He kept coming back to see her, and when he did, he'd tell her what troubles he was having with the girl he intended to marry. He knew it was thoughtless, but who else should he have talked to? She'd been his best friend. For seven years, they talked only to one another.

"Find another best friend," she told him.

The ring in the lake, the stereo in the lab assistant's apartment.

Why did she want so much of everything? She was always rapacious, a female Attila the Hun. So many things.

Then he spotted something small and brown in the back, and before he reached out to pick it up, he knew how it would feel in his hand. It was the little wooden Eeyore he had carved for her that first Christmas in 1958. No legs. Its little string tail was missing. It wasn't like her to be careless. For twenty-six years it had gone with her from place to place. As he would have if he'd married her. She did not give up on people easily. But she hadn't loved him, although she always said he hadn't loved her.

He kept looking at the shining clutter on her dresser, doubled in the beveled mirror behind him, and saw himself plain, drably colored, incapable of the illuminations and transformations achieved by the light in the room. He placed his hand on top of a tray of rhinestone pins; they were cold to the touch, but inside themselves they blazed with light. Like atoms, he thought. And then the objects changed and he was looking at a different order of things, the small mosaic pieces that made up her soul. It was not the surface of a dresser. It was a landscape. Other people hoarded food. She hoarded beauty, things found in dreams. There was nothing on the dresser that was not beautiful and old and shining.

The spirit too can starve. In times of famine, the spirit could come here. She would give away whatever she had. She was never practical.

If you need it, take it.

She had made sure there would be enough.

Of course, if she died, getting rid of all this would be a nightmare.

He put Eeyore back, grazing just behind the pink marble jewel case. Apparently, he was beautiful in her eyes.

He picked up the red notebook, open on the table next to her bed, and sat down with it. Cornwall! She was writing about Cornwall! His first wife's family had come from Cornwall. He began reading the entry.

What was the point of coming here on vacation in the first place, and at such great cost, so that returning is an extravagance that cannot even be considered? The physical beauty of the place, the rumor that seals could be seen from the cliffs, the idea of a change so complete that the mind would go blank, all made it seem so probable and desirable. The day before yesterday, I was told that the concrete posts don't mark anything historical and in fact I should stay away from them, since most of them show where mine shafts sink into the earth. What an appetite for human bone the land must have.

He closed the book and looked at its red cover. *Challenge* read the brand name in the bottom right-hand corner. She must have bought this book in England, a huge notebook, two inches thick, meant for businesses. On the bedtable were nine or ten such volumes. How could anyone have so much to say about life? When did she have time to notice so much, much less write it down?

When he met her, she was sixteen and a freshman, and he was twenty-one and beginning his Ph.D., and they used to walk over Hyde Park while he marveled at her ignorance of things, her dullness of vision. She couldn't tell a Jaguar from a Volkswagen. He'd ask her to close her eyes and tell him what color the house they just passed was and she couldn't do it. How many floors did it have? She didn't know. But she learned quickly, and then she tried describing how things looked to her. "Don't say it's a black fence," she said. "Say it's a black fence that's *like* something. Try." He couldn't do it. If her stomach hurt, she didn't say she had a stomachache. She said she felt as if she'd swallowed a squirrel. *Metaphors are equations. You do all your work with equations.*

Then her dresser was an equation. Here is a stretch of wood like a plain, a country where everything is beautiful and a cause of wonder. If this small country can be beautiful, so can the large one. The large one may be the country of the mind.

In the months before he decided to come here, he had sat in his study, empty except for an armchair and an electric teapot, and he would hold the teacup in both hands and stare at the wall, remembering. For hours. A kind of compulsive remembering brought on by realizing that he had already lived many more years than he was going to live.

He had remembered everything; waiting for the city bus when

70

he was three years old, so short the bus driver couldn't see him through the door's window, standing there half frozen while bus after bus went by, until the woman in the house on the corner realized what was happening and flagged down the bus for him. His mother was busy with the two younger children. He had been so proud to be independent.

He remembered the house at the lake, and the summers there, their sailboat, their cat, and his mother. He didn't like to think about her. One summer, a friend came to the lake with him and they were sitting at the kitchen table talking about physics, and his mother said she was just a stupid woman and went out of the room crying. His friend followed her. He watched from the window as his mother entered the woods, followed by his friend. When his friend caught up with her, his mother told him that she was going to throw herself under a truck because nobody cared about her. Into the woods or into the lake. Whenever she was displeased.

Iris never liked his mother.

He thought about his daughter in the hospital. He thought about his first wife. He thought about his brothers, but rarely about Iris, who, except for his daughter, had been the most important person in his life. He tried thinking about her, but whenever he did, he became angry. She had overwhelmed him. When he was with her, he felt blotted out. Yet here he was. If he wrote down all he thought about, he would fill five, maybe six, examination booklets.

"What are you doing?" Iris asked suddenly, waking up.

"I was reading about Cornwall," he said. "We went there two or three times. I thought it was beautiful."

"Those journals," said Iris, "are private. Put it back."

"Do you remember my cat? Moonshine?"

"Put it back."

He did.

"I think about Moonshine all the time."

"I'm tired," said Iris.

"You don't remember," John said sadly.

It was their first summer at his lake house, the first house his father had designed and then built with the help of his three brothers. It was a beautiful house, three A-frames connected together, from the front resembling three pyramids, and on the lower level a huge sun deck on which everyone sat and watched the sun rise and set. He told her she would love it there: the quiet, the smell of the pines, the sound of the wind in the trees, the raccoons who came to the door every night. It was a family tradition. Every summer, they all came.

He had neglected to mention the mosquitoes, fat as bumble-bees, which bit both of them so violently that after their canoe trip down the Cabbage River they spent two days in bed, swallowing antihistamines, swollen and feverish. He had also forgotten to tell her, or perhaps he had not known, how much anger there was in the house.

One day, all the men in the house got up early, leaving Iris with her book and his mother, who proceeded to clean the house in a kind of religious fury, saying, as she dusted, that only a fire could get the house really clean. Iris tried to help with the dusting and vacuuming and was sent back to reading *The Good Soldier*.

The men came home, mosquito-bitten, fish-laden, and happy.

In the morning, his mother took the fish she had been skinning since sunup and fried them all in bacon grease.

"Isn't it good?" said John's father.

They nodded their heads violently. John's mother didn't touch her food.

Moonshine was a family legend. He was a wonderful cat because he was beautiful, a Siamese, more intelligent than any other cat, more fierce. He had more nicks in his ear than a hired killer had notches in his gun. But his prime virtue was his independence. He didn't like attention. He wasn't the kind to get on your lap and sit on your book. He was always off by himself, hunting.

After everyone ate the bacon-flavored fish, they decided to go out and practice archery. Faced with John's mother, Iris found a place to hide. Above the linen closet was a crawl space big enough for her and a book. She climbed up, using the shelves for a ladder, and inside she found Moonshine, lying sphinxlike, watching her out of wide blue eyes.

He's going to scratch me, Iris thought. He could. They say he's a mean cat.

But no animal had ever hurt her before, and she didn't want to go down. She said hello to the cat. She curled up in the small space, her back to him. Eventually, she thought she heard purring and turned to face him. He was watching her, his head tilted, puzzled by her. When she started to pet him, the cat became ecstatic, flipping from side to side, finally lying on his back so that she could scratch his stomach. He had the loudest purr she'd ever heard. Eventually, her hand got tired and she stopped petting the cat and lay with her face toward him. He pressed his cold nose to her nose and reached out a paw, his nails retracted. Iris thought about covering her eyes, but closed them instead.

The cat sat on her shoulder and tried to wash her hair, which was long and covered with hair spray, and as he drew a strand of hair through his mouth, his face contorted. He must not have liked the taste, but he continued, determined to wash her. When she came down, she was covered with silver fur.

"Where were you?" asked John's mother.

"Oh," she said, "reading."

"Have you seen Moonshine?"

"No," said Iris.

Evelyn thrust her head into the room. "Mr. Stone," she said, "it's time for dinner. I hope you like steak."

7

IRIS LOOKED OUT the window. The snow was gone. How was that possible? It was still very cold, and when she had last looked, the trees and the roofs had been covered by inches of snow. Now the yard was filled with little mists, which seemed to be steaming up from the ground and thickening with each second.

She found she could get out of bed without touching the floor and floated toward the window, passing easily through the glass louvers. She was not surprised to learn she could fly and hovered in the air until she saw a strange little house built in the middle of her yard. She let herself down through the air so that she could look more closely at it.

It was not a little house after all, but a large granite mausoleum built in the Victorian style. She walked around it, found a cracked wooden door grayed by the weather, and went inside. There was a little flight of stone steps, and she went down, holding on to the rough stone walls. When she got to the bottom, she found herself in a large room, and in the middle of it, all her family were sitting at a long table, eating dinner. When they saw her, they asked her to come over and join them, but she didn't want to do that because she knew they were all dead, even her mother and father, who were living in Florida. While they were in this room, they were also dead. She didn't recognize some of the people at the table, but she knew she would eventually.

Her mother kept motioning to her and pointing at the two pairs of white candles, one at either end of the table. This puzzled her because her mother had always been so afraid of fire she never lit a candle in the house, not even when the lights went out.

Then she was outside the mausoleum, although she could still see them inside. Her mother was bending forward, trying to blow out the candles, but she sat straight up and motioned to Iris to come down.

She found she could float back and forth through the granite walls and stood watching them eat, and they again began asking her to join them, more and more insistently. She was frightened of them and floated farther outside, but no one else was left in the world. Everyone and everything but the people in the mausoleum had vanished.

Mike awoke and found his wife pressed against his back, her arm around his shoulder and across his chest. He was lit with pleasure, a kind of heat that started in his stomach and spread throughout his body. For the last four weeks, his wife had slept with her back to him on the rim of her side of the bed. In the mornings, when he awoke and was taking his underwear out of his top drawer, he looked at the bed and wondered if he shouldn't put something like a small couch up against it. She slept dangerously near the edge. He assumed his wife did not want physical contact, so scrupulously did she avoid it. Often enough, he'd slept in his study.

Slowly, to avoid frightening her back to her side of the bed, he turned over and found himself staring into her terrified eyes. She hugged him, or grabbed him, and her flesh was sweaty and cold. He extracted his left arm from beneath hers, turned over, and put his arm around her shoulders. She pulled her left hand from beneath his neck and began stroking his forehead and then stopped, lying back exhausted.

"What happened?" he asked. "A bad dream?"

She shrugged her shoulders.

"Have you been having bad dreams?"

She shook her head. Before this, as far as she knew, she hadn't been dreaming at all.

"*I* was dreaming all day yesterday," Mike said. "I dreamed that man, John Stone, was staying at the house." He watched his wife's face. "I'm sorry I yelled at you," he said. "Maybe that's why you're having bad dreams." He tended, as Iris had repeatedly told him, to assume responsibility for all difficulties in the lives of the people he loved.

"It's not your fault," Iris said.

"Eggs for breakfast?" he asked.

"How are you going to put up with him?" his wife asked.

"Will he do you any good?" Mike asked.

"I think so," she said.

"That's how I'll put up with him," Mike said.

"But he makes you angry."

"So?" said Mike. "So I'll be angry. Eggs for breakfast?"

Iris fell back asleep. She awoke to find a plate of cold scrambled eggs on top of her notebooks, a pitcher of orange juice set on the windowsill. The snow had stopped, the sky turned blue, and the light was brilliant. The orange juice blazed on the sill. She lay back against the pillow, thinking about last night's dream. She was accustomed to interpreting her own dreams, but she could make nothing of this one. Then she heard the sound of pages, turning. She sat up. John was sitting in the peacock chair, reading her journal.

"I told you," said Iris. "Leave those alone."

"I just wanted to finish the part about Cornwall."

"Finish it and put it back. Please."

He had never been aware of other people's feelings. Now that he was dying, he wouldn't see any reason to be.

"Don't worry," he said, reading her mind. "I'm not expecting special privileges."

"Good," said Iris.

"What's wrong with you?" he asked her. "You seem nervous."

She was surprised. When they had lived together, over twenty years ago, he would try to carry on an interesting conversation with a person in a straitjacket. "Didn't his outfit give you a clue," she'd ask, "that maybe he didn't want to talk?"

"My wife said I changed after my daughter died," he said.

Apparently he wanted to talk about his daughter. She didn't.

"I had," she said, surprising herself, "a frightening dream. Terrible."

Now she expected *him* to change the subject, ask where the morning copy of the *Times* might be, express astonishment when he found out they didn't take a daily newspaper, or ask her what she thought about the famine in Ethiopia. Instead, he asked her what the dream was about.

"A mausoleum. Terrifying, but it didn't seem like my dream. It didn't seem to have anything to do with me."

"It wasn't your dream," he said. "You had my dream."

His dream!

"I have that dream at least twice a week. When my daughter died, I started going to groups studying extrasensory perception. After two weeks, I had an out-of-body experience. Everyone was surprised I had a gift for it. You must have a gift for it as well."

For out-of-body experiences? Evidently extreme grief could drive people crazy.

"Why," she asked cautiously, "did you want to have out-of-body experiences?"

"To find my daughter," he said impatiently, as if the answer were obvious. "Death takes the spirit out of the body, so if I could get out of mine, I could find her."

"Did you?"

"Yes."

"What was it like?"

"Good. You float above your body. It lies there in the bed or the chair and it looks like a corpse, but while it's happening, it's funny. Then you hear voices murmuring, colored shapes circle around like flowers, and one of them starts getting closer and pretty soon you can talk to her."

"What did she say?"

"Mostly that she didn't blame me."

How convenient for him, thought Iris, who wondered if, while she was still alive, he'd told *her* he didn't blame her for dying.

"What was her name?"

"Celia."

Cecilia was the title of her second novel.

"That's a nice name," she said neutrally.

"Well," he said, "your novel. It came out the year before she was born. That's another tie."

"Did she have a middle name?"

"Sylvia."

"Was she named for someone in the family?" She didn't remember any Sylvia Stones.

"No, but my wife liked Sylvia Plath's poetry."

Why not Antigone or Medea or Cassandra, thought Iris, who kept quiet.

"How do you know I had your dream?" she asked suddenly. "Describe it to me."

"It starts out with a fog or a black slab, and sooner or later I go down into a mausoleum and my family's eating there, and they keep asking me to come and eat with them. They don't actually speak but I know what they're saying, and I float back and forth and wake up frightened. I hate that dream."

It was the same dream.

Iris wanted to know when he started having the dream. If he began to have the dream after he knew he was dying, perhaps it was a premonitory dream. If she had the same dream, perhaps she too was dying.

"I started having that dream a long time ago," he said. "Not long after you left me."

"After *you* left *me*," said Iris.

"Mother," said Evelyn, appearing in the doorway, "would you mind if I borrowed Mr. Stone? I need help with my physics homework."

Not again, thought Iris. *That* was how *she* had fastened John to her. No one else had ever been tutored so long, to so little effect. By the time she was doing well in the course, they were engaged.

"Wait!" she said to John.

She motioned him over to the bed.

"I want you to tell me," she said, "what happened in Chicago. I want to know what it was like from your side. I *have* to know."

"You always ask me for things I can't do," he said.

"You can."

Evelyn shifted restlessly, obtrusively, in the doorway.

"Maybe," he said, thinking, "if you wrote down what you thought happened, I could tell you what was wrong with it."

Iris raised her eyebrows.

"I could tell you what I didn't agree with," John said.

"All right," said Iris. "If that's the only way."

She wrote all afternoon.

In the beginning, they loved one another's bodies.

Only later came the talk of souls. Untrammeled countries,

mysterious caves, voices always on the edge of hearing. Later still, she came to feel persecuted by his body and her hunger for it, which seemed to her all there was, as if her mind, which she had once valued so highly, was now an unwelcome, obtrusive guest.

Much later, when he wanted to leave her, she felt his words, his movements, as murder.

She had climbed down the evolutionary ladder, rung by rung, out of the animal world into the world of plants. She was rooted in him, depending on him for light. He said this was a sin.

A writer is a thief, and when I think how much I stole from him, I see how ruthless a thief can be. We plunder our own lives and the lives of everyone around us, and the better we are, the more we take, the greatest of us reaching right through the walls of this world and lifting object after object from the shelves of the next one while the police in that world rush frantically about; and everywhere, the sound of sirens. Sometimes a writer is like a thief who arrives with a huge van, disguised as a mover, and does not stop until he has taken everything, perhaps even the roof and the windows, and the building is left lidless, open to the weather. The writer may not know he is stealing. But at some point I think he does. At that point, if he is honest, he will want to put things back. But how to find the plundered building, which, in any case, existed in the past? How does one make reparation to something that has already gone?

In the beginning, they loved one another's bodies. That was true. True, too, was how they loved everything around them, and after a short while they could not separate themselves from what surrounded them, not even from the fortresslike granite walls of the buildings in whose corners they huddled to keep warm and out of sight. They were part of the old cathedral, and its long-throated spire was their throat, and when they made love in its cold shadows, and the wind blew cold from the lake, they spoke with its great brass tongues. The bars of the fire escapes in back of the old dorms where they pressed against each other in the endless cold that came skating down the streets from the north became bars printed on their souls. They knew early they would never be free. But they could not admit it.

Eventually she took pills and they parted. Which one of them lived happily ever after? A meaningless question, except to two ex-lovers. They both had tragedies. But even a quarter of a century after they met they would examine one another's lives with jealousy to see who had the better time of it. That, of course, was in the beginning.

When they met, they were clear as glass, and when they walked on the Midway, the falling snow fell through them and they were like the moony night, blue and unearthly, and their souls drifted like light snow whirled by a sharp wind which was never as sharp as their feelings. They wore the great gothic domes of the reading rooms as if they were their own hats. These things, dome, wind, snow, spire, slid in and out of each other, wove around them and in them. They were absolutely incapable of seeing things as they were, and there was no price too high to pay for this partial blinding.

Later, they would learn the price and it would be too high. But now they are the carillon ringing out over the snow-covered streets of Hyde Park; everyone else is asleep in the gray stone buildings, but the two of them are on their way to his laboratory. And they are the spires towering over themselves, and they look at each other and are the sleepers in all the rooms on all the blocks around them, safe behind blinds, curtains, and shades. In the lab, they will find a table to make love on, and later they will lie on its cold narrow back, on their backs, facing the ceiling, arms folded on their chests like a dead king and queen on their catafalque. But they are not dead. They are magnificent. And they are not magnificent because now they have bodies whereas before they did not. Before, they had been trees in a forest, perpetually frozen in place. Then they saw one another and began to exist.

Does the great clock hate the faithful man whose fingers, numb with cold, wind it into life? Everything wants to believe itself glorious. Eventually, they wound one another like clocks and learned to hate one another as day by day, everything, every leaf against the sky, every breeze in the wind, said the same thing: together they were everything. And then the subtext became the text. Apart they were nothing.

The great sin they committed was bringing each other to life. They could not forgive each other. Clocks can tire of ticking. They heard the sound of their hearts and that was more than they could bear. She would have faced down the fear. She did not then see the world holding a bloody sword in one hand and a severed head in the other. She thought she would have faced down the fear. She might have fled first. But she always loved him.

And they left each other, and the carillon was far away in its spire, and the spire became itself, cold, separate, and distinct against a distant, enigmatic sky. And when she said everything in the world had become alien and always would be, he did not disagree with her. Instead, he said something about how all things had purposes of their own, and when she asked him what he meant, he couldn't tell her.

Utterly lost. They had had no pasts before and they had none now. Swallowed by the earth and its many mouths.

She put the notebook on top of her journals and stared out the window. Rooftops against the sky. The same sky that had canopied over them twenty years ago.

When he came into the room, she handed him the pages. She listened to the slow, steady sound of the pages turning.

"No details," he said at last. "I used to think about us together. Sometimes one of us was a pile of blocks and the other one would build the blocks up into some kind of structure, a tower, whatever. Then whoever'd done the building would knock the blocks down. Then we'd switch places. I'd be the builder. You'd be the blocks. I think all human relations are like that."

"My God," said Iris.

"What you wrote," he said. "Those two people. They didn't have any pasts."

"No," said Iris.

"But we did," he said.

"Yes," she said. "We did." And she waited.

"I'm not sure I understood what you wrote," he said finally.

"You understood it."

"You usually write in a much plainer style," he said.

They were standing outside the movie theater, waiting for the people in front of them to push out into the clear black-glass cold. Five of them had come to see *Wild Strawberries,* and none of them had a word to say.

"The camera angles are remarkable," said John. "How do you think he photographed the watch?"

They stared at him, amazed.

"Did you like it?" Iris asked.

"The cutting and the themes—" he began.

"Oh, shut up!" everyone said.

"I did what you asked," Iris said. "I wrote it down."

"I get tired more easily now," he said.

Iris lay down, turned away from him, and looked out the window. She, too, had a repeating dream and could conjure it up at will. She was in her house in the country, or in this house, and she would go up to the third floor and stand still, looking at the door to the storage room. If she opened it, she would see something she had been promised long ago, but because she didn't want to be disappointed, she hesitated.

On the other side of the door were empty, brightly lit rooms, and she could see right through their walls. She could see all the way to the white beach beyond them, and to the white shells on the white sand. It was the purest joy, the most marvelous thing, discovering these new rooms which had been there all along. How could she have not known they were there? Why had she never looked for them before?

And the terrible disappointment when she awoke, expecting to see the empty rooms filled with light and knowing they existed only when she dreamed.

She dreamed of extra rooms filled with light. He dreamed of a mausoleum, a world in which everyone was dead, or dead and alive at the same time, as if he didn't know the difference between the living and the dead. As if he didn't know whether he was alive or dead.

"Go over to my dresser," she said. "In back of the little pewter vase. The things that look like little leather books. Look at one."

"What is it?" he asked. "A mirror? Oh, it's a picture. A photograph."

"A daguerreotype," said Iris. "Keep looking at it."

What would he see in it? Tilted one way, it was a mirror, reflecting your own face. Tilted another, it was a photograph of a woman long dead, her cheeks perpetually flushed by the photographer's red dye, cheeks which testified to the blood's once wild, mindless will. Tilted another way, your own face was superimposed on the face of the woman in the little, plush-lined case. There it was, all at once, one generation moving through another, the ghosts underneath everything staring out of one's eyes, the two of them, the living and the dead, one's own face the image that flesh spins for a short time over bone, the embossed leather cases like coffins, the red plush lining inside, protecting the fragile face on the glass, the tributes to the mind's stubborn refusal to let the soul go. The velvet, which feels like moss on a warm stone come upon suddenly in a clearing when the sun's long hand draws the dark wood aside as a hand yanks back a curtain, flooding a frightened room with light.

Those serene faces staring trustingly at whoever opens their cases, just as they once stared at the photographer, entrusting the viewer with their very selves, and at the border of the photograph, the margin of greenish-blue iridescence, the tarnishing of the silver emulsion that keeps their image there, those margins of tarnish moving relentlessly in, like algae on the border of a pond. A band of color that can only widen in the light, beautiful but deadly. Your face, the faces of the dead, the dead and the living together, and the mirror, moon-silver, completely empty.

"Pictures on metal plates," said John. "I read about these when I first got a good camera. It's amazing they can last so long."

"You can have it," Iris said.

"Would you like to see a picture of my daughter?" he asked her.

The child resembled him. She had his cheekbones and his green eyes, but her hair was blond. She was also excruciatingly thin. There was an eagerness about the face in the picture, as if the child had been about to tell someone something when the picture was snapped. In the background were trees and a blue sky. Unreal. A photographer's backdrop. She turned the photograph over. Someone had written, *Celia. Age 8. Class picture.*

Little voices, little bits of souls, trapped in these pictures.

"You can keep it," he said.

She would have handed it back, thinking, No, it was his, what else did he have left of the child? when she thought, If he dies, no one will keep the picture; the child will vanish altogether. She put the picture between the cover and the first page of her notebook.

"Tell me what happened," she said. "Why you left me."

"No," he said. "Tell me about the hospital."

"I can't."

"But," he said, "it's the same thing."

She looked at him, looked away, and was about to drift into the half-sleep that lately swallowed her so easily when there was a knock at the door, urgent and loud.

"Mother," said Evelyn, "I think I'm pregnant."

"Oh, God," said Iris.

"The one hundred and fourth false alarm," said Nate, who was in the hall with her.

"When your daddy come home, he'll take care of this," said Etheline, propelling Evelyn back to her room. Evelyn let herself be dragged off, her eyes fixed on John, not her mother.

"Her mother's daughter," John said, smiling slightly.

"*I* never got pregnant when I was with you!" Iris said. The possibility of catastrophe seemed to have loosened her tongue.

"You never wanted to," he said. "You never wanted to have children with me."

"I was seventeen! *You* didn't want *my* children."

"I always wanted children," he said.

"Anyone's children would have done, even mine. Is that it?"

When had she last felt such fury? Not since she had taken to her bed.

In the silence, Iris felt her body stiffen with fear. Evelyn did not sleep with Justin, who was only fifteen. She couldn't be pregnant. It was impossible. God only knew what strength she thought sperm had. Perhaps she thought they had wings.

"No one," said John, "ever wanted my children. They had to be talked into it."

It's starting again, Iris thought. He's come here to drive me mad. She had taken one look at him and dreamed of having children who looked just like him, her children and his, her life justified by bringing forth such magnificent creatures.

"I wanted them," she said. "You didn't want me."

Outside, the snow was falling forever. The window looked like a television screen that had lost its signal. On very foggy days in Cornwall, the television screen had looked like that: snow and more snow. Was he here, really, or had she conjured him up?

"The reason I can't tell you what happened," he said, startling her, "is because *I* don't know why you didn't love me."

"I adored you! *You* were the one who left *me*."

"I left you because you didn't love me," he said. "Things aren't always the way they seem."

"I took sleeping pills because you wouldn't marry me!"

"By then," John said, "I was only a habit. Everyone told you I was wrong for you. I was a scientist. I was cold. *You* said I didn't have a soul."

"I was angry!" Iris said.

He was silent, accusing her.

"Did *anyone* ever love you?"

"No," he said. "They never did. They pretended to, but they didn't."

"Not even your precious mother?"

"Especially not my mother."

"What about your daughter?"

"She was only a child."

"Did you love her?"

"I'm glad she was alive," he said.

"Can't you say you loved her?" Iris asked.

"I loved her and look what good it did," he said.

Iris sat up and looked at him. His cheeks were wet.

"The worst thing you can do to a person," she said slowly, "especially a woman, is refuse to believe she loves you. You take everything away. If you do it long enough, they're not women anymore. Why do you do it? Why do you still have to do it?"

"The truth is the truth," he said.

"You never knew what the truth was!"

"Then tell me," he said.

"Tell you why I didn't love you?"

"Yes," he said. "Tell me that."

"But I did!"

"You thought you did," he said.

This is what he does to women, she thought. He makes them feel needed, he comes in and says he's dying and he has no one else, and as soon as they begin to respond, he turns on them and tells them they don't know who he is, he's only a poor substitute for someone else, he doesn't know whom he's substituting for, but he's not the one who's wanted. He waits until he holds your heart in his hand and then says it isn't a heart at all, it's fake, it's counterfeit, and he hands it back to you.

No, that's wrong. Before he tells you you've never loved him, he tells you he doesn't love you. He waits to see what you'll do. He tests you. Can anyone ever cry enough?

In the dormitory laundry room, in the basement of the old dorm building, she was sitting on a table waiting for their clothes to finish spinning in the dryer, and tears were pouring down her face. She had been crying for over an hour and showed no sign of stopping. She cried as she breathed in and out.

"Change your mind," she pleaded with him. "Last week we were so happy. You said we were!"

He took out the clothes and began folding them.

"When you're finished, can we go for a walk?" she asked. The crying continued, rhythmical, eternal. He handed her a handkerchief taken from the pile of clothes.

"What changed?" she asked. Sorrow had driven her out of her body, and she sat, a tiny doll, high above herself, looking down, asking herself how she could so humiliate herself. She was young, and young in the relationship. She had not yet learned to ask herself how he could so humiliate her.

Such humiliation, such weeping, was worth it. Anything was worth it because the week before they had been so happy. So arbitrary, so unexpected was his announcement that things had to end, as if the happiness itself was the reason behind his decision. Because nothing else had happened but the happiness. How could that be a cause for bringing things to a stop? She cried until three or four in the morning, and he sat next to her, ostensibly waiting for her to stop, to calm down, so he could, in good conscience, leave her. But by two o'clock, she knew he had changed his mind and she knew that the extravagance of her grief had changed it. Thereafter, the scene would be repeated, more and more frequently as the years passed, and finally tears were not enough to impress the fact of her devotion upon him, and she swallowed sleeping pills.

That, she thought bitterly, should have impressed him. But she had made the mistake of not dying, and so he could tell her she hadn't been serious. Even if I had died, Iris thought now, watching him, I would have failed his test. If he could have spoken to me, wherever I was, he would have told me I hadn't loved him enough to stay with him.

To be compelled to test people who loved you, as he did, it

was a kind of death, wasn't it? No one could pass the kind of test he set.

She looked out the window again, and the windows became two large eyes, and she walked into one of them and found herself in the first of many huge abandoned rooms. No one had been in the room for years. All the furniture was covered by white sheeting and dust was thick everywhere, a heavy blanket on all the surfaces, turning grayish-black what had been white. Streamers of dust hung down from the beams on the ceiling. They gathered in the corners of the room and hung down against the walls. There was a fine webbing of dust strands between the beams, thin, thin lines like fine quilting.

She walked toward a mantel, high and mirrored, but the silver backing had pitted and the mirror reflected nothing. On the top shelf of the mantel were two bronze urns, dust covered. There was no sound here and no possibility of sound. She went into the next room and found the same thing: furniture covered with sheets, dust and silence. But now the things in the room seemed to be saying, in faint, strained voices, *People lived here. Once people lived here.* It was a terrible place. She had walked in through the doorway of his eyes and was standing in the middle of his soul. She was also in Riverdale Hospital, in her hospital bed, the striped yellow and orange curtains drawn around it. The two things were the same.

"You got too close," he said. "You started to cross over."

"What?" she said.

"In the hospital. You were there too long and started to cross over. I know hospitals. You should tell me about it."

Did he also know what she had seen when she looked out the window, how his soul had appeared to her?

"In my other dream," he said, "I'm in a house full of empty rooms and I go from one to another trying to find someone but they're all empty. Empty and dusty."

Iris began to cry.

"Tell me," he said.

She said she would imagine the last thing he wanted to talk about was a hospital.

"The worst already happened," he said. "Tell me."

Once, she had been the one to coax, to insist: Tell me. Talk. You wouldn't have those headaches if you'd talk.

"I tried to raise the dead," said Iris.

8

IN THE MONTHS before the publication of her last novel, Iris had become more and more nervous, a kind of perpetual agitation that caused her to jump into the air whenever anyone opened a door to her room. To others, she seemed to be waiting for something. She knew she was really concentrating all her energies on a problem for which she had no solution. She had no idea what she thought about during the many hours she spent in her study. She told her husband and friends that she was in a peculiar state, and everyone, including Iris herself, assumed this state had something to do with finishing a novel and awaiting its reception. "You're always crazy when you finish a novel," Mike said. "You're always crazy before you begin one."

Then there had been a period of unusual peace, during which Iris began to make frequent trips into the city, particularly to Central Park, where she would sit on a large granite rock and look back at the corner of Eighty-sixth Street and Central Park West, the block on which she had lived before moving to Brooklyn. She sat there and thought how well she was surviving, although, until that moment, she wasn't aware of anything menacing her or of the need to survive.

Across the street, near the entrance to the park, some men were tearing up the asphalt, and the yellow sawhorses made all the cars crossing town veer out of their lane, so that there was an endless flurry of honking horns and shouts from drivers rolling down their windows to yell at the drivers in cars going the opposite way. It was a beautiful day, and she was feeling sorry for herself because she couldn't stay and watch the wind blow the dull gold leaves that escaped from the park across the road and under the wheels of the cars. She had mystical tendencies when it came to autumn and dry leaves blown by the wind, little mummies, dry bodies of tiny animals whose souls flickered in the light and then fell back to the browning grass, where they turned to a kind of ash and rose in the air like pollen.

She waited for the bus, still thinking about how well she was surviving and how curious that was, since nothing unusual had happened. She had promised a friend to visit her studio and look at her paintings before they were exhibited, but at the last minute she changed her mind, decided to go later in the day, and went back into the park.

She found her rock. The sun was still warm, and she leaned back, running her fingers over the rock's pocked surfaces. She thought, The city never changes. And then two middle-aged men, both bearded, both wearing horn-rimmed glasses, jogged by in ink-blue suits trimmed with white stripes. Ten years ago the city had sported few joggers. She looked after the jogging men and thought, What a melancholy sight. How much everyone wants to stay alive these days. And then she thought, Why shouldn't they?

Two men walked by, their arms around each other's waists. One man had his thumb hooked through a loop of the other's corduroy pants. A young man hurried across the park, looking from side to side, turning to look behind him. Clouds were boiling around the sun and the trees cast longer shadows. Why shouldn't they all expect to stay alive in an age like ours? The age promised such miracles. *Lucky to be alive in such a glorious time. Such wonderful things happen. When we're learning so much.* Phrases from a conversation she'd had with a friend who worked at the Rockefeller Institute.

She thought about a friend whom she had not seen for almost a year, and the test her friend had just had because she was pregnant and over thirty-four, a test that allowed the doctor to determine if the unborn baby was healthy; a sonogram located the baby so that the surgeon could safely guide the needle into the womb. *It was wonderful. You could see the baby on the screen. He had his fist in his mouth.*

Iris said it was wonderful. It was too bad you couldn't keep such pictures forever.

But, said her friend, you *could* keep them forever. She had them. She took out three pictures and handed them to Iris.

There was the baby, he or she, they didn't know yet, floating in a sea of dots, barely visible, as if dreamed, as if forming himself out of the dots, as if one's eyes were bad but, if you squinted, if you knew how to look, you could see him clear and shining, his fist in his mouth, already chewing on the world. In the second picture, the baby stretched out his arm. *How much room is there? How much room is there for me?*

The results came back and the baby had to be aborted.

Sitting in the autumn sun, Iris thought about the pictures and what happened when civilians dabbled in the black arts. Seeing into the future. Promising immortality. Little Fausts in white lab coats. Then she thought about her novel, soon to be published, in which she told the story of her grandfather's life. The terrible silences in her house when she was a child, of which she understood nothing, the silences from which her grandfather, dead now for thirty years, had rescued her. Soon there would be no one who would remember him. All writers try to stop time, to prevent the erosion of memory. And what did they get for it?

94

What had Faust gotten for it? In the end, they were ripped apart. In the last act, their arms and legs were thrown onto the stage through a trapdoor.

Because she had written a book in which she had tried to raise the dead, something was going to happen.

Artists and scientists locked themselves in book-filled rooms, while on the floors below their families burned with fever, looked up the stairs with longing or hatred, called them out of their studies or laboratories at their peril.

Too many things waved and stepped off the edge of the world.

Wives of scientists she knew looked for their husbands as ancient people were said to descend into Hades seeking their beloved dead. Artists, scientists, they came out of their sanctums unexpectedly, at odd hours, muttering about hidden variables or perspective or point of view. At times they were glad to see other humans if they happened to be in hallways into which they had come to clear their minds. The work had to be done. If someone was stabbed in the hall, they called a doctor, but the work waited. A week later, looking up from a typewriter, a computer, a microscope, they might ask, *What happened to her? Did she die? Who stabbed her?*

The first review of the book was unfavorable, and she appeared to take no notice. She came down with a fever, retreated to her study and its bottle-green velvet fainting couch, a couch with carved animal feet, and let herself be tended by Etheline. She spent hours on the couch, staring across the room at the family photographs on the wall, running her fingers over the quilted pattern of the couch fabric. Then she would suffer sudden attacks of fury and her body would go hot. She would wait until the house was quiet, get up, and begin pedaling on her exercycle and wail. She saw herself in the reflection of the mirror. She heard her voice. She was a wolf in a trap.

She threw things. She pounded on things. She burned with a

shame so intense it left her weak. She learned to cry quietly so that no one else in the house could hear her, and while she cried, she invented voodoo rhymes about the reviewer of the book, the editor of the book review section, and finally about herself. She did not talk to anyone because the rage was too great, and rational words of comfort would only drive her into incoherent bouts of screaming for which no one would ever forgive her.

It was an obituary, not a review. She had not brought her grandfather back from the dead. She had not vindicated him. She had held him up to ridicule, disgrace, criticism, worse than anything he had ever known in life. The book could not bring back the man he was. It was a horrible caricature, a travesty. She had dug up a grave and left the body exposed to the crows and the weather. For this attempt to resurrect the dead, there would be a terrible punishment.

She spoke to no one because she knew no one who had committed the crime of which she was now guilty. Her fever rose. She continued riding the exercycle. The dog and the cat stayed in her room constantly, leaving only when called down to eat. They stayed with whoever was sick. Why were they with her? She was merely sick with rage. When they lay on the couch with her, she cried into the dog's side, sobbing so violently he would get up, stand over her, and lick the top of her head.

No one in the family knew what was happening.

Eventually the crying stopped and the bouts of anger became less frequent. She looked around the study unperturbed, thinking how nice it was to be in it, how nice a room it was, how nice it was to be going nowhere, not having to go anywhere, how nice to have no one expect anything from her.

Friends called and asked her to visit but she refused. She was ashamed to be seen. Inside, in her room, the wild shame was tamed by the familiar things around her. She had found a safe place, which she could only leave for another safe place.

Her fever, which had been 99 degrees, climbed slowly until it reached 102. She noted the climb with satisfaction. The rage that filled her, that took the place of skin and bones, of mind and heart, was burning up her body. When the rage died down, the fever would go.

Etheline, who brought her lunch and dinner, thought otherwise. Mike called the doctor, who warned that if the fever continued she would have to be admitted to the hospital for tests. She paid no attention. Of course it would rise. It would rise and then it would go away altogether. In his own study, Mike thought about his wife. What was she suffering from, really? Overwork? She overworked herself. Criticism? She was used to that. She had, he thought, a virus, which was producing a black mood. She would get over it. He told her so. But if it was something more serious? His mother had died of cancer. Could they begin with fevers? He called the doctor, who said, Yes, they could.

Then, said Mike, he wanted her in the hospital.

Let's wait a few more days, the doctor said.

Iris, who had ears like a fox, heard every word her husband said.

In her study, she watched soap operas, thought vaguely about writing an article on them, and did number stumpers on her daughter's computer. Between four in the afternoon and eight at night, when her fever rose to 104, she did nothing but huddle under three blankets and listen to her teeth chatter. This was fine. This was what she wanted, suffering that led to absolution.

The doctor continued to threaten; Mike continued to worry.

"It can't be her state of mind," said the doctor. "States of mind don't cause fevers that high. I have other patients who get bad reviews and ride exercycles. No temperature, no tests."

What exactly, Mike asked her, was she unhappy about?

She didn't know.

After he left the room, she cried into the dog's stomach. Another sin, this time one of omission. She knew more than she had told her husband. For this, too, she would be punished.

She had always assumed she had a happy childhood. Now she was no longer sure. Those terrifying silences, unexplained, waiting in the corners of rooms. But even if her childhood had been terrible, hadn't she long since concluded that all childhoods were terrible?

The doctor said she had to go to the hospital.

She was glad to go. She thought of it as a place of refuge.

"A place of refuge!" said John. "Ha!"

"Didn't they take good care of your daughter?"

"If she complained," he said, "they said she was a spoiled brat. That's what they called her. A child with bone cancer."

"When I complained," Iris said at last, "they sent a psychiatric social worker to see me. If adults complain, they're crazy."

"Yes," he said, "well."

I should never have left that study, she thought. I would have gotten well there. She thought about her study, glowing strawberry red, and it seemed far away, as if it were not merely on another floor but floating somewhere in another life.

"Would you like to see my study?" she asked.

Was she really planning on getting out of bed?

When she was twelve, her grandmother, who had been senile for years, was admitted to a teaching hospital. At family get-togethers, everyone lamented her senility because she had been so intelligent. She was admitted when she was ninety-four, and as soon as she was wheeled into her room, she began shouting in her thick accent, "No students! No students!" Senile as she was, the sight of a hospital restored her senses. For one hour, she shouted, even through her daughter's fingers, "No students! No students!"

98

"I should have known what to expect," said Iris.

"Were you ever on a medical floor before?"

"No. Always surgery. I thought I'd be out in two or three days. All I took was a nightgown."

"I'd like to see the study," he said.

Iris sat up and swung her feet to the floor. "The floor's cold," she said, astonished. Why hadn't she noticed when she'd gotten out of bed before? Thick socks. Usually Etheline put heavy socks on her unresponsive feet. All the socks must be in the wash.

"When did you get sick?" he asked her.

"November. Sometime around then. It wasn't cold."

"It's the beginning of February now," he said. "It's been cold a long time."

"February," said Iris. "Are you strong enough to walk upstairs?"

"I'm very strong," he said. "Still."

The long muscles of her legs were unaccustomed to bearing her weight. Her legs felt porous, her bones heavy. Suppose she fell on the steps? He had never been able to tolerate the sight of weakness.

Under the eyes of her astonished family, including the possibly pregnant Evelyn, the two of them left the room and walked to the stairs.

"I'll go first," said Iris.

The study was just as she had left it. The dust, which in the winter settled heavily on everything as soon as the oil burner was switched on, covered every object. Standing in the doorway to her own room, she felt as if she were trespassing upon someone else's grave. Naturally Etheline had not touched it for months.

John had never seen such a room. It was like the surface of her chest of drawers, only far more elaborate, more layered. Except for the ceiling there was not an unadorned inch of space. He recognized the strawberry pink of the walls immediately. When they were living together in Chicago, Iris had painted their dining room that color. On one wall she hung the rug her grandfather had given her for an engagement present.

A beautiful bookcase with leaded glass doors ran the length of one wall, and above it hung a tapestry, a copy of a Breughel painting he remembered seeing, although he did not know where. Oh, he did. His sister, who was an art historian, had once hung that picture in her bedroom.

The top of the bookcase was so covered with things that there was no appearance of clutter. Instead the objects formed something solid, a painting of sorts, made up of found objects, all of which somehow blended one into another. At either end of the bookcase were brass statues of women dressed Turkish style, their arms stretched out toward one another. In between the two statues were dozens of antique dolls, meticulously and fantastically costumed, some sitting in doll-sized peacock chairs, others standing up. There were ivory figures, of people, of fish turning into people, of men riding strange creatures that resembled dogs but were not dogs: these stood among the dolls. He walked closer to the bookshelf and saw a small display cabinet with a mirrored back mounted on the wall above it. On its small shelves were tiny cloisonné boxes, an inkstand carved to resemble a walnut, and what appeared to be several lead spiders. He took one down and turned it over. Little Russian letters were engraved on its body.

He had seen the large rolltop desk when he walked in, but it was covered with things, not meant for use, and the child's oak rolltop desk across from Iris' fainting couch was used as an end table. She had banished, he saw, all modern things except appliances from the house.

"Where's your desk?" he asked.

She pointed across the room at the window. In front of it was a small square black-walnut table. Something covered by a quilted sheet sat on it. He went over to look at the desk. Its top was covered in red velvet, and on top of that was a thick protective pane of glass. Under the glass were old photographs.

He remembered that she could never work unless she was looking out a window, but her window was filled with geraniums, all in full bloom. He touched a pink blossom gently. *Geraniums are such fine flowers. I don't know why no one appreciates them.* His mother had always said that.

"If you're going to stay in the room," said Iris, "sit in the chair. I'll sit on the couch." He was sick, he was dying. Someone would have to call their doctor and ask him questions. What should they do? What should they expect?

He sat in the chair, a high-backed oak chair, carved, as was all the furniture in the house, and was surprised when his feet barely touched the floor. He was a very tall man. Someone had put large gold casters on the chair's feet. Otherwise it would have been too heavy to move about the room.

It was an L-shaped room, and the couch, in the small part of the L, gave the impression of a pallet in a den or a cave.

He looked out the window through the geraniums. Across the narrow corridor of air separating her house from the next was another window, the shade dirty and pulled down. From one of the geranium's clay pots, a pitted metal face of a doll stared at him, eyeless. "A mold for a face," said Iris, who had been watching him. He turned his head slightly and found himself looking at a stained-glass lamp.

"You've still got it," he said.

They had gone to the Loop for something or other and then begun driving around when Iris started screaming and pointing backward. He turned the car around and they stopped in front of the store. She jumped out before the car came to a stop, and when he caught up with her, she was staring into the closed store window, her hands splayed against the storefront glass as if they had frozen there.

"Look!" she said. "There!"

"At what?" he asked finally.

"At the lamp! How can I find out how to get it? I'll borrow money from my grandmother for it! I've never seen anything like it!"

He looked at the lamp. It was only stained glass. He saw stained glass in church every Sunday during his childhood in Nebraska. He said something to that effect.

"If I ever have a lot of money," she said, "I'm going to build an entire room out of stained glass."

They found the phone number of the owner written on the awning. Iris called him, and the price of the lamp was set at forty dollars.

"Forty dollars!" said John. "For something like that!"

After she called, she wanted to go back to the store immediately, before someone else had a chance to buy it. He said he was sure the lamp had been there for months and would be there for months if not years. She was not to be pacified. *When* could they leave to get the lamp? *When* could he be out of the lab? She asked these questions as she cleared off her desk and made a space for it.

On the ride back from the store, the stained-glass lamp in a carton in the back seat, Iris hung over the front seat, holding it. If the car stopped suddenly, she said, the lamp could slam forward and break. There would never be another one like it. It was not a lamp but a dream.

In the end, she didn't borrow money from her grandmother. He gave her the lamp as a present for her nineteenth birthday. Her twentieth birthday was the one that upset her. They had walked the streets for hours while she said again and again, "This is the last day I'll be a teenager." She had her aging crises earlier than anyone else. She was always, as she herself said, ten years ahead of other people, in her hopsacking dresses, her stockingless legs, her long hair. Ten years later, everyone looked as she had looked a decade before.

It was a beautiful lamp, dull when unlit, but when lit, its green panes glowed like the leaves of the geraniums with the sun behind them. A rim of orange and red flowers amid dark green leaves waited to show its splendors. He remembered the lamp. When he left her, he had taken nothing. When he left his first wife, when he left his house to come here, he took nothing. Nothing seemed to belong to him.

Today the lamp was priceless.

"You're the best known of all of us," he said aloud.

"I wish I were better known," she said.

"You were always ambitious."

So was he. He had begun as a physicist and told her again and again that all great discoveries in theoretical sciences were made by men who were twenty-five, twenty-six at the latest. When he reached his twenty-fourth birthday, he said he saw the writing on the wall and was changing to molecular biology where he would still have a chance. He had not accomplished great things. But then neither had she. And even if she had, she wouldn't know in her own lifetime. It took a hundred years to sort out the great from the non-great.

"I never knew you wrote," he said. "I never knew you *wanted* to write."

"At the time," Iris said, "you were the only creation that could get my attention."

He looked at her, sitting on the fainting couch, her back against the wall, under a copy of a primitive painting: a small girl, holding her cat. The face of the cat and the face of the child were almost identical.

Perhaps she had been writing while they lived together. She had never seen him as he was. She had been creating the character she needed, her own version of him, working without words. At twenty-one, he had not seen himself as he was. He had begun as a character in a novel neither of them knew existed.

He looked at the legal bookcase to the left of her desk. The top shelf was filled with doll house miniatures, little couches that resembled pieces of furniture he'd already seen in the house. The furniture sank beneath a crowd of miniature dolls surrounding them. Other dolls, only a few inches taller, towered over them like giants. There was no sense of scale in this room. Everything echoed everything else. Themes were repeated. Things changed from themselves into ideas of themselves. The room erased boundaries.

"What's under the blanket?" he asked. He pointed at the desk.

"You can take it off. It's a word processor."

"Do you use it?"

"Yes."

It had taken her five years to learn to change the ribbon in her electric typewriter, almost as long to set the margins. He remembered the frantic calls to the lab for instructions. Did you or didn't you cut off the metal tab at the end of the ribbon. You didn't. But she already had. When was he coming home? The ribbon was winding out of the typewriter like a thin black tongue.

"Who taught you?" he asked her.

"My husband."

There was a silence while he studied what appeared to be shelves and shelves of literary magazines and learned journals. Finally, he picked one up and scanned the table of contents. There was her name: Iris Otway. She had written more than he thought.

"How is it with you and your husband?" he asked finally.

She didn't know how to answer him. If she went into details, if she said how happy she was, he would think she was taunting him with his own failures. She had been married almost twenty years. Writing, children, the house, her life, all branched from the same source. When she and Mike quarreled, she fell asleep and dreamed she had her arms around his waist and was leaning back, looking up at him, and he was smiling down at her, and the feel of his body against hers, the sight of that face, made her resolve, each time, upon waking up, to apologize even if she were not at fault. She could rarely keep such resolutions, but no matter what the argument, she woke up flooded with love.

Over twenty years ago, rage had been at the heart of what lay between them.

She loved this room and its timeless quality, each of the artifacts from a different period of time, mixing zones of time in the dusty air.

She looked at the lamp and tried to think back to what had gone wrong between them. But she would go back through her memories, and when she came to the time they no longer made one another happy, it was as if she came to an empty space, as if the film in the camera had failed to record images. There was a blank space in the past, in her memory of it. She remembered instead family arguments, long discussions of whether or not a woman ought to go to graduate school, the day her father had brought her to the university, two days before school opened, and left her in a hotel overnight. She had never been away from home before.

It was impossible. In her memory, they had been completely happy and then they had been utterly miserable. There had been no transition.

"We love each other," she said at last. "We did from the beginning."

"You don't *adore* him?" John asked. He could not keep the sarcasm out of his voice.

"Sometimes," she said.

"Does he adore you?"

"Sometimes."

"Does he think you're perfect?"

"He did in the beginning."

"And did you like it?" John asked.

"I took care to disabuse him of the notion," Iris said.

"Some people refuse to be disabused."

"It took me some time," Iris said. "Of course, you wouldn't understand that. I was always unsatisfactory to you, never what you were looking for. I was too fat or too short or had too much hair or too much temperament or was too dependent or too independent, whatever."

"You were never too independent," he said.

"I was. In the beginning."

"Did you ever get your Ph.D.?" he asked her.

"Many years ago."

He made a face, as if to say he was impressed.

He had been competitive all along. She'd never suspected that. He always told her he wanted her to do well. If his sister had only gone to college before having children, he used to say, she would have been so much happier.

"I knew I wanted to marry Mike," she said, "because as soon as I saw him I knew I wanted to have children."

"Things like that are important," he said.

Now he was angry at her.

"He's very stubborn," Iris said, "and he's a much better person than I am. He does his work. He's not terribly ambitious when it comes to the world outside this house. He'll do anything for the family. Most fights here seem to start because he won't say what he wants to do. I don't know what to do with that kind of goodness. Selflessness. Whatever it is."

"You never had any experience with that kind of thing before, I take it?" John asked her.

"You were the one who asked how things were between us," she said.

He didn't answer her.

"Do you want to use the word processor?" she asked him.

"I barely know how to use it."

"Do you *want* to use it?"

"To do what?"

"Write something. Anything."

He laughed. "Do you really think I'll write something? Do you really think I can?"

"Try," she said.

"Write about what?"

"Anything. I'm going downstairs. I'm tired."

Several hours later, she heard her printer clattering.

When John came downstairs, he saw Mike sitting on the edge of Iris' bed, stroking her hair. While he watched, Mike picked up the brush and starting brushing Iris' wild blond curls. Apparently Iris didn't like it, because she took the brush back and brushed her hair herself.

From the little room that held a television, a couch, and many chairs came the sound of crying. Evelyn. She saw him, sat up, and patted the space next to her. Why, he asked her, did she think she was pregnant? Because, she said, she was two weeks late. Girls who were fifteen, he said, were often irregular.

She dried her eyes and looked up at him. "If I'm not pregnant," she said, "will you come with me to celebrate?"

"Like where?"

"The coffee shop at the Junction."

"It's a date," he said.

"I feel better already," said Evelyn.

Why bother figuring out what women wanted? he thought. They always let you know. He thought of Mike, brushing Iris' hair. The man must be hopelessly stupid. Women were like cats. You didn't touch them until they let you know how they wanted to be touched, and even then you checked to be certain they had withdrawn their claws. And you didn't check once. If you valued your life, you checked every few seconds.

In the morning, after everyone else had gone, John came into Iris' room. She was sitting up, her back against the headboard. "Here," he said, handing her a piece of paper.

These days I observe how archaic are the icons of my youth. I still reread my old orange volume of Arthur Waley's translations of Chinese poems, and one I often think of, as I walk each morning from my house, across the Methodist church's parking lot, and past the Episcopal cathedral to my four-story modern lab, is a poem which Po Chu'i wrote to the friend of his youth, Li Chien, in 818:

> The province I govern is humble and remote;
> Yet our festivals follow the Courtly calendar.

But you don't have the same calendar I do. I clung to my peculiar religion fairly quietly during our youth, going out early on Sunday mornings to the chapel while others slept. My church is one which keeps a calendar, and soon now Advent, the penitential season before Christmas, will open our new year.

Po describes how he celebrates, in his rural province, the same ceremonies in which he and Li used to ride their horses together in the streets of Peking. Your calendar has continued to be the calendar of a person surrounded by a family, and mine whatever I can maintain in the midst of an isolated life in this remote, empty province.

Before setting out to come here, I did regular Saturday chores all afternoon, and as I drove home from the drugstore,

the last stop, the sun came down under the clouds and il-
luminated the flat, gently sloping city in gold, and trails of
mist floating beneath the layer that shadowed our day. Now
the crisp little crescent of the new moon is setting in the west
against the last dark turquoise and orange after the sun's
departure, and I will listen to tapes of The Midnight Special
and make the rest of my dinner. At night, the last traces of
the clouds will stripe the sky, hiding stars behind them.

"You're a better typist than I am," Iris said, looking the page
over. "Did it take you long?"

"It took me *three* hours!"

"You get faster with practice."

"You didn't like it?" he said.

"Like what?"

He didn't answer her.

"What did you copy it from? I don't remember reading that
passage."

"*I* wrote it."

She slid down in the bed, staring at him.

"Well, you ought to remember the book of Chinese poems,"
he said. "You gave it to me."

"Good Lord," said Iris, picking up the sheet of paper and
rereading it again. "You wrote it?"

"I told you."

"It's very good," she said at last.

"Do you mind if Evelyn takes me to a coffee shop?" he asked.

"No, go ahead," she said.

"When she comes home from school," he said. "If everything's
all right."

"If she's not pregnant?"

"Yes."

"She's not pregnant," Iris said.

"I know."

"Look," she said, looking down at the sheet of paper, "would you mind leaving this here and going out for a while? Just out of the room?"

There was something wrong with her eyes. Wherever she looked, a crack ran down the middle of things. The peacock chair he had been sitting in was cut in half by a broad stripe of light. The image of John sitting in the chair persisted, cut in half by a stripe of light. Life had split him open. Perhaps the death of his daughter had done it. Something had.

She read the page, read it again, put it down, and read it again. When things had ended between them, she'd told herself he had no soul and would never have one. But someone with a soul had written this page. She sat still on her bed, as if the bed rested not on the floor, but on top of a high, swaying pole. Her assumptions about the world were cracking, as walls crack in an earthquake, chunks of plaster falling away, leaving the lathing, and then the lathing crumbling, the weather outside roaring in, always cold weather.

When he left me, she thought, I believed he was dead. I had to believe he was dead. There was no other way I could go on. It had seemed a sensible way to proceed.

Now she understood that, for her, he had never died. Daily, her memory resurrected him, making him sacred and powerful. Yet her memory of him grew weaker as years passed, so that every day he died, slipped farther from her, and this was a new death every day because she had only pretended to accept his absence. There should have been a death when he left, but there had not been one because she could not accept it.

But she had believed he had no soul. When did she begin to think that?

In the hospital, she had seen her own soul recede from her. At times it seemed to float above her bed. At other times, it hovered just outside her window, between the hospital and the industrial buildings, which changed only in hue, at times taking on a brilliance more vital than flesh—oh, yes, brick was capable of that—but there was nothing human in what she saw as she looked out of the window day after day. In the hospital, she saw so many people preparing to die she came to think of her floor as a railway station to which you came, bought a ticket, and waited until the train arrived to take you. Once it arrived, it was no use deciding you didn't want to make the trip.

She began to remember them, her roommates in the hospital, one terminally ill patient replaced by another—the first, who had brain cancer and was scolded by the nurses for soiling the bed; the second, a Chinese woman who had ovarian cancer and came every two weeks for chemotherapy; a Haitian woman who had come in for dialysis and suffered complications and was now holding her head with both hands; a young Spanish girl who had a scar that ran from the middle of her chest to her armpit because of open heart surgery done when she was twelve—and they all wanted to tell her about their children.

But she was in a protective cloud. She admired the striped orange and yellow curtains which could be pulled and seal off her bed. She spent two happy weeks running errands for the women in her room, calling nurses for patients whose rooms she passed when walking through the halls, fetching pitchers of ice for anyone who wanted them. Almost no one on the floor was ambulatory, and she remained convinced there was nothing wrong with her. She was merely suffering from rage. Her fever rose to 104 at eleven in the morning and stayed there until three in the afternoon, when it fell to normal and did not rise again until midnight, and by two A.M. it was gone. She had an explanation for this: the fever rose during the hours she would normally be writing.

III

"A fever of creation?" her doctor asked her, his smile beginning to erode.

"Exactly," she said. She was delighted. He was beginning to understand.

As she learned later, the doctor understood that he'd better talk to Mike, since Iris was, in his opinion, temporarily unbalanced. That fall, cases of fever that abruptly ended in coma or sudden death had been reported by most of the Manhattan hospitals, but Iris did not know anything about this, and lived on, briefly, in an ominous state of bliss. The medical students were clouds on the horizon of the refuge she claimed to have found in Riverdale, but even they were acceptable. They took her case history again and again until she asked them why. How many times could they ask her if she'd been to any exotic places lately? Had she been bitten by a parrot? A snake? Oh, one of them told her, she was so articulate, they were sent to practice on her. That was when she first realized she was a curiosity on the ward, an educated white woman.

"You better watch it," one of the two white nurses told her. "They'll think with your money you ought to pay for a private nurse. They'll let you lie like a dog."

Iris ignored the warning. She was enjoying the doctors' confusion. Just as she had predicted, test after test showed nothing. After two weeks, everyone agreed it would be best to treat her for an infection of the heart, because if they couldn't be sure she had endocarditis, they couldn't be sure she didn't have it either. Six weeks with nothing to do but watch television while an intravenous measured out powerful medicine, one drop at a time. She was delighted.

She had not counted on the diabetic woman who came to share her room, the casual cruelty of the hospital, the eventual erasure of her faith in the world outside her hospital room.

The diabetic woman was poor and black and had gone untreated for too many years. She was long and thin and wrapped her small head in a turban and sat up in the bed swaying like a snake. Her toes had rotted on her feet and were to be amputated if they did not fall off first. Friends came to see her and read to her from the Bible. A faith healer came and prayed over her.

Terrified by her, Iris pleaded with the doctors to change her room. When they refused, she turned off the television and lay in bed reading. After a while she took the phone off the hook and read. By the fourth week, she had drawn the curtains around her bed and stopped reading. She stared out the window. Days went by and she spoke to no one but Mike.

The nurses began to ignore her. She was not critically ill and she could walk. They would forget to change the bottle of the intravenous, and sooner or later the fluid that fed the tube going into her arm would run out, and the rubber tubing would fill with her own blood, climbing higher and higher in the tube, as if the blood itself wanted to escape from her body. As if the blood were ready to ascend, to leave this earth. Nothing she could do, not even setting her alarm watch so that when the fluid was about to run out she could get up and find a nurse, did any good. In the middle of the night, they did not exist. When they came, they complained that her veins were too small for the needles and about how much time it took to change them.

She began to collect cruelties as if she were collecting evidence, cruelties inflicted upon herself as well as upon others. At the same time, she began to worsen. She could not lie comfortably in bed. When she stood up, the room tilted and did not right itself, and one night, after getting some ice from the other end of the floor, she was too dizzy to walk back. She collapsed in the chair of another patient's room.

"Nerves," said her doctor. She knew better. In the beginning, she had insisted she was perfectly healthy. Now she believed she was dying. As her fever dropped, she grew weaker.

During the seventh week, she pulled the curtains back and began to talk to Mrs. Smith. The nurses were delighted by this new, healthy attitude. But Iris had become reconciled to Mrs. Smith because she now saw nothing in the woman to frighten her. They were both dying.

During the last ten days she spent in the hospital, she and Mrs. Smith became good friends. Mrs. Smith began to include Iris in her prayers and Iris was grateful. She let Mrs. Smith give her advice.

"If I had eyes and could see," said Mrs. Smith, "I'd grab hold of that book and I wouldn't let it go."

Iris began to read. She swallowed the tranquilizers the doctor prescribed for her. When Mike came in, he would find her listening to Mrs. Smith's stories of her childhood in the South, and she was annoyed if they were interrupted before the story ended.

"It's nice having you in this room now that you've come out from behind them curtains," said Mrs. Smith, "but get out before you worsen more. You stay too long, you die even if you're well. I've seen it happen. I've been in here again and again. I know every nurse on the floor."

If Iris didn't leave, she would certainly die.

Her temperature dropped to 100 and her doctor was easily persuaded to let her go. The last time he saw her, she was unable to fasten the buttons of her nightgown, and when he did it for her, she began weeping and could not stop.

After it was over, and Iris came home and took to her bed, she began to see it for what it was. She had begun to adjust to a country where everyone was dying or about to die. Like the dying who surrounded her, she turned her face away from the living who were mysteriously free to come and go on the other side of the glass. When the nurses talked about going out for pizza, she heard them and thought how wonderful it was to eat pizza, how wonderful to get dressed and go out for a walk.

Then she stopped wanting to walk, to go outside, even to go home. She had discovered the black border around life's calling card.

She had always known that border, and she had been terrified of it all her life, but she had always been able to look away from it, to tell herself it wasn't there. Once she set foot in that black land, it was too hard for her to come back into the light. Returning from the black land was a cruelty and a temptation. There would be a brief respite, a teasing, and then the blackness would close over her again and she would never be able to return. In some corner of her mind, she decided dying was easier than living. Pushed into the black wall of the hospital's fifth floor, she was forced to ask herself what meaning her life had, if it was to end, as everyone's around her was ending, in isolation, in dizziness, in pain, surrounded by people randomly but effectively cruel, in the slow failing of the senses. And when she looked back at the life she led before coming to the hospital, something was missing. When she asked herself that impossible question, Why live?, she did not say, as so many others do, Why not? She had no answer at all. And without an answer, she could not make herself get up. She could not, as she wrote in her notebook, go through life as a living corpse, which was how she had come to see herself. When routine tests found a simple explanation for her dizziness, for all her aches and pains, she looked around her, decided the world was an untrustworthy place—it was not worth the effort to live in it; she could not make the effort—and she stopped talking.

She answered questions. She spoke in monosyllables. She got up and walked around her room as the doctor ordered her to do. But she was not there. She was waiting for someone to tell her, or teach her, why it was she had to live.

Iris sat back, propped up against the headboard, and looked over what she had written. When she looked up, three unusually plump squirrels were jumping from snowy branch to snowy branch, sending flurries down. Their fur was thick and lustrous. What did they find to eat in the winter? Usually she fed them the end pieces of loaves of bread, but she had not been feeding them for some time now. They must have been raiding the bread crumbs the priest in the house behind hers threw out every morning for the birds.

The black calling card, the black margin. She had lived, temporarily, in the country of John's childhood. It was terrible, looking back. Understanding came too late to help anyone. Looking backward, seeing herself, seeing John as they once were: It was like watching Hansel and Gretel set off into the forest, and because you know what awaits them, you tell them, "Watch out for the crows! Watch out for the crows!" But they cannot hear you and they enter, stepping onto the dark carpet of shade flung down thick in front of the huge trees, and they pause, holding up their fat bag of crumbs, smiling happily, waving goodbye, goodbye, saying, "Oh, the crows! There's nothing to worry about! We have all these crumbs!"

When the window is frosted over, and a finger is pressed to the glass, a little circle, like a porthole, opens the eye to another world.

The soul was so loosely stitched to the body. It could come undone. It could turn away from the light and into the dark and it was only protecting itself. It meant no harm. There was no thought in it.

They were living in Boston, in an apartment they subleased from one of her high school friends, and they had virtually no money. He was working as a research assistant and she was a secretary. Her salary, after taxes, was thirty-five dollars a week. She still loved him then, or she was determined to believe she still loved him. He worked late in the lab, and she came home and cooked dinner. Every so often, she would open the refrigerator and decide that something special was necessary, something to commemorate the fourth or fifth or sixth month of their exile from Chicago, and then she would scour her bookshelves, decide which books she was least likely to want again, take them to the used bookstore across the street, sell them, and with the money she would buy the fantastical cakes sold by the bakery across the street. If they were a day old, which was possible, she was no less happy with them. At night, when she set the table, it did not look so desolate. The individual lemon meringue pies sat in the center of the red-and-white oilcloth like the promise of a better life.

She thought he was happy in his lab. She believed there was nothing else he needed. She marveled that he had found a use for her in his completed world.

Then came the piano. In the middle of a rainstorm, he insisted they go to a piano store and rent some kind of piano, any kind. He settled on a dark brown upright and sat down and began playing scales in the store's dim light. The piano was not tuned, and the distorted sounds gave her a headache.

"How much is it?" she asked.

"Six dollars," said the owner. "That doesn't include tuning. You'll have to get yourself a piano tuner."

"Six dollars a month?"

"Six dollars a week," said the owner.

She pulled on John's jacket. She tried to tell him they couldn't afford a piano, and in any case he couldn't really play it, and by the time they found a piano tuner, they wouldn't have any money for food.

The piano was delivered early the next morning and installed in their bedroom, the only room in the apartment capable of accommodating it. The piano practice began shortly afterward. While she was brushing her teeth, the apartment filled with awful sounds. He had decided to practice on Bach's Two Part Inventions.

Oh, God, she thought, my favorite music. She stopped brushing her teeth, the toothpaste frothing in her mouth, while she listened to the silence, which meant he had made a mistake and was soon to repeat the phrase. He began again and she began to relax until he hit the wrong key and stopped.

Please, she pleaded. Play something else. Play something I don't like.

He practiced relentlessly. She would awaken to the Two Part Inventions, which shook her, headachy, out of bed. She told friends he was doing it to torture her. He knew how she loved the music and how she hated hearing it mangled, and yet he would play nothing else, over and over again, the Two Part Inventions, which she would never again be able to hear without stiffening with suspense, waiting for the mistake, the long, agonized pause, the resumption of the horrible, out-of-tune playing.

She began to sleep on the couch. Before the piano came, they slept happily on a narrow single bed. After the piano came, the bedroom turned alien. She would stare at the piano as a crazed mother might stare at a baby she intended to strangle. She had tormented him over the piano.

He was not playing the piano but looking for himself, a small self, but essential, and she had stopped him.

Later, she insisted he had no soul at all. When they fought, she said that, over and over.

At that time she could not afford the luxury of complexities. There was a villain and a victim and she was certain she was incapable of villainy. She had sensitive ears; she couldn't stand playing off key.

What had she done?

In the beginning they were absolutely clear, like glass so clean it shimmered like air. Terribly fragile in their newness. Clear sheets like clear pages in the photographer's solution, which have no images at all. That magic instant before the lines the camera has caught imprison and set the image on the page forever. That instant in which the past is erased and all that exists is the present. Clearer and more blank than a newborn infant still rocked by the sudden starting up of the genes, the influx of air, the shock of the airy world, the intolerable memory of the watery one left behind, mourned, howled for.

In that magic time, they created themselves. They were beings whose existence depended on one another. They were mirrors whose faces reflected the perfection of what they had just created. Caught by perfection, they stumbled through their days as if shackled by hand and foot. The progress they made exhausted them even as it transformed them.

She was younger and believed she could live forever in that still, clear moment. He began to have doubts. A parenthesis, a respite, a brief glimpse of purple clouds rimmed in gold—it was more than he hoped for.

Images began to shadow the clear glass. The past returned. He avoided her eyes, and the person she had become, the person they had made, began its slow inevitable crumbling. It was a horrible thing, as creatures preserved for centuries under hundreds of feet of ice begin to decay when the ice melts or when someone finds them and brings them up later into the air.

It was soul murder. They had placed their souls in each other's hands and he tried to give hers back. She couldn't forgive him. The voices came back, her mother's, her father's, the strange cavernous voice of her house in the East. She became as she was then, walking through carpeted rooms, green walls, green carpet, underwater. The silences, too, came back. There was no describing her terror, or the murderousness of the grip with which she held on to him.

He remembered a tantalizing, frightening world. Wonderful things had been given to him and then taken away. They would be given again, ever more wonderful, and each time he would be allowed to keep them longer. Just as he thought they were secure in his hand, his fingers would be pried open, and whatever it was would be taken away, the woman who took it, smiling. *Oh, you won't mind.* And *No one will ever be faithful to you.*

She had promised to be faithful. He began to test her. He would leave and come back. There would be days of perfect happiness and then he would turn dark. *This was not what I wanted.* She passed the tests. But there is only so much energy in the world; there is only so much energy in a soul. Hers was ebbing. When she looked in the mirror, she saw something sallow, hollow-eyed, a simulacrum of what she had once been. She knew his fears and began to use them. In the end, she was the first to be unfaithful. She turned from him and then turned back. When she looked in the mirror afterward, her eyes were even more hollow, and her hands perpetually cold.

They turned on each other in a purity of viciousness. They did not survive their own tortures. The fragile present, the sheets of clear glass, shattered and were swept under the rug. Every now and then a piece would work its way up through the carpet and lodge like a splinter in the skin. Then they would pause and look at each other as if nothing had ever gone wrong, as if nothing could ever go wrong. Eventually, the splinters were swept up or settled into the cracks between the floorboards.

They were possessed by ghosts infuriated by improper burials, souls which had not found rest and hoped to rest quietly in them. There is nothing like the energy of the dead, the unquiet souls, who now took possession of them.

They fought each other. They hated each other. And
yet they were caught in the trap of perfection, the
memory of it, stronger than any steel trap. Still, they
wanted to live, and like two animals caught in the same
trap, two animals who grow confused, they tried to free
themselves by chewing off each other's arms and legs. In
the end, they were utterly ruthless, and their only hope
of escape became each other's pain. When the pain
became incandescent, it was like a light, and because it
was the only light they had, they found their way by it.
From then on, they could not go back. The pain was all
they had.

She looked quickly at the page, out the window, and began
writing again:

On the other hand, I have seen enough of artists trying
to lug themselves into the next century, that round,
faceless silver door, like a worn coin, or one so ancient its
worth has been spent by time, bag and baggage into the
next century, blind to the marvelous engines of the day
waiting on the silver tracks, orange sparks shooting high
into the blue sky, then falling back to earth, engines that
let loose white clouds of smoke, as if to say, *I am the
earth's factory,* while the artists, typewriters in hand,
sketchbooks under their arms, rush by sightless.

She stared down at the page, bewildered. Bag and baggage into
the next century. Outside, a loud engine started itself up as if the
world were grinding into motion. It was time to think about
getting up.

Halfway up the front stairs, Evelyn paused on the landing and
looked around her. Webs everywhere, fine strands connecting

this place with that, one object with the next. Eyestrain, she thought, or the pattern of the capillaries in her eyes suddenly visible because the darkness inside followed too quickly after the glare of the sun outside on the snow. It was intolerable, being pushed out of her mother's life this way.

"Mother," said Evelyn resolutely. "I want to talk to you."

"Come in," said Iris, patting the bed, her eyes startled, as if she were seeing her daughter for the first time.

"I want to talk to you about John."

"Oh," said Iris wearily. "John."

"It isn't exactly responsible to have a sick man here and not know what to expect. I called Dr. Chipwitz and he'd like to talk to you."

"What did you tell him?"

"I didn't tell him anything. We drove over with John's medical records. That's another thing. You can't expect him to stay in the house forever. He has to find things to do."

"What did Dr. Chipwitz say?" Iris asked. Evelyn had called John a sick man. She thought of him as a dying man, someone who was soon to be a problem, but was not now suffering from anything in particular.

"He agrees with the diagnosis, but he says the clinical picture isn't really consistent with it. If he has amyotrophic lateral sclerosis, he should be having more trouble breathing and walking. He thinks maybe there's something like multiple sclerosis in the picture."

Was this Evelyn, who could not remember her own phone number?

"Tell me, Evelyn," she said, "will it make any difference if he's dying of amyotrophic lateral sclerosis or if he's dying of two diseases at once?"

"No," said Evelyn, her voice cold.

"I'm sorry," Iris said finally. "That was a cruel way to put it."

"It's just that facts—well, they give you a feeling of power."

"It's a terrible thing," Iris said.

"Mother, it could take months."

"I know," Iris said.

"Or weeks."

"I know."

"I'm not pregnant," Evelyn said.

"I know."

"Why are you in here?"

"I don't know," Iris said.

Evelyn started to cry.

Mike came home late, found Iris asleep, saw her notebook on the windowsill instead of the end table, and took it with him into the bathroom. Where was the rest of the world? Where had it gone? This fascination with the past, this obsession with it, what did it mean? She spoke to John most of the day, and when she wasn't speaking to him she was writing about him. What was so interesting about John? Everyone had first loves that ended badly. Mike slept in the same bed with his wife, but he wouldn't know what she thought from one day to the next if it weren't for her notebooks. He was tired. His patience was exhausted; his work was not going well. People stopped him in the corridors and told him he looked terrible. The secretaries and the students brought in things for him to eat, and his wife lay in bed and smiled at him when he spoke to her and perversely refused to get better. A pest, that was what she was. Then he felt ashamed of himself. A friend of theirs, a psychologist, had tried to warn him. "When she gets better, everyone in the house is going to be furious at her. She's not going to understand it. But you better understand it, because if you don't, she won't forgive *you*."

"That's hardly fair," he said.

"Life's not fair," said the psychologist. "Look at you. You're angry already."

"I'm not angry," Mike said.

"Have it your way."

He wasn't.

And what did this mean, *bag and baggage into the next century?* Tired of people with their eyes on the future when the present was standing in the doorway to their house, screaming like a madwoman demanding entrance: that was all well and good. But his wife was standing in the present, her back turned to it, staring like Lot's wife at the past. There were times he thought she had found a doorway into it and left her body behind as a snail leaves its shell.

The soul inching its way out, as if from under mountains, that was what he was watching. Or reading about.

He was starting to sound like her. She was reducing them all to the status of readers, not family members. Writing was not supposed to take the place of normal human conversation. Yet she was getting better. That humorless, hopeless creature in the bed might yet turn back into the woman he had known before the fever. His jealousy of John was ridiculous. The man was no threat. He was dying. But Mike was jealous. This stranger, an ex-lover, was all his wife thought about.

She must be getting better, Mike thought, if I'm angry at her. Automatically, he knocked wood.

The next morning, John came into the room before Iris awoke, picked up the notebook and read what she had written. She had described the hospital as it was. But a tantalizing world! Soul murder! His fingers being pried open! The past shadowing the clear glass!

Every word made him furious. He read the last line—in the end, the pain was all they had—and he closed the notebook and went upstairs to her study. There were homes for the ill. There were resorts. Why hadn't he gone? Why had he come here? There was her computer. He took the pillow cover from her word processor and turned it on.

PART TWO

The House

9

THE SNOW HAD stopped and the phone was ringing. Iris heard Nate answer it on the landing and knew immediately he was talking to her mother. "No, no, she's *fine*. She's *fine*. She's talking. Not to us, to some man she used to know. His name? John Stone."

Oh, no, Iris thought. She'll be on the next plane.

"*I* don't know what he's doing here. You better ask Dad about it. I don't think I'm supposed to talk about it. What do you mean, don't talk to him? He seems OK. I *can't* put her on the phone. She won't talk to you."

Silence. "All right, I'll get her. Hold on."

"Ma," Nate said, opening Iris' door, "Grandma wants to talk to you."

Iris shook her head no.

"That's what I told her," he said, turning around.

"She doesn't want to talk to you," Iris heard Nate saying. "Sure I love you. . . . You want me to tell her what? That she doesn't care about you? I'll ask Dad. We're not supposed to upset her.

"Dad!" Nate shouted.

Iris waited.

"Don't worry about it, Frieda," Mike was saying. "He's perfectly harmless."

129

Now her mother would say that the last time her daughter spoke to John Stone, she had swallowed sleeping pills.

"Frieda," said Mike, "she's been *sleeping* for over two months. *How* can he push her over the edge? She's *been* over the edge! Well, if you want to, you can come see for yourself. He's not so bad."

Her mother would now be saying that neither was Bluebeard or the Boston Strangler.

"You're exaggerating, Frieda," he said. "No, *don't* put Lester on the phone."

Her father would get on the phone and tell him a man ought to be strong and protect his family from outsiders.

"No," said Mike. "I don't think that would be strong at all. If he seems to be doing any harm, I'll throw him out. I *know* you wouldn't do the same thing. Don't you want to talk to Evelyn? Later?"

In disgust, her father would hand the phone back to her mother.

"This *is* the strong thing to do, Frieda," Mike said. "Believe me, it is. Don't feel sorry for me. Why not? Because you'll make me start feeling sorry for myself. Evelyn wants to talk to you."

Iris listened, smiling.

"Oh, he's very nice, Grandma. He helps me with my physics homework. Daddy told you he's dying? He doesn't seem sick at all.

"Daddy!" Evelyn shouted. "Grandma wants to talk to you again."

"No, Frieda," he said wearily. "It's nothing contagious. Yes, I *do* know. He and Evelyn took his records over to Dr. Chipwitz. Frieda, I have to go to work. 'Lightning always strikes twice'? The saying is, 'Lightning *doesn't* strike twice.' If there's something to cry about, I'll let you know."

Look what I've been missing, Iris thought.

"That was your mother," Mike said, coming in. "She's buying a black dress to celebrate our divorce."

"Don't worry about John," said Iris.

"I do."

"When will you be home?"

She hadn't asked him that since she'd come back from the hospital.

"About seven."

"Good."

Upstairs, she heard her printer clattering away. Apparently John was still an early riser. She heard Evelyn telling Nate she'd be down in a second, and then her daughter's footsteps running up the stairs. "It's only a half day today," Evelyn was telling John. "We can go as soon as I go back."

Go where? wondered Iris.

She looked around the room and sat up, staring at two framed needlepoint pictures, both done by her grandmother: a house in winter, a house in spring. The patience of that woman and her silver needle, thread by thread filling the holes in the honey-combed canvas, the landscapes solid, the matrix behind them hidden, stitch by stitch, eliminating the small holes in the fabric backing of this world. Outside it was winter but soon it would be spring. How was that possible? How did one season change into another? It was frightening, that transition. And yet it would happen, whether or not she lay beneath her white sheets, as if she had fallen asleep in deep snow.

Two meetings were canceled, and Mike came home early. Iris, wearing blue jeans and a purple velour pullover, wearing the same clothes she had worn the day she had gone into the hospital, was standing looking out the window.

"Are you going out?" he asked her.

"I'm thinking about it," she said, sitting back down on the bed.

"Where's Evelyn?"

"She took John to the eye doctor. He needs a new prescription."

"How did they get there?"

"He drove."

"Where's Nate?"

She shrugged.

"You up?" Etheline asked, coming into the room. "What do you want to eat?"

"I'll come down and eat something," Iris said.

"Why's that man writing up there in your room?" Etheline asked. "The doctor says he needs his sleep. Ain't no one in this house but you gets enough sleep these days."

"I think," Iris said, "Evelyn is interested in John."

"A passing fancy," said Mike. "Look at it this way: We won't need paid mourners."

"That's not funny," Iris said. "How long does it take to get glasses, anyway?"

John appeared in the doorway. "I'm sorry," he said. "I didn't mean to interrupt a family discussion."

"We were just wondering where you were," Iris said.

We, thought Mike, we. A wonderful word.

"You're dressed," John said, staring at Iris.

That night, watching Iris take off her pullover, then her jeans, then her brassiere and pants, Mike smiled, carefully keeping his arm across the lower half of his face. Next she would put on her nightgown, disappear into the bathroom, brush her teeth, and then sit down on the edge of the bed, swing her legs up onto it, and lie down. She would turn to him, put her arm around him, and wait for his breathing to become deep and regular. Then she would turn to face the door and lie on the bed, uncovered. After ten minutes, she would pull the covers up and in seconds be sound asleep. It was a miracle, this return of the ordinary. Progress, once it began, was as inexorable as decline. It was always forward or backward. There might be some kind of trouble now, but he would no longer awaken in the middle of the night, terrified, listening for the sound of her breathing. He breathed deeply and fell asleep before she came to bed.

Iris awoke to complete silence. Ten o'clock. The children were in school. Etheline didn't arrive until eleven. The printer upstairs was silent. Where was John if he wasn't upstairs writing a history of his past dissatisfactions with her? She thought she heard a noise on the sun porch that adjoined her bedroom, but the bed was warm, and the cat and dog had taken up their places, the dog sleeping on Mike's side of the bed, the cat on her hip. Everything in its usual place. Where in the world had the world gone? Since she had been home, she had taken little notice of the animals.

She got up, put on her robe, and opened the door to the sun porch. John was standing there examining the collection of little glass animals which stood on the shelves of a small china cabinet she had found on the sidewalk and rescued from a sanitation truck.

"That's no place for you," she said. "The room's unheated."

"I never minded the cold," he said.

"No," she said, remembering how, in Chicago, in the middle of the winter, he would run from the dorm to the lab without a jacket while she moved clumsily inside three layers of clothing. "Do you still have those plaid flannel shirts?" she asked him. His mother and sister made his shirts. Every Christmas and every birthday, he was given two. Until Iris discovered Oriental rugs, she had never seen such beautiful colors as those in his shirts.

"Do you remember the little saw your parents gave me when I first visited their house?" he asked her.

133

"No," she said. "I don't."

"I kept it for years."

"I can't remember it at all."

"I thought you remembered everything."

"It must have been my grandfather's saw. He was the only one in the family who could do anything with his hands," she said.

"It was a good saw," he said.

"I suppose it was," she said. Why didn't John say he was sorry she'd forgotten about the saw which had been so important to him? She was sorry.

"Do you remember the ice-cream parlor in the little town near our lake house?"

"No," said Iris. "I don't."

"I saw a copy of your last book there. I thought it was a sign."

"Of what?"

He hesitated. "Of connection. It's just an ice-cream parlor. They never have books there. Some picture postcards of the lake, that's all."

"I want to talk about why you came back," she said. "Why you came here. I have to understand it and I have to be able to explain it."

"I've already explained."

"You know perfectly well that was no explanation."

"You're sure?" he asked, smiling slightly.

"I'm sure," she said.

He sat down in the chair and she watched him.

He was puzzled. He never knew why he did anything, or so she had always believed.

"It's beautiful outside," he said. "You always liked snow. Is there anyplace to go?"

"Are you supposed to be out in this weather?"

"Nothing makes any difference," he said wearily. "You always had favorite places you went to again and again. Like a Catholic. Catholics are inclined to ritual."

"Well," she said, "there's Hopwood Cemetery. It's famous for its Victorian statuary and stained glass. I've got a card giving me permission to drive the car around the grounds. It's run by the Mafia or something. Someone told me they bought it so that they could dispose of bodies quietly."

"Let's go," he said.

"Outside?" Iris asked weakly.

"I'll drive."

She remembered that he was the worst driver she'd ever known, making U-turns on the Dan Ryan Expressway when he passed his exit, then driving backward into oncoming traffic, telling her not to worry, there were no other cars in the lane. But it seemed somehow fitting that her first trip out of the house should be to a cemetery in a car driven by a maniac.

She'd better get her raccoon coat in case he got lost and trapped them in a snowdrift.

"Where you going?" Etheline asked.

"Hopwood Cemetery," John said.

"What you two need with cemeteries?" she asked. "Don't the movies have afternoon shows?"

"We'll be home by five," Iris said. "If we're not home by five, call the police."

"Don't *you* drive," Etheline told Iris. "You're still weak and it's been months since you drove anything."

Iris opened the front door and hesitated, but John was immediately behind her, and she went down the steps. The world flung itself on her like a white leopard leaping from a tree. Houses, cars, bushes covered with snow, children trudging down the block slowly, their khaki book bags on their backs, late for school, the mailman approaching in the far distance, still a small figure. Her throat tightened and she began crying. Wire fences, a white picket fence around the neighbor's garden, garbage pails: it was all so beautiful it stunned her. She had never expected to see any of it again. The world had faded so fast. In the elevator with Mike, coming down from the fifth floor, on their way out of the hospital, she saw the lit number 5 that marked her floor change to 4 and she began to sob uncontrollably into his jacket. The other people in the elevator looked at her with sympathy and then looked away. They had all come from visiting someone made shockingly unfamiliar by tubes in their noses or needles taped to their arms. But she was crying because she was leaving and had not expected to.

"What's so special about this cemetery?" John asked her.

"It's huge," she said. "Fifty acres. You can forget you're in the city while you're there. In the summer, the place is full of pheasants. If we're lucky, we might see some rabbits. I like the stained-glass windows in the little houses."

"Mausoleums," John said.

"That's not how I think of them."

"That's what they are."

"Fine," said Iris. "Let's not discuss it. I hope it's open."

"Cemeteries are always open."

"This one isn't. It has tall iron gates, and they lock them on Sundays."

"They were probably repairing something the Sunday you were there," he said.

"Have it your way," said Iris.

"Is it frightening, going out?"

"Only because of your driving," she said. "Yes, it is."

They were driving in a fog of irritation; it felt dreadfully familiar, and this caused Iris to ask herself, again, why she had agreed to let John stay at the house, and what she had done by allowing it. With each block, the panic she felt grew stronger and stronger, and with the panic, memories returned, like broken pieces of a globe, which, if she collected enough of them, would form together into the same world she once had such trouble escaping. It could reclaim her. She remembered setting off for the movies and having to stop at the drugstore to renew her prescription for tranquilizers. She remembered coming back to the house, skidding over five icy, windy blocks because she stopped, halfway to school, and realized the little bottle of pills was not in her pocketbook. She remembered walking out to the Point and sitting in the middle of a patch of daisies while he set his camera and took so long at it that she thought she might get a chance to see the sun set and not have to go back to the lab with him after all. She went with him to arcane lectures in physics and listened to a professor from Berkeley explain why, in terms of particle theory, if everyone drove at the posted speed limit, no traffic would move, while she asked her professors for permission to bring him to her classes in Shakespeare and Faulkner. From the moment they got up in the morning, they were together. When she had a class, or when he did, she would tell herself it would only be an hour and forty-five minutes before she saw him again. When she went to the school cafeteria after class and arrived there first, she sat at a table facing the street so that the instant he appeared she would know he was coming. In movies, she watched him watching the films, surprised at how he sat forward, as if what he saw upset him terribly. She remembered the first time she found the courage to put her hand on his shoulder, and how he jumped, startled, and looked quickly at her and then back at the screen.

Locks on doors were never a barrier to him. He let them in to the gymnasium in the student union, and they sat in the balcony's bleachers, and when he finally kissed her, he placed a band around her heart which could only grow tighter. She remembered his first apartment, a room painted lime green, in high-gloss paint that shone in the light, and a tiny kitchen, sleeping there every night after signing out of the dorm, and on Mondays, walking thirteen blocks to the supermarket to buy the week's food and have it delivered, coming back, ringing the bell, and walking up five flights of steps, her eyes fixed on his face as he leaned over the banister, watching her, smiling.

She also remembered the arguments in the apartment they took after coming back from Boston, the day he told her he'd decided he would not marry her, the stone statue she'd picked up and thrown at his head, missing him, but taking a sizable chunk out of a solid wood door. Such rage! She remembered lying in bed, shaking so hard the bedsprings rattled, while he insisted there was nothing at all wrong with her and if she wanted to come with him, she could.

The car skidded slightly and she remembered his red Porsche and sitting for enraged hours in the car while he adjusted the twin carburetors. That little red car, symbol of futility, which started out bravely but never got more than a mile and a half before John's ear detected some lack of synchronization and he would stop, while she sat still, in summer, watching his feet protrude from beneath the car. She remembered the day he left her, and thinking, when she heard the door click, *How strange when death is only the click of a door.* If her body had obeyed her, she would have watched the red car out of sight, but her fever was 104 and she could not get up.

Thinking about upsetting things made her feverish. She was feverish now.

They turned into Hopwood Cemetery, going through the gates, the guard nodding at her and smiling, recognizing her.

"It's all Victorian rococo," John said, looking at the red-brick castles on either side of the gates.

"It's all very nice," she said sharply.

They drove through the cemetery, a park filled with statuary, and John exclaimed at the marble dogs on either side of an even more enormous urn. He stopped and rolled down the window to get a better look at a fifteen-foot statue of a woman smiling down at a baby in her arms. She watched him, knowing what he was thinking. "The folds in the toga are well done," he said. "There was something clumsy about the dogs' noses, did you notice?"

She sighed. This, too, was familiar, listening to what he said, then translating that into what he meant or felt and explaining it to him.

"How long did it take to get over it?" she asked. "Your daughter's death?"

He looked at her, surprised. "You never get over things like that," he said.

"Never?"

"Never."

"What was she like?"

"Smart. She looked like me. Thin, dark-haired. After my wife died, she went everywhere with me. She used to come to the lab and do her homework by infrared light. I asked our pediatrician about it and he said not to worry about her eyes; if she could see well enough to read in the dark, let her."

"Your parents must have been excited," she said. "A grandchild."

"Actually, they didn't pay much attention. My sister already had four children, and I didn't have Celia until I was almost forty."

"What became of your parents?" Iris asked. She imagined them swallowing poison together at the lake house, leaving behind a note asking the children to bury them in the same grave.

"You don't want to get out and walk?" he asked her.

"I can't," she said. "I'm not ready."

"I'll stop the car here," he said. They were parked in front of a remarkable statue, a man in uniform holding the reins of a horse on which a naked woman rode, hair streaming over her breasts, looking straight ahead at the industrial skyline and across the water to New Jersey.

"What do you suppose that means?" he asked her.

"God knows," she said. "Lady Godiva in the Civil War."

"It must mean *something*. Come on, Iris. Jack would have known."

"Jack," said Iris dreamily. "I thought about marrying Jack."

Jack had been part of the group they formed in Chicago—not a group, really, but a family—the only trouble with the family being, as one after another pointed out, that Iris was the only female in it and since she was constantly falling in love with one after another of them, or they with her, it was a family headed for the troubles of Agamemnon and his relatives.

"He would never have married you, Iris. He drank because he didn't like thinking. Especially about himself. Compared to him, I was an analyst of human behavior. He would have killed himself after a week with you. You analyze every word anyone says."

"He did kill himself," Iris said. "Six months ago. Ed sent me a clipping."

"I didn't know that," John said, looking straight ahead.

"Yes," said Iris, "well. Sometimes it pays to think."

"Coming in from the airport, from LaGuardia," he said, "we passed an enormous cemetery. Do you know which one I mean? It had an impressive skyline of its own. Two skylines: the skyscrapers and a skyline full of angels."

"As if the city of the dead were waiting for the city of the living," she said.

"Or guarding it," he said. "All those angels. All those lives going on in back of it. So much energy. In the city, I mean. *You* know what I mean."

She did. All that energy beating inside the walls of the city, surely some of it spilled out and roamed the world, disturbing the inevitable sequence, life followed by death. Perhaps it could even enter into the dead and revive them. It might bring back their words, their promise of reunion.

"A child doesn't just die," he said. "If it's your child, you think about it and think about it, every word you said, every move you made, every one you didn't make. You try to find out how you murdered the child. How you could have saved her. You join groups of other parents who've lost children and you learn to say it wasn't your fault, but you never believe it. You join groups to reform the treatment of children in hospitals because you never believe it wasn't your fault. You go to the child's grave and try to apologize in every way you can. You think if you find the right way to say how sorry you are, the guilt will go, but it doesn't go. The dead don't accept apologies. You can't forgive yourself for a crime you've committed against someone else. Some days start out well and then the bottom falls out. It's a roller coaster. For a long time it's that way."

"You didn't commit a crime," Iris said.

"No?" he said, smiling strangely. "All my life I've felt I did."

"All your life?"

"From the time I was a child."

In the hospital, after she'd swallowed sleeping pills, the college psychologist interviewed John and asked him if he felt responsible for what had happened. He said he didn't. Iris wanted him to be unhappy. He hadn't made her take the pills. He didn't know she had them.

"That time I was in the hospital?" Iris said. "Because of the pills? It wasn't your fault. Not really."

"It was," he said. "I saw what was happening. I should have left you alone from the beginning."

"But I wouldn't leave you alone."

"I was stronger," he said.

"Yes. But the weaker are always strongest in the end. You can't break their hold."

"Did you forgive me?" he asked. "For leaving?"

She thought. "No. I don't think so. But eventually it became irrelevant. Or I thought it did."

"Nothing ever becomes irrelevant," he said.

"Did you ever forgive *me?*" Iris asked.

"You? You never meant any harm. You didn't do anything wrong."

"I did. I couldn't let you go."

"That's what you were writing about. Soul murder. Traps. People who love *are* like that."

"I don't think so," Iris said. "Don't make excuses for me."

Two large birds flew over the naked woman on the horse and into the trees beneath them. They were parked on a high hill and below them the lake was iced over.

"Geese," said John. "Everything gets confused in a city. People here must feed them and so they stay."

"I suppose," Iris said. "What *did* happen to your parents?"

"It's a terrible story. How well do you remember my father?"

She remembered his father very well, an older version of his son, hands twisted by arthritis, those same green eyes, always coming into a room, standing there awkwardly, smiling at everyone as if to wish them well, nodding once or twice, and leaving without saying anything. She had liked his father, a man happy to be in the world but not at ease in it either.

"He had a stroke about ten years ago. He was twelve years older than my mother. He would get better and then he'd get worse, and then he'd have another stroke, and after a while, my mother couldn't wait for him to die. It's understandable. She spent her life raising seven kids and then just when she thought she'd have some time, he got sick and kept getting worse, and he didn't want a nurse. He wanted his Emma. He was Emma's man. That was his purpose in life. He had to take care of Emma, so he kept hanging on and she couldn't stand it and he couldn't see that she couldn't stand it.

"Meanwhile she started designing fabrics with another woman from town, someone she'd grown up with, and the woman moved into the house with her and they both took care of my father. She wanted him to die so she could get on with things. She and the woman were very close. After a while she didn't need my father. But he couldn't see it or he wouldn't see it. Whenever we came to see him, he'd say he was hanging on for his Emma. He should have let go.

"Anyway, she finally couldn't take it and put him in a rest home, and he realized his Emma didn't need him anymore and he died two days later."

"Your mother did that?"

"*He* should have let go!" John said violently. "He could have seen what was going on."

"Why do you make excuses for her? You always made excuses for her."

"She wasn't to blame. She didn't make him sick."

"She didn't take care of him, either."

"There's a limit to everyone's patience."

"Was there a limit to yours when your daughter was dying?"

"No."

"Did you wish she'd let go?"

He wouldn't look at her. "Sometimes," he said.

"You're not like your mother," Iris said.

He turned and looked at her, tears in his eyes.

"You're not," she said. "You never were."

"She told me I was."

"She said a lot of things."

"You wrote things about the past shadowing the present," he said. "Do you believe that?"

"Of course. Everyone does."

143

"Then," he said, "if you don't understand your past, you don't understand your present?"

It had always amazed her how, when it came to human things, he sounded like such a child.

"That's right."

"Do you understand yours? What happened before?"

"After a quarter of a century, I do better at it," she said.

"*You* always thought you had a happy childhood," he said.

"I don't anymore," she said slowly. "I always had to know the truth. I wanted to know why they cried in their rooms. I watched changes in their expressions. And when I thought I knew the truth, I'd tell it. It must have been like living with Snow White's mirror. Anyway," she said impatiently, looking at him, "the truth can be a terrible thing. When Nate was nine, he came home with a box of colored pencils and we knew he stole them. Etheline—well, you've met her—she's very religious, and she kept telling him to tell her the truth. *The truth never hurts.* So he admitted he took them from his friend. I didn't scold him, but I had to tell him how wrong it was to steal, and he ran up the steps and when he got to his room and was safe, he was crying and shouting as if we'd ruined his life. '*You said the truth doesn't hurt. But it does!*' "

"It does, it does," John said.

"Well, I was perfectly willing to tell the truth before I knew how it felt," Iris said, "but it's one thing to know the truth and another to accept it. I never could accept the truth of loss. So I started writing. It's all an attempt to rescue—yourself or someone else. You can save some things from time, maybe, but not yourself, not people you love. In the hospital, that was all there was. Loss. It"—she hesitated—"it *broke in.*"

She looked at John.

"Whoever said people become artists to defy the world was right," she said. "Anyway, the world is always stronger. No, I didn't have a happy childhood. By the time I met you, I believed there was something dangerous about me and no one would ever want me. Not really."

"Families," said John.

"And you?" she asked. "Do you still think your childhood was happy?"

"Wasn't it?" he asked.

"No."

"I thought it was," John said, "but I've been thinking about it more. Since getting to your house."

"*You* decided to come," she reminded him.

"I suppose I wanted to know the truth," he said.

"About what?"

"About what? About everything."

"Good luck," Iris said. It was getting dark. "You know," she said, "we better start back or we'll get locked in."

"No one locks cemeteries," said John.

"John, they lock this one," Iris said nervously. It was getting darker and she knew that set expression, his lips pursed as if he were considering whistling, an expression which meant he knew what he was doing and had no intention of listening to uninformed amateurs. "They do more than lock it. At night, it's patrolled by armored cars and guard dogs. John, it *is.*"

"Just a few more minutes," he said.

She sighed and sank back against the car seat. She hadn't sat up straight this long in three months. She was tired and, sitting overlooking the city, she was reminded of how much of the world there was.

"All right," she said irritably, "why are we staying here?" She was restless, nervous. She had called him by his first name, one of the things she thought was forbidden to her. Touching him, even on the wrist as she wanted to do when he spoke of his daughter, that was forbidden to her.

145

He began fumbling in his pocket and took out a sheet of paper. "You want me to read it?" she asked. He handed the paper to her.

It is more than four years now that I keep thinking, "In the middle of the journey of this life, I found myself in a deep forest, where the straight way was lost." I am still deep in the forest, trying to find my path. I had been feeling particularly lost after I learned the diagnosis for my disease, and I sat in my chair, thinking all afternoon, before I could get back to work. I began to lay out records to play while I worked and thought, as I always do, of an evening at the T-Bone Steak House in Farmington, New Mexico, where we used to stop on our trips out west, a big L-shaped space with a concrete floor, picnic tables where strangers shared the benches, and walls of rough-sawed lumber lavishly ornamented with popular tapestries: a big scene of polar bears, one with peacocks and a castle, another in an older tradition, based on Watteau. Running horses, elks, moose, a tiger, and a lion. We would stop there for dinner on the drive back to La Jolla from skiing in Aspen or Durango, many miles still ahead on the narrow icy highway south across the reservation. The night I remember, a little boy of four was putting quarters into the jukebox and playing "Witchy Woman" over and over: "See how high she flies . . . she's got the moon in her eyes." I suppose Celia must have been four or five, still just a sleepy baby.

Iris shook her head and stared out at the skyline, beginning to light up, turning into a network of lights honeycombing the solidifying dark. "Are you writing your memoirs? Is that it?"

"There's so much of my life no one knows about," he said. "There are times I think I'm already dead."

"You ought to write an autobiography," said Iris, looking down at the page. "I think you could."

"Would you do it?" he asked her.

"Me? How can I write your autobiography?"

"Oh, well, for obvious reasons, I can't. Write my story or your story, in the end it won't make any difference. It's the same story."

"I don't begin to know what you're talking about," she said. He looked at her grimly, as if to say she'd understand what he meant soon enough. "Look, I'll think about it, we'll talk about it later, but let's get out of here. They'll lock the gates."

"No one is locking the gates, but if you're so worried, we'll go."

"Thank you," Iris said, "and be careful going downhill. It's steep, it's icy, you were never careful on ice."

They drove down the little winding path, barely wide enough for a car. It must have been narrow even when horse-drawn carriages brought people there. At the bottom of the hill, he asked Iris which way to turn, and she couldn't tell him. There was something about the place that erased all sense of direction. "That way," she said, pointing to the right. "I think."

They began driving, looking for an exit. "Drive faster," Iris said, but he was in no hurry. Finally, they saw a gate, not the main one, but a gate all the same. When they pulled up to it, they saw it was closed. "I'll get out and open it," John said, climbing out of the car, through the snow. Iris glared at him as he tried to unfasten the bolt across the cast-iron gate. "Well," he said, "this one's locked, but the main one will be open." He began driving again, taking a different route.

"It's *six* o'clock!" Iris said. "They're going to be worried sick." He said they would find the main gate. "There it is," he said finally.

"Locked," said Iris. "I told you. Now what do we do?"

"Go back to the other gate."

"Why?" she asked. "That's going to take ten minutes."

"Once we get there," he said, "we can call through the bars. Someone on the street will see us."

Iris crossed her arms over her breast and glared through the windshield, refusing to look at him. When they got to the gate, she knew, no one would be there. And it was too late and too dangerous a neighborhood for people to be out walking. "Now what?" she asked. "What's that barking?" She looked out her window and saw five German shepherds clawing at her window, barking their throats out. The patrol dogs. If there were patrol dogs, she thought, there must be patrol guards. She took a piece of paper from her pocketbook, started writing, finished, and began rolling down her window.

"Don't touch that window!" John said. "Those aren't tame dogs!"

But Iris was calling to the dogs, who had retreated and from ten feet away from the car were barking at them. "Come on, doggy. Nice, nice doggy. Come on, come on and take the note."

"Iris," John asked, "what are you doing?"

"I'm trying to get one of them to come over here and take a note to the guards. There have to be guards here somewhere."

"Shut the window!" John shouted.

"Don't shout at me! I told you this would happen. Do you have any better ideas?"

"If we have to, we'll turn on the heater and sleep overnight in the car."

Iris lunged across him and slammed her hand down on the horn.

"Iris," he said, "what good is that going to do?"

"I'm honking for the guards, you idiot!" Iris said. "What's Mike going to say if I don't get home? He's not going to be so happy if he hears we slept overnight in the car."

In the rearview mirror, Iris could see headlights. "Oh, thank

God," she said. "Human beings." Then two guards, heavily armed, were walking through the deep snow toward the car. "Oh, Mrs. Otway," said the first one to reach them, "got yourself locked in, did you?" Iris, who was afraid of losing the card which allowed her to bring her car into this sanctuary, apologized profusely and began explaining she had tried to give a note to one of the dogs so he would get them, when something resembling a small tank rolled up on John's side of the car. "It's all right, Sam," the guard said, "only Mrs. Otway and her husband.

"Look," the guard told Iris, "it isn't safe in here after the gates are locked. They turn the dogs loose and we're supposed to bring in anyone who looks suspicious." He flushed. "We've had too many robberies, you know; some of the young ones aren't too careful before they start shooting. We'll watch you out."

"I have never," said Iris, while the men opened the gate, "been so glad to get out of a place in my life."

"I've never heard of anyone locking up a cemetery," John said. "You know the old joke. Why don't you see ladders up against cemetery walls? Because no one's dying to get in."

"Don't talk to me," said Iris.

"And where'd you get to?" Etheline demanded, pulling off Iris' boots as she sat on the kitchen chair. "Your first time out, you stays out so long and scares us all to death." She clamped her palm over Iris' forehead. "Clammy," she said. "Get back in bed."

"The back of your hand, not the palm," said Iris for the hundredth time.

"The palm works just fine for me," Etheline said. "Where were you?"

"Locked in the cemetery. Guards let us out. Did anyone call?"

"Did anyone call? You pick up your blue telephone book and start with A and just go through to Z. That's who called."

What an unlikely pair, thought Mike, who had just come in, yet the two women were close. Whenever he got a chance, he eavesdropped on their conversations, which were always about their view of men. His wife, who had long fingers he sometimes thought capable of reaching right into people's minds and taking their thoughts out for further study, was, like all women, capable of forgetting there were such things as individual members of his sex.

Etheline was a heavy, comfortable black woman from Haiti with a penchant for goat meat, religion, and scheming against her estranged husband. After one of Iris' miscarriages they'd hired her on a neighbor's recommendation to stay at the hospital with Iris during the nights.

Settled in her chair after visiting hours, Etheline said, "This is how I likes it. No men. Men is trouble."

"Why are men trouble?" asked Iris, wrenching herself awake. There was no human being whose story she didn't want to hear.

"They ain't trouble," said Etheline. "They's disaster. Why you think I'm sitting up here with you in the dead of night if they ain't disaster?" Iris pressed a button and her bed lifted her up. She leaned back and closed her eyes.

"Your man treat you good?" Etheline asked Iris.

"He doesn't eat goat meat," Iris said sleepily.

"What man do have sense?" asked Etheline.

When Iris awoke the next morning, she decided that Etheline was just what they needed in a housekeeper, and a week later they had hired her. She'd been with them for sixteen years.

"And you," Etheline said, turning on John, "you a sick man. You got no better sense than staying out all night in a cemetery waiting to see things coming up out of the ground? You go to bed yourself."

"I'm fine," said John.

"Dinner on a tray coming up and you get up there first," Etheline said.

"Don't argue with her," Iris said.

"Sick people and children," Etheline said to Mike after they'd gone upstairs. "I don't see what is the difference."

"Come into the living room," he said.

Etheline sat on the velvet couch straight up, patted the kerchief that covered her hair during working hours, and then folded her hands in her lap as if in church. Mike sank into his wing chair, picked up his phone, and turned it over. "I don't want to be interrupted," he said. "Do you think I'm doing the right thing? What do you think of this John Stone business?"

"Well," said Etheline, "it isn't bad. Your wife isn't the kind to run around with anybody. When you is away for a few days, you ever see a chicken getting ready to lay an egg? She's like that, man: here, everywhere, waiting on your call."

"What are people going to think?" he asked. "Her mother's furious. And her father. He called me at the office to tell me he wouldn't let his wife wear black lace stockings a couple of years back, because the next thing he knew, she'd be standing on street corners holding a red pocketbook. Iris' friend Lily said it was the most bizarre thing she ever heard of, an ex-lover moving back in with his ex-fiancée over twenty years later while her husband and children were in the house with her."

"You listening to that flea-brain Lily now?" Etheline asked. "She see a person bleeding on the sidewalk and she worry the blood get on her boots and ruin them. That Lily the most selfish person on this earth."

"But it *is* bizarre," Mike said.

"Tell me something that ain't," said Etheline, shifting in her chair. One of the oil portraits on the wall opposite her was crooked. She'd straighten it later. "I married to Lafayette fifteen good years, and we had us two fine children, and he runs off with a car. That ain't bizarre?"

Her vocabulary, Mike noticed, had improved in the last sixteen years, as had her grammar, and he often suspected her of speaking as she did only so she would continue to fit in with the people she met when she left their house.

"Bizarre is Mr. Lafayette, man. He come back two years ago, his head hanging between his legs, saying all his bad days is over, all he want is to raise his children and stop his drinking, and I want to know what he talking about now, the children all raised, and he go on and on about how we were married fifteen years, and we still married in the eyes of God and he have nowhere to go, and I tell him stay, and he lie around all day in front of the television with his bottle in his hand, and my great big ugly son throw him out of the house when he raised his hand to me. If anyone ever told me it would come to that, my son raising his hand to his father, man, I would have slapped them down where they stood. He got a woman here, he got a woman there. He came and he went again faster than you can turn off a switch. What you care what people say?"

"Her parents—" Mike began.

"Her parents *married* to her, man? Her parents in Florida have eyes big enough to see what going on in this house? He won't cause no trouble. That's what my mind says. When she walk in the door today, you know what she ask me? She ask me if anyone called. You know how long it been since she ask if anyone called?"

"They seem so close," said Mike.

"Two books on a shelf close," said Etheline.

"It worries me."

"Look, man," said Etheline, taking the kerchief from her head, "see these gray hairs? I older than you are. They close. They closer than they think. Siamese twins is close. She doesn't love him like married people. When she sick, she feel guilty until she make herself hot. She need to talk to somebody. Me and my friend Irwin, we so close my husband couldn't stand it. One day he picked up a pot and came at me with it over Irwin, and I grabbed up a knife and told him, he come any closer, they search the house for his nose. Men is always jealous of the wrong party."

"When he gets worse, it's going to mean a lot of work for you," Mike said.

"When you hear me complain about work, man? Dying is something we all come to," she said, tying the kerchief around her head. "Dying and sickness is harder for men than anybody. He brave, man, to come here and come out with it like he done."

"Should we call the doctor? Get him to come over here?"

"Leave that up to Evelyn," Etheline said, bending over and picking a notebook up from the floor. "She made him her special project. She know everything he do. She know when he cough and when he don't."

"He's coughing?" Mike asked, patting his shirt pocket.

"You not looking for cigarettes?" she asked him. "You forget them cigarettes."

"Coughing?" Mike repeated.

"Last night, at three A.M. and the night before two times, at twelve and two A.M. I seen Evelyn's chart."

"You wouldn't happen to know what became of a letter I got that came from California last week sometime?" he asked her. "I put it down and I can't find it. I turned my office upside down."

"A long brown envelope? With some bird stamps on it?"

"That's it," Mike said.

"I went to get that envelope when I washing up the kitchen floor. That last Monday. I took the mails up with my mendings. Then Evelyn go out for a sweater and come home with a skirt and I hemmed it up. Nate's friend came to the house for supper and I saw the letter when I bring the food up to them in front of the television. Then I pick it up and put it somewhere. Iris' mother call and I wrote down her aunt's number on something. My mind tell me I wrote it on that brown envelope with them bird stamps. Where I put it? If it have a number for Iris, it on her windowsill under the wood clock. You need it?"

Mike nodded.

"I'll get it," she said.

Women, Mike thought, are like peasants. They had inexhaustible memories. They could replay the past as if they had it coiled inside them like rolls of film. They were impossible to argue with because their version of what had happened was always so much better documented than yours could ever be. If they suffered more than men, which he doubted, their memories were to blame. If they were more vindictive and petty, it was because they remembered more circumstances, more petty details. If they were not quick to forgive, it was because they remembered the details of their suffering so well. He wondered how John Stone was likely to fare with Iris, who was, according to her notebooks, so determined to excavate things that happened over twenty years ago. *He* hated arguing with his wife. Scenes from the beginning of time were brought back onto the stage, dusted off, and held up before him as evidence. If he bought something she didn't like, she'd be likely to tell him that was all right; he'd done the same thing on her twenty-seventh birthday, when he bought her that blue vase covered with art deco dancers. "I told you then," she'd say, "that I don't like everything just because it's an antique." How did you argue with a memory the size of a whale?

He saw Etheline standing in the doorway, staring over his head. "This room dusty," she said. "No one come in here much anymore. Here," she said, handing him the long brown envelope. "Under the brown wooden clock, just like I said it was. Iris is sound asleep, man. She didn't hear me come in and I rattled around enough to see if she sleeping or she pretending. Man, she sleeping. *He* in his room sleeping too. Locked in a cemetery! Just when I sure the children know how to get from here to there, she start getting herself lost."

"You know," said Mike, "I don't think that was Iris' fault."

"You been eating candy kisses?" asked Etheline, who had apparently spotted something silver and shiny under his chair. "No? Then I better search Nate's bed. He getting too fat."

She came back downstairs ten minutes later with a fistful of tinfoil. "Talk to that child, man. He eat too much sugar and he get diabetes like that lady in the hospital who used to call Iris."

He was surprised. "Did Iris talk to her?"

"Once," said Etheline. "No, twice. Then she call her at the hospital and they say she move her room. Iris think she died because they always said someone move his room when someone died on the floor. She say she use to ask them where they move to, and when they don't tell her, she know they dead."

"I thought," Mike said, "I knew everything that went on in that hospital."

"She know better than to worry you with everything," said Etheline.

"What do you think they talk about all day?" Mike asked her.

"They don't talk all the time. He writes and she reads."

Good grief, thought Mike, isn't that backwards?

Evelyn stood in the doorway and saw a conference in progress. "Dad," she asked, "can John take me to Fort Tryon Park some Saturday?"

"Not on the subways," said Mike.

"Can we take the car?"

"Take the car. Make sure there's gas in it. Check with your mother."

"Don't you go wearing that man out," Etheline warned her.

"Don't go getting too attached to him," Etheline called after Evelyn's retreating back.

"Talk to the wall," said Mike. "Like mother, like daughter."

He went upstairs to the bedroom. Iris was lying across the bed, on her stomach, one arm flung above her head as if it were reaching toward the windowsill and the world beyond it. This was how he used to find her asleep, when, tired of waiting for him to come to bed she would lie down, "just for a minute," and awaken again in the morning. He sat on the foot of the bed, watching her. She lifted her head, saw him, and told him to come back to bed. He told her it was only nine o'clock and she said to come back to bed and then fell back asleep herself. Before she had gotten sick, before she had taken to her bed, he had known they were happy, but he hadn't given it much thought. Now he regarded that time as the lost paradise and wondered, again and again, if they would ever get back to it. For the first time, he believed they would. He didn't understand the source of the weakness that afflicted her, but he could see it was losing its hold. When he asked the doctor how long it would take before the weakness was gone, all the man could say was that since he didn't know what was causing it in the first place, he didn't know how long it would last. "But look at it this way," the doctor said. "When she came home, she could do nothing. Now she can do *next* to nothing. That's progress." From John's room came the sound of coughing.

He went out onto the landing, hesitated, and looked into the guest room. John was coughing in his sleep. From what he had seen, the man appeared to have no fear of death. Mike was terrified of dying, so terrified he was surprised his fear of death hadn't already killed him. He couldn't say he liked the man— he barely knew him—but there was something about him that commanded respect. He radiated vulnerability. His eyes, when they were on you, were wide as a child's, and his lips always seemed about to quiver. Strength and weakness at once, that was what his wife said women wanted in a man.

Then she ought to want him and not bother with this John person. When Mike was an infant, his mother looked into his crib and decided he was dead, screamed, and called the doctor, who said she'd overfed him. She used to tell this story repeatedly, that's how funny she thought it was, but Iris didn't think it was funny. "You mean your own mother couldn't tell if you were alive or dead?" she asked him. He started to cry.

He looked at the walls as he climbed up the stairs. *He* couldn't stand the cruelty of separateness, which was what his wife was inflicting on him. He was angry. He paused on the landing and looked up at the moon. It would be wonderful, he thought, if I could take a rock and throw it at the sky and break it and see what was up there behind it. Some cogs and wheels probably, not much, but maybe there was something, something else.

He ought to start writing down *his* dreams and memories. When he was a child and went fishing, he used to think a giant would come along and fish him up using a candy bar for bait just as he fished up the flounder. It was intolerable, being so small and insignificant and separate in the world. When his mother was dying, he stayed up late at night so that he would fall asleep exhausted because otherwise he would have to think of her having to die, bit by bit, alone in a hospital. He hadn't thought about these things in years. Iris' illness was bringing all these memories back. He supposed they were always there, like stars you couldn't see in the city because of the smoke-clouded air, but he didn't want to think about them now. If you were going to manage, to get from day to day, jumping from one to another without looking down, without losing nerve, it was better not to be too aware.

Who was he kidding? He was aware of everything and he wanted to talk to his wife, who was, instead, talking to John.

Should he talk to John himself? He was absolutely sure John didn't want to talk to anyone else in the world but Iris.

He sat down in his desk chair, switched on his desk light, and pulled the schedule sheets toward him. All he had to do was wait. Waiting was what he did best and hated most.

10

THE SNOW HAD begun to melt. Iris looked out the window and saw black patches and unraked leaves from the previous fall emerging from what had been an expanse of white waves. Time was passing and dragging its engines into life through the sky, pulling the buds out of the sterile limbs of trees, sending messages to the birds, telling them to return, turning the buds on the rosebushes bright red, like nipples, and tugging the insides of crocus and tulip bulbs out of their protective Russian-shaped domes six inches under the earth. What was pulling on everything was also pulling on her. John had settled into a routine of his own, coming into her room in the morning and reading in the peacock chair while she lay in bed, writing in her journals and trying to ignore him.

When they lived in Chicago, he constantly complained that she gave him no privacy. She always wanted to be with him, even when he was sleeping. Turnabout was fair play, she supposed, even if it was over twenty years later.

Now, at noon, they would go downstairs and eat lunch. Neither of them ate very much. After lunch, he would walk restlessly about whatever room she was in until she would ask him if he didn't want to go out. He could take the dog, who needed exercise. He would start for the front door, change his mind and come back, and repeat the performance four or five times until she asked him if he wanted her to come with him, which he did. "Exercise is important," he'd say, "especially after you've been inactive for so long. You have to build yourself up gradually."

After a week, she could walk around the block without shortness of breath. After two weeks, she could walk three or four blocks, and then they would walk to the Junction, have a cup of coffee and a bran muffin, rest, and begin the walk back. "I don't understand it," she said. "*Why* am I still so exhausted?"

"You're making progress," he'd say.

The walks exhausted her, and she would get back in her bed, or go up to her study and watch television, uneasy the whole time, as if it were wrong to let John out of her sight. He was bringing back old memories of the children when they were babies. She remembered how, when Evelyn was born, she wanted the child attached to a cardiac monitor, how she safety-pinned the blankets to the side of her bassinet so they couldn't slip and cover her face, how she watched all night when the stump of her umbilical cord, which had dried, began detaching itself and she was afraid the child would bleed through the abdomen, so she got a lamp, rigged it up so it shone on the child's navel, and watched Evelyn all night. In the morning, after Etheline swabbed the baby's stomach, the little shriveled sign of Evelyn's previous waterly life detached itself and Etheline said, "Well, she's here to stay now." But Iris, who had read about crib death, didn't relax until the child was nine months old.

"He's a nice man," said Etheline.

Iris looked up at her. She relied heavily on Etheline's judgments of people. "It's the calm before the storm," Iris said. "He causes trouble. He wreaks havoc. He can't help it. He doesn't do it on purpose. It's part of his nature. If things go too well, he has to smash them all up."

Etheline snorted.

"Just watch it," Iris said, going back to writing in her notebook. "Tell me if anything strange starts going on."

"Anything strange? Iris, you been in that bed too long. Your imagination climbing the wall. You should get out more. When John finish fixing them bicycles, you try them out."

"What bicycles?"

"Your bicycles. Them two in the garage."

"I'm not ready for a bicycle," Iris said, turning to the window.

Nate and Evelyn began to fight over John. Nate told Evelyn that John had promised to go to a heavy metal concert with him, and Evelyn said first he had to go with her to Fort Tryon Park. Later, when Evelyn and Nate came in and asked her what the hospital had been like, she told them little stories and they listened to her with the same intense attention they had paid when she had invented bedtime stories for them.

"Tell us about the time you fell into the wastepaper basket," Nate asked.

"Again?" said Iris.

"Again," Nate said.

They were enjoying it, this reliving of childhood times when their mother told them stories of her own misdeeds, and every morning and night afterward they wanted the same story repeated, exactly, in precisely the same words, and would stop her if she altered a detail or a phrase.

"Well," Iris said, "I was writing a letter and I put the pen down on my stomach and it fell off the bed, and I thought, Why get up and walk all around the bed to get the pen and have to drag the intravenous after me when I can just lean over and get it? So I leaned over, and the nurse came by and said to be careful before I fell out of bed, but I was holding on to the side of the mattress with my other hand and I leaned over, and then I leaned over a little farther and then a little farther, and then a little farther, and the next thing I knew, my head was in the wastepaper basket and I had fallen off the bed. I pulled myself back up and sat down on the bed, but when I fell off, the big needle pulled out of the intravenous and it was lying on the bed, and when I sat back down on the bed, I sat right down on that needle, and it stuck me in the bottom and I had to pull it out, and the liquid was spurting out of the disconnected I.V. and blood was dripping out of my bottom, and I went off down the hall to find a nurse, and little drops of blood kept spattering on the linoleum as I walked."

"You fell into the wastepaper basket?" Nate asked.

"Into the wastepaper basket," Iris said.

"And we thought you were suffering," Evelyn said.

Ah, Iris thought when they left, I'm learning to be happy. She looked around her room and thought she was a lucky woman; she was surrounded by things that were beautiful to her. She recovered in a bed with a sunburst on its headboard, a huge dog asleep, his head on the pillow next to her, and a cat on her stomach or her hip. A woman with a cat on her lap and a book in her hand, Iris thought, can never be poor. Even John's presence could be regarded as a blessing. He was her great luck, her chance to right past wrongs. In the present, it was always possible to make reparation, while the past, frozen, painted in its brilliant colors of guilt and regret, followed you like an avenging angel, glimpsed now and then in the tall stocking-capped figure of a mugger, heard in the odd noises the house makes when you're alone. Once she had done terrible things to him because she'd known no other way to survive, and she had never forgiven herself. Now she had another chance. She hadn't believed in second chances. Well, then, spring could come. It had her permission. It might not be such a disaster after all, the starting up of the cosmic engines.

She was smiling idly at a sun spot moving along the wall above the peacock chair when John came into the room and began walking restlessly about. "Look, Iris," he said, "when you wanted to know what went wrong all the way back then. What went wrong was that I never loved you in the first place. You fell in love with me. I didn't fall in love with you."

She stared at him, speechless.

"I didn't want you. You didn't give me a chance to want you. What you wanted came first. It was always a question of my autonomy. I never had any when you were around. I never knew what I wanted. I never had a chance. We spent seven years together because you wanted to. I didn't. You knew that but you insisted. If I'd left you earlier, I would have gotten married earlier, I would have had children earlier, I wouldn't have wasted so much of my life."

"And your daughter wouldn't have died," Iris said. The shock of it, the change of mood, the deliberate erasing of happiness: oh, she remembered it well, she remembered sitting in their living room, in their apartment, in the morning, after staying up late the night before hanging the hopsacking curtains she had made herself, how happy he was with her, with the curtains, with everything, how she fell asleep while he stroked her hair, and in the morning, he sat in front of the curtains, the light illuminating them so that they looked like gauzy panels of stained glass, and said gloomily, I don't think this is going to work. Why not? Why not? she cried frantically, and he shook his head: I don't think this is going to work. Then came ten days of misery, of pleading for explanations, of finally resolving to live on her own, of telling herself people recovered from these things, of beginning to make inquiries about other apartments she could live in until he left this one, and as soon as she had accepted the fact of his leaving, he would look at her and ask her if she wanted to go to Nebraska to see his parents or did she want to go to Starved Rock for the weekend, or was blue the color she wanted when he bought the Volkswagen they wanted to have as a wedding present.

She sat still, her face white, saying nothing.

"You were upstairs, weren't you?" she said. "Were you writing something?"

"You were the one who decided when we slept together. *I* didn't want to sleep with anyone until I got married."

"That's all true," Iris said. "Are you about to leave and go somewhere else?"

"Leave?" he said. "I didn't say anything about leaving."

"What were you doing up there?"

"Writing."

"Writing what? Can I see it or will I be infringing on your autonomy?"

"Thank you, Iris," he said. "Thanks a lot." He walked out of the room.

A few minutes later, he walked back in. "Here," he said, handing a sheet of paper to her.

> In spite of what people think, I had a happy childhood. I came from a large family of six brothers and one sister. I was the second child, and my mother always told me how much I was wanted because it was a family tradition to name the son after the father, and if she had a boy I would be John Robert Stone the Fifth.
>
> Midwestern and western families are said to be reserved, even cold, but our family was very close and our mother was right when she said we would never find better or more understanding friends than we had in our own home. A mark of this closeness was my mother's ability to talk to us about the most intimate things. From the time I was twelve, I knew that my mother and my father, who loved one another as much as two people could, were having sexual problems. My mother frequently confided in me about the suffering my father's

impotence caused her. Later, my sister also confided in me. Her husband, who was almost fifteen years older than she was, had low blood pressure, which made it difficult for him to sustain an erection, and to remedy this he would fasten a rubber band at the base of his penis once it was erect, and this would solve the problem. It was my sister who warned me that delaying too long in consummating a sexual relationship might end in the woman's inability to experience an orgasm during intercourse, and when I became involved with a woman myself, I worried about this.

What was remarkable about my family was the freedom they gave all of us. I remember how casually my mother took injuries, so that in the end all of us became daredevils. Once, I fell out of a tree near the lake house and nearly bit my tongue in half, and my uncle, who was a doctor and staying with us at the time, sewed it up without giving me an anesthetic. My brother ripped his arm open when we were driving past the mailbox and he reached out to open the door and instead gashed himself on it, and my mother, who was driving by, simply wrapped his arm in a handkerchief and drove on to the hospital. We learned the virtues of courage and fortitude, and we enjoyed our lives.

"Why are you giving me this?" Iris asked. "I know all this." He asked her what she thought.

"What do I think? What do you think? You had a child. Did you discuss your sex life with her? Autonomy! Observing boundaries! Your family belongs in Krafft-Ebing!"

He said, as he wandered around the room, that he thought she liked his previous attempts at writing.

"*That* was writing!" she said. "*This* is nonsense! Propaganda!"

He said he thought it was pretty good. "We were a happy family," he said.

"Is that why you came down with headaches whenever we went to see them?"

"I always had headaches."

"Not when you lived with me, you didn't."

"I must have been allergic to something in the lake house," he said.

"Oh, yes," said Iris. "The people."

He coughed, startling her.

"Look," she said, controlling her temper, which had gone from the size of a small sparrow to a great goose and now threatened to hatch itself out through her rib cage, "I'm not interested in fighting." That, of course, was a lie. What she wanted to do was kill him. "Take this document and go for a walk with it. Leave me alone."

"That's what I always wanted from you," he said, his voice thick with bitterness. "To be left alone."

"Fine," said Iris. "Good. Out."

But why, really, was she so angry with him? That house of horrors, his childhood, was familiar enough to her. When she thought about his house, designed by his father, protecting the family he insisted was perfect, she did not see people walking through the halls or the rooms, she saw wolves, wild and hungry, blood on their jaws, so hungry they would devour one another.

All this nonsense about what his mother and sister confided in him! He wanted to remind her of her passion for him, to imply that she had never felt anything like it since. He had been reduced to seeking sanctuary in her house. He was going to make her pay for his humbling of himself by humbling her, remind her of how things had once been and how, whatever she did now, she could never recapture the colors of it, the purity of it, the splendor. The conceit! On the other hand, he was right. Were all young girls like Sleeping Beauty, afraid their passions would never be awakened? In her teens, she had watched couples, the girls hungry for the bodies of the boys they were with, the male, the female, pressed against one another so hard, as if they wanted to obliterate any differences, as if they aspired to complete union, an androgynous state. Was it a sickness? And if it was, how did one catch it? She would observe them with a clinical eye. That could not happen to her. She conceived a profound dislike of Jane Austen, mystifying her teachers, but she knew here was no sweet, gentle woman observing family life through her embroidery hoop: here was a woman like her, unawakened, hoping to be awakened, bitter, aloneness cutting into her wrists like a razor, the world burning itself painfully onto her hopelessly open eyes. She lay awake, eyes wide open, knowing she would close her eyes, having seen nothing, soon enough. She was sure Jane Austen was an insomniac.

"What makes you think it's love?" a friend asked her. "You two are completely unsuited."

She knew it was love because, after she saw him, her body gave her no peace. She was tormented by her body. How was it possible to read through that fever? Conrad, James, and Faulkner had to be gotten through, because if she didn't pass her courses she would be separated from him. Shakespeare was an obstacle, taking up time she could spend with John, although she had some small sympathy for Othello, with whom she identified.

He wanted to remind her that he had been her first love and that first loves cannot be equaled. He wanted to make her unhappy with what she had. She flung the covers back and sat on the edge of the bed, looking out the window. Massed crosses. The mad passions of plump gray squirrels, pursuing each other across the network of branches. It was comical. No more comical than she had been. They had made love everywhere: she still remembered all those places as if they were bathed in the strange blue-white light of the moon, as if none of the rooms had ceilings, as if they had tumbled from the earth and were swimming in the stars. After they made love, she could study.

She thought about her husband, angrily, because she knew that was exactly what John wanted her to do, compare them. To compare them and conclude that what she mistook for marital happiness was some kind of empty compromise, as a hunter, falling asleep on a freezing night, believes he loves his dogs, his furs, whatever keeps him warm.

She thought, If I were a tree and felt fire for the first time, the shock of it, the fear, all of it would be indelible. If I felt it a second time, the fear would be back, the pain, but the shock would not be the same. The first time a sensation travels along a nerve it must burn itself into the mind forever. He had set the first fire, unwillingly, since what he wanted was to be a virgin when he married. He knew, he said, it was old-fashioned. Not old-fashioned, merely irrelevant and ridiculous. How could he put her in the position of the sex-hungry maniac from whom he was protecting *his* virginity? In the end he gave in, not, he insisted, because he felt any great passion for her but because he didn't want what happened to his sister to happen to her.

He would never admit to feeling any passion for her. That was how he had tortured her, how he had maintained his loyalty to his family. Was there anything more painful than that refusal, that attempt to make her unwomanly, to make her feel ugly and earthbound amid flights of swans? Oh, she should tell him what it was like between herself and her husband; he had asked once, he would ask again. She should tell him that the first time she saw Mike, she wanted children; she should tell him about their trips to the city, interrupted by sudden visits to his apartment, the exquisite torture of drives back from Manhattan to her apartment, both of them impaled on the force of their feeling.

After nearly eighteen years, things were calmer but not calm.

After making love, she would fall into a deep dreamless sleep and wake up boneless, absolutely boneless, her body melted, her spirit free in the room. What would he know about that, changing wives as he did every ten years? The unbearable intensity of beginnings was his. And she would envy him that, if she could envy the ability to go back and do things again. But there was no part of her life she wanted to repeat. An angel poised on a razor: an instant in life. Go back, lose your balance, the beauty is overwhelmed by pain, the balance is gone, it's impossible to go on to the next moment, the next balancing act.

But there are patterns, things to guide you, thin ropes you can hold, invisible to the eye, which make possible the progress from one sharp instant to the next. Only with age do you find them.

"Ma!" Nate bellowed from the foot of the first-floor stairs. "What's the myth of eternal return mean?"

"Look it up," she called back. An encyclopedia costing over one thousand dollars sat unused in his room; he preferred to have his parents look things up in the unalphabetized caverns of their minds.

"Look it up where?" asked Nate, appearing in her doorway.

"You figure it out," she said, lying back against the pillows.

"Want to read this?" Nate asked, tossing a book across the room so that it landed on her stomach.

"Don't *do* that!" she said. "You can take a person's eye out."

Children were the best contraceptives for the mind or the body; they short-circuited thought. They made intimacy impossible.

"The Unbearable Lightness of Being," she said. "Is it good?"

"It's OK. It starts out talking about the myth of eternal return. The teacher's going to ask us what that is. Don't you want to read the book? It's by the same man who wrote *The Book of Laughter and Forgetting.*"

Iris reminded her son that she hadn't read that book either.

"Ma," he said, "give me a clue! Is there a myth of eternal return?"

She raised her eyebrows.

"Come on," he said. "Read the book. You'll like it."

She shook her head and told him to call someone else in his class.

"I thought we weren't supposed to read translated books in an *English* class," he said. "The parents should complain."

Iris pointed to the door.

Later she heard Nate talking to John. "The myth of eternal return?" John was saying. "Let's look in the encyclopedia."

Iris thought of Dr. Johnson, refuting the theorists who claimed human senses could not give an adequate picture of the world as it was. The objective world and the subjective world. "Thus I refute you," said Dr. Johnson, kicking a stone. Thus did John, standing out there, prove the myth of eternal return. Why was it a myth and not a true description? If she had believed in the myth of eternal return, she would never have taken to her bed.

"Ma," said Nate from the doorway, "if John went with me to a heavy metal concert, *then* could I go?"

"He says you think they're dangerous," John said, standing behind her son, holding a tray. "How can they be as dangerous as all that?"

"They are," said Iris, accepting her plate, knife, fork, and a can of soda, while John sat in the peacock chair and began eating his own dinner, sociably, pleasantly, as if he had not that very afternoon implied that she had destroyed his life by insisting he live with her for seven years. As if she had physically confined him to their apartment, raped him, had her will of him.

"What's this book?" John said, picking up the same book her son had thrown at her earlier.

"If you want to read it, take it," Iris said. "I can't concentrate on anything."

"I'm reading something else," he said.

Why didn't he tell her what? Why was he being so secretive? She had no intention of asking lest her question turn into, according to him, an invasion of privacy, an abridgment of his autonomy.

He was getting closer to the children, who seemed to be competing for his attention. What could she expect? She was still too weak to walk more than a few blocks or sit up straight for a few hours. It made her uneasy. John's great gift was for turning people against one another as if, should two people form a friendship, they would turn against him and outnumber him. Still, he seemed to like children. She was worrying about nothing.

11

THE SOUND OF rain woke Iris, who thought, The snow's gone, the winter's going, in the country the snow will be letting go of the earth, and it is hard for the frozen earth to feel the sun on it, to hear the thousands of little engines, the hearts of crickets, the sputtering inside the bulbs, the sap beginning to move in the trees. It was too early. She was not ready. She wanted snow and more snow. A warm spell, that was all it was, a warm spell that would end and the snow would return, the whole earth like a bed into whose white sheets and quilts everything would again sink until things were ready, prepared, warned that the cold was going.

And then the snow was back and it was very cold, and she heard the radio announcer saying it was too cold to snow, but it was snowing all the same. She was fully dressed and in the middle of a frozen lake and there were holes cut in the thick ice that covered the surface of the lake, and a person's head stuck up out of each hole. She was surprised that her clothes were dry even though she was underwater. She looked at the others and saw they were all looking away. This, too, seemed normal. Perhaps they were ashamed of being trapped. She began to worry about fish nibbling at her toes, but her toes were safely encased in her leather moccasins. Overhead, a helicopter was flying as if it were considering rescuing them, but she had no idea if the helicopter pilot could see them and in fact the helicopter appeared to be stuck in the sky just as she was stuck in the lake. She was very warm in the frozen lake.

She awoke drenched in sweat, her teeth chattering. Her hand was shaking. She had a fever. She took the thermometer from the windowsill and put it in her mouth, watching the clock. Seven minutes later she took it out. One hundred and four. It was starting again. She turned on her side and lay still. It was an hour and a half until Etheline arrived.

"Can I come in?" John asked from the doorway.

"It's starting again," Iris said. "The fever."

He asked her what her doctor's number was and called it. Did she have any other symptoms? No, she didn't. No, he wasn't coughing much himself. Yes, he'd tell her.

"He says there's a bug going around and you should be back to normal in twenty-four to forty-eight hours."

"A bug," said Iris, through chattering teeth.

He asked her where she kept her extra blankets, went into the television room, came back with three, and covered her with them. "Your hands are like ice," he said, tucking the blankets around her.

"I had a dream," she said through chattering teeth. "About being in a lake."

"With only your head sticking up?"

She nodded.

"It's like the other dreams," he said wearily. "It's my dream, not yours."

"Oh, no," she said, trying to stop her teeth from hitting together. "It's *both* of ours."

He asked her if she wanted him to talk to her. She did. He talked to her until she fell asleep, and then he sat in the chair, watching her, thinking.

Lately, he thinks, he looks back all the time, and looking

back is like watching a film that was savagely edited. Children's laughing faces turn suddenly into crying faces. What happened? What was the instant the change took place? How did he find it? Why was there an instant like that, a turning point? Time splits. People split. But people should be immutable, like physical laws. He walks down the street and thinks that if he suddenly turned right or left the world might disappear and he would know he was no longer alive. He loved his Swiss Army knife, the red one, he still has it because it has a screwdriver and if anyone put him in a coffin by mistake he could unscrew the lid. Years of it, walking down the street, and the windows suddenly look as if they're painted on and he hesitates at doors, afraid to open them, because the rooms inside might be filled with dirt and people could be buried in them. Should he talk to her about that? Probably not until she stopped shaking. Should he tell her he was coughing more at night, that he tired more easily? Probably not. What was the point? Discontinuous time, as if his study of quantum mechanics had corrupted his thoughts, some perverse kind of mimesis. He felt less discontinuity here, if only because Iris' presence served to splice his past and present together.

On the windowsill was a book popularizing theoretical physics. He should read it to her. No people, no emotions, pure theory. It was what she needed.

He went down to the kitchen, filled an empty pitcher with water, and brought it upstairs. He told her to drink it. She picked up her head and obediently drank.

Did she remember when he taught her physics? During her first semester, she would put the numbers into an equation and then not know how to solve for t because she didn't know how to get it out from the denominator. By the second semester, they were on optics and she cried in frustration. Who cared where the focal points were? The third semester was quantum mechanics and he felt despair. He would have to drop out of his own courses to tutor her adequately. But she was one of three students in the college to get an A that semester.

How had she worked out the math? Oh, she hadn't. She would read the problems, look at the numbers, think about what events must be taking place, and she'd see the numbers getting bigger or smaller. When she was finished, she'd look down at the choice of answers and her pencil would point at the right one. He suspected her of having copied the answers from someone next to her or in front of her, so he made up new problems. She read them, stared into the distance, then looked down at the page and pointed at the answer.

He asked her how she did it.

The same way he did, she said. She pictured things.

If the subject hadn't frightened her so, she might have been as good as he was. Or better. But she hated to hear him say such things. It was luck. It was thinking in pictures. She couldn't think any other way. But there was a limit to what that thinking could do when you couldn't add two and two and when you weren't interested, not really.

She had to believe he was better than she was. *He* had to believe *she* was better than *he* was. They needed one another to be perfect.

"Oh, man," said Etheline, standing near the bed, "I had enough of this fever, man." She announced she was going downstairs to make a drink of boiled grapefruit skins.

"Does it work?" John asked Iris.

"In the hospital, Mike brought me a jar of it every day. Doctor Chipwitz said it was nonsense and it couldn't do any good, but when my fever went down suddenly, he told me to stop drinking it."

"You should have gone on drinking it and left the hospital," John said.

Iris kicked at the blankets until her feet stuck out. Her feet, she said, were hot. He felt her head. She was cooling off.

"It's a virus," John said.

Whatever it was, she did not get out of bed for three days and their walks together were discontinued. Evelyn volunteered to keep John busy. That Saturday she would take him to Fort Tryon. If no one minded. Iris, who was again sleeping all day, was not consulted.

The weatherman predicted a return of cold weather, but spring was in the wind, hauling up windows to air acrid rooms, bring newly washed laundry up from basement lines to fly like victorious flags over the wet black earth of the backyards, calling the men and women out with rakes and shovels, causing housewives who were devoted to their rosebushes to stoop over them with puzzled expressions: Was it time to begin pruning away the dead branches? It was time to rake away from the budding plants any renegade leaves which had escaped the fall cleaning. The crocuses were beginning to point their green potato-peeler shapes up to a vivid blue sky. Hoses were attached, water was turned on, cars were parked in driveways and washed in the middle of the day while the gray and black winter dirt streamed from their metal sides and poured down the grates in the cement. Afterward, the cars stood clean, groomed like well-kept animals, ready to be turned out in the peculiar long black narrow pastures of the city. The days were getting longer, and in the mornings when people got up for work they did not have to switch on lights to find their eyeglasses or their clock radios. Laughter came into the house on the waves of cool, moist air. Snatches of conversation bubbled up from the sidewalk to people sitting on their window seats. On Ocean Parkway, the benches, deserted all winter, were filling with the old people who lived in the grand apartment houses that belonged to another time, of doormen, of safety, of a domestic routine so precise it was in itself graceful and elegant.

Different ambitions grew up with the crocuses—to get out of the house, out of the office, to start roaming—atavistic urges to go on to the next pasture and see if the grass there had returned and was sweet to chew on. Nothing wanted to stay still.

Iris began to sense the resolution that lay behind her inactivity, the beginnings of regret, a premonition that what prevented the new current, which was running through her as it ran through everything else in the world, would refuse to be blocked and would find new pathways, driving her, like the plants on her windowsill, toward the sun; and the more she sensed this, the more tightly she hugged her quilts to her.

John watched her and watched the world outside quicken and felt himself pulled along by the returning waves of energy but he could give the current no help. Increasingly, he felt like a sentient piece of wood afloat on wide water, unable to use the force of the waves to propel himself toward the shore. If the waves wanted to bring him in, they would do it of their own accord. He had little strength of his own.

To die like this, slowly drained of energy—he thought of himself as a car battery, running down—in the middle of his own family, had it been possible: that would have been unendurable. They placed such a premium on physical strength, while Iris, who had always loved to walk, was content to admire strength in others and slow to notice its absence. Spring had brought Nate's friends and their basketballs to the hoop over Iris' garage door, and John would play with the boys until he was exhausted, a few minutes, five or six, but the boys never said anything to imply he was old or weak or sick. His family would have treated him with equal doses of contempt and sympathy, and then it would have been contempt and more contempt until all the sympathy was gone.

He was glad that none of them had been there when his daughter was dying. A machine running down. It was an appropriate death. Iris would say so. What was it she used to say? People don't drain you. They're sources of power. When you have no energy of your own, you can borrow theirs. They don't mind. There were two kinds of energy, individual and communal.

Her source of energy had also been cut off.

Evelyn's, however, had not. The clearer, bluer skies, the noise of the birds returning to the trees, not many birds, but enough to mark the change in the season, excited her. She wanted to go to the park. What about her boyfriend? Oh, she said, waving her hand, he has something to do. Basketball practice. Let's go.

He drove down the FDR Drive. She apologized for taking him on a circuitous route, but she only knew one way to get there. A dark blue tugboat was pushing a huge garbage scow through the grayish-green water. So does the heart push the body through life. He drove carefully. Iris had a low opinion of his driving skills. In the beginning, she had admired his daring. Later, she saw it as something evil, intended to frighten her or to destroy him. He used to walk on the railing above the four lanes of traffic between the Science Museum and the lake, one step, then another, balancing with his arms as if he were on a tightrope, while Iris would not only refuse to look but sit down on the top step to the overpass and cover her face with her hands until she was sure he was safe on the other side.

His family had encouraged such displays of courage.

No more of that now.

Evelyn showed him where to park, a typically gray city street, gray stone buildings, none more than five stories high, gray cement sidewalks, trees still gray from winter, that was part of city life, one of its attractions, hiding the rhythms of nature, lulling everyone into a sense of sameness, erasing the evidence of change, the remorseless eruption of the season, the remorseless obliteration of what had erupted, an eternal sameness that could be mistaken for eternity. There was evidence here and there, little tufts of grass shooting up between hairline cracks in the cement, but evidence easily ignored, easily eradicated, the bark peeled from trees, which died and were not replaced, flowers torn up and left to die on hot sidewalks, an insistence on sameness, on refusing to feel the implacable forward motion. Or perhaps a rebellion against this kind of eternity, gray, cold, hellish. He had lived in cities so long now, more than thirty years, that his seventeen years in Nebraska had come to seem a kind of interlude, and yet he had never accepted the city. He averted his eyes when he walked as if he were walking through a bombed-out place.

"This way," said Evelyn, going through a metal gate and making her way across a playground to a narrow path through the bare trees. "This way. It's a long way up." She was carrying bags of sandwiches and cans of soda. He followed her up the hill, along the winding path, while she stopped frequently to look back down, exclaiming at how small the benches and the swings looked from up above, but really pausing to give him a chance to rest. They climbed up and up until they could see a wide river, a dead gray-silver flashing in the light, and he asked her what river it was, but she didn't know—maybe it was the East River, maybe it was the bay, maybe that was New Jersey on the other side, maybe it was Staten Island—just like her mother, imprecise about everything. "On our way to Boston, we could stop sometime in Washington," she used to say. Things like that. Maddening.

He climbed and controlled his breathing, making it regular: a deep breath in, slowly; a deep breath out, slowly. Enraging, this tyranny of the flesh, enraging too that the flesh would give up its hold on the spirit, letting it go without a battle.

"I climbed a mountain with your mother once," he told Evelyn.

"Was it fun?"

"She didn't think so."

"Why?"

"I didn't want to stop until we got to the top."

"The view's almost always best from the top," said Evelyn, leaning her back against a tree, saying how warm it was in the sun; wasn't it warm? You couldn't even see the playground anymore.

"She was furious because when we got to the top, in fact before we got to the top, it started getting misty, and we climbed most of the mountain in the middle of a thick gray fog, and when we got to the top we couldn't see our hands in front of our faces and we had to hold on to each other if we wanted to stay together. It was like walking through a rain cloud. Your mother went on strike. She wouldn't climb any more mountains. She went back to the tent and convinced her friend not to cook dinner and we all had to go out to a restaurant. Women. Revenge."

"On the other hand," said Evelyn, "it must be disappointing to climb a whole mountain and not see anything. All that effort for nothing."

"The effort was the point."

"I'd want to look down and see things," Evelyn said.

"So did your mother. She said the whole thing was an allegory of my life. Rushing up a mountain to see the view and finding myself in a cloud."

"Mother is hard on people."

He looked at the girl.

"Not really," he said.

They began climbing again. Finally the barges on the river below were the size of dominoes.

"Here we are," said Evelyn.

He spread the tarp on the damp ground and the plaid blanket

180

on top of that. They sat on the blanket and rested their backs against a large elephant-skinned tree.

"I love it here," she said.

She was only fifteen, but she looked seventeen or eighteen. She looked exactly as Iris had looked when he met her, Iris who had been dating his roommate, and who had come into their apartment with a dog she'd found on the street, pleading with his roommate to keep it until she could find a home for it. Pets weren't allowed in the undergraduate dorms. Ed, his roommate, loved her, her unpredictability, how she seemed to read his mind, her fear of labs, her hatred of routines; all of it intrigued him. He sat on the edge of his desk, watching the two of them fuss over the dog. Did John want to eat dinner with them? He couldn't decide. His roommate became impatient. Iris' green eyes fastened on him and he felt the heat of it, that stunning curiosity. No one had ever been so curious about him before. No one had ever known there was anything to be curious about. The more he hesitated, the more intently she watched him. From that minute, she said later, she loved him. For his part, he wanted to know what about him caused her to watch him with those wide green eyes, green planets, green seas. For an instant, he saw himself outlined in a haze of green light like the light in the fluoroscopes the shoestores once used to see if their shoes fit his feet. He took up space in the world.

The myth of eternal return. His own daughter had taken after nobody, a great relief to him. He had put off fatherhood out of inadequacy, sure he could not meet the needs of a child.

Physically, Evelyn differed from Iris. Her waist was smaller, her hips fuller, her breasts larger. Two hourglass-shaped women, but this one more perfect, her legs longer, her ankles slightly thinner, her thighs, too, he imagined, leaner and stronger. Only her hands were inferior to her mother's, her fingers shorter, almost stubby, her nails bitten. She was a child, after all. Iris never

181

bit her nails. When he met her, she was sixteen and had long polished nails, which she seemed to think went perfectly with her blue jeans and college sweatshirts.

Tired? Evelyn asked him.

He was, he was. And confused too, in a strange city, sitting with a girl who looked exactly like the one to whom he had gotten engaged almost twenty-five years ago, full of the knowledge of his dwindling present at the precise moment the past seemed to be returning, as if the passage of time had suddenly been decreed unlawful and had been annulled by the severe green engines of spring. The girl was saying something about what a beautiful flannel shirt it was, you didn't see ones like that in the stores, and he was too tired to tell her that the shirt was older than she was, his mother had made it for his twenty-first birthday. He was dizzy with the tenderness in her voice, which was no longer a voice but tenderness itself, which wrapped him and warmed him as it had a quarter of a century ago, those years that were gone now. Her hand was on his shoulder, gentle, tentative, she was leaning forward to look into his eyes, was he asleep, was he breathing, her green eyes wide, no pupils at all, she didn't blink, she was like a cat, he had taken her to an eye doctor when she complained her eyes were dry and the doctor said, You don't blink often enough; are you aware of not blinking? Of how you stare? No, that was Iris, not Evelyn. Like cats, eyes wide open as if blinking were a risk they were not willing to take, the unexpected thing happening just as the lids dropped for an instant, over with when the eyes opened wide again. Her face so close to his, such white skin, its features out of focus, that heart-shaped face, those wide cheekbones, those preposterous lips like the lips on Valentine cherubs, all out of focus and coming closer, he bent forward slightly and kissed her on the lips and she slid her arm around his shoulder and kissed him back and he kissed her again.

"No," he said, "I can't. It's wrong.

"Don't cry," he said.

Evelyn said she was crying because she was happy.

"Your mother wouldn't like it," he said.

"She won't care. And if she does? She's *married*. To Daddy. Even if she seems to forget."

"Seems to forget?"

"About us. About him. In that bed. All the time."

"No," he said. "Something happened to her. She's trying. She hasn't forgotten."

"Well, I don't understand," Evelyn said.

"Why should you? You're too young."

"I'm not young," she said, stung.

"Your mother was never young either."

"Forget about my mother! She wouldn't care."

He moved forward so that her arm slid down his back. He looked at her and she withdrew her arm and folded her hands in her lap.

"I love you," she said.

He sighed. "You don't. It's the drama of it, an older man, a dying man, someone foreign to you. It's not me you love."

The same words, more or less, he'd said to her mother repeatedly in the past.

"It's you."

The same words, said with the same intensity, the same absolute belief.

"I love you too," he said. "But not in that way."

"What way then?"

"As a friend. Don't cry. I'm not worth it." He heard the weariness in his voice. "I inspire love. I don't give it."

"I don't believe it!"

"Let's go down," he said.

"If I behave, can we stay?"

183

He nods. They sit there quietly, watching a barge move from the left to the right of the painting the river has become.

"What kind of mother is Iris?"

"She has no patience," Evelyn says. "Lately."

He is surprised. He would have thought Iris had all the patience in the world. After he left her, he went back to Chicago because there was no one else he could talk to, and he told her he didn't understand why, but whenever he was in bed with his wife, he had to pretend she was someone else. He'd thought that happened when he was with Iris because she wasn't what he wanted.

He asks himself now how he could have done that, why she listened to him, patiently walking by his side, not touching him, but her arms around him all the same. She was better than I thought, he thinks. Is better.

The sun is dropping and the air turns chill. He tries to stifle a cough but it pushes at the base of his throat. Impossible. Evelyn hears the cough and gets up. *We better go back.* Two women, he thinks, born to be nurses. Burdened down with such fine minds.

They drive back slowly, in the right-hand lane. He wants to watch the river, and in any case the traffic is heavy and brings the car to a stop before the Sixty-third Street exit. Evelyn is rummaging in the glove compartment, looking for a tape by Bruce Springsteen, whoever he is. She finds the tape and rewinds it until she finds the song she wants. The words: "Everything dies, and that's a fact, but maybe everything that dies still comes back."

"I'll *always* love you," she says, looking out the window.

"Good," he says. "People need love."

She looks at him as if he's said something cruel.

Iris awoke much later and found her daughter sitting on the edge of the bed.

"Mother!" said Evelyn. "Are you awake?"

She nodded.

"He kissed me!"

"Who did?"

"John."

"What!"

"He's the most marvelous man, a really wonderful man, it's horrible what's happening to him, I'd wait for him forever! How could you have let him go? I don't mean there's anything wrong with Daddy, it's just—"

"Evelyn," Iris interrupted her, "stop. Now!"

"But Mother," her daughter whined.

"And stay away from that man!"

"Ma!" said Evelyn.

"Out!"

"You want everything for yourself!" Evelyn said.

"Out! Go!" said Iris.

When he came into her room at ten the next morning, he found her sitting up, lips a white scar in a white face, a look he remembered all too well.

"Evelyn said you kissed her."

"*I* kissed her *back*."

She started raving. It would be useless to try stopping her. He sank down into the peacock chair.

"What do you think you're doing? Don't you think I know what you're doing? You're trying to humiliate me by taking up with her. *My own daughter.* You want me to feel old and unattractive and you pick on my own daughter! That was always your idea of love! Humiliation? Torture isn't a way of life here. If you go near her again, I'll kill you with my bare hands! I'll tear your eyes out!"

She would have continued repeating that forever, but his face, stunned, his eyes half closing, the way he picked up his hands as if to ward off an attack, stopped her.

"I want," she said coldly, "an explanation."

"I was confused," he said. "I was tired from the climb and she looked so much like you. I kissed her back."

"Confused! Confused about what? You always said you never loved me, *I* seduced *you* by loving *you,* I never gave you a chance to find out how you felt! Don't tell me Evelyn did all those things to you while you sat on that damn hill!"

"You were never what I wanted," he said slowly, "not physically. I wanted a woman with no hips, small breasts, dark hair. You were never what I wanted." He got up slowly and sat down on the side of the bed. She did not move away. "I *learned* to love you. I got used to you. I always loved your eyes. Your face, it was such a dramatic face, like the face of an actress. Everything you thought or felt was written on it. I disappointed you all the time. I remember the first time you came back from the supermarket and you looked up at me from the bottom of the steps, and I thought, I love her. I love that face. It was the first time I let myself think it. So then I thought, If I love her, she'll promise me things, I'll start to want them, I'll depend on them, she'll take them away. You used to talk about how we were happy for ten days and unhappy for ten days. During the second ten days I paid for the first ten days. *You had to pay.* Do you understand?"

She understood.

"What," she asked, "does this have to do with Evelyn?"

"Nothing. Except she's like you were then. She'll grow up to be what you're like now."

She says nothing. Time has collapsed for her. She has waited over twenty years to hear him say he loved her. What has enabled him to do it? The passage of time, the visible end of it, as at the edge of a cliff, one sees the end of all solidity, one sees it is possible to fall off the edge of the earth, first waving, goodbye, goodbye; is this his way of waving goodbye before leaving? Is this the only time he can tell her he loved her?

"Your wives," she asks. "Did you tell them you loved them?"

"I couldn't. They knew. I hope they knew."

"Your daughter. Did you tell her?"

"I told her. She knew."

He stood up and went back to his chair.

"How did she die?" Iris asked finally.

"The cancer moved into her liver. She was so emaciated she had to lie on a bed covered with inflatable cushions, but when the liver went, she bloated. In the end, she looked like something that had drowned and washed back up to shore."

He looked into Iris' green cat's eyes, saw the wrinkles at their corners, they didn't belong there; when he wasn't looking at her, her face was unlined, sixteen years old, her throat was unlined, there were no deep frown lines, two of them between her eyes. He saw the tears in her eyes and began to cry.

"I understand about Evelyn," she said.

"You do?"

"I do. She loves you. I love you. People should be more careful about love. You can't stop it. It's like death."

"Like death?"

"Yes."

He looked away, out the window.

"It feels like death," he said.

"Oh, yes."

"I wish," he said, "we weren't in the city. I miss the country. I should never have lived in a city, not for so long."

"Ambitious people," she said, "go to cities."

He said he wasn't ambitious now.

She thought about their house in the country, shut up now for months because of her illness. Up there, it was probably still snowing. She leaned over, picked up a book, flipped through it until she found the photograph she was looking for, and handed it to John. Pictures of glass trees, covered with ice. She told him to look at the date: April 27.

He looked at the picture and remembered walking down the Midway with her in the middle of March, stopping in front of Rockefeller Chapel, the trees glistening in their skin of glass, the sun turning the winter-worn trees to alien beings dressed in crystal. She was wearing a maroon corduroy coat with a hood, and with one hand she clutched it closed because otherwise her ears would become infected and she would end up sitting for hours in Student Health waiting for a chance to see the doctor. Earaches, cold weather, coats with hoods, he had been happy then and he hadn't known it.

"Would you like to go to the country?" she asked him. "We have a house there. Mike could probably take the time this weekend. Or we could drive up on a Wednesday and he could take the bus up on Friday."

"The country," said John.

She looked at him and smiled. It was painful, remembering how perfectly ecstatic making him happy had always made her. And how desperate she became when she could not do it.

"It's not fair to let you take all the blame," she said. "There was such need on my side. No one could have met it. I couldn't tell it from love. I thought the two things were the same."

"You didn't mean any harm."

"I caused harm all the same," she said.

"Yes," he said. "You did."

"We both did," she said. "Let's go for a walk later. Let's go to the country. Would that make you happy?"

"Oh, yes."

She loved the country.

Two fingers of sun were running up and down the windowsill as if the white painted surface were a keyboard and the sunbeams were playing a tune she could not hear.

"We have to do something about Evelyn," Iris said at last. "Or *you* do. She's not going to listen to anything I have to say about you."

"I'll be careful with her," he said. "I won't go near her. You were right to be angry with me."

"Right, wrong," she said, her voice desperate.

"What you have to do," she said, finally, "is pretend to love her. Tell her if you weren't dying you'd wait for her, but it isn't fair to her. Tell her you're giving her up for her own good. You know how to do it. Remember what you used to tell me. It will come back to you."

"Iris, I'd rather tell her the truth."

"What truth?"

"I'll tell her I mistook her for you, it was all a mistake, I thought she was someone else."

"You're going to tell Evelyn you kissed her because you mistook her for her mother?" Iris asked. "Do you want to kill her? She's my *daughter*. She's a normal child! She thinks I'm an old hag! You can't tell her you thought she was me!"

"But it's the truth!"

"Oh, forget the truth!" Iris said.

"You were the one who always said there was nothing more important than the truth," John said.

"I didn't know what I was talking about."

"In other words," John said slowly, "you want me to take her aside and tell her I love her and I'd wait for her if I weren't dying?"

Iris sighed.

"Don't take her aside anywhere," she said. "She'll find a way to take *you* aside. She's precocious."

"I could tell her," said John, "that if it weren't for your being sick, it would be different."

"Oh, fine," said Iris. "She's mad enough at me already. She's never been sick for more than three days in her life and she doesn't understand why I couldn't just tell my fever to go down. She certainly doesn't understand why I didn't get out of bed."

"Iris, be reasonable. If I tell her I love her, she's not going to care whether I'm dying. If I tell her I can't do anything that might make you sicker, she'll respect my principles. I can't think of another way. Either I tell her the truth or I tell her it's a matter of principle. Loyalty. To you."

"All right," said Iris. "She's already mad at me." She looked up at him. "Love, love, love," she said. "Yuk."

Mike was delighted to hear that she wanted to go to the country. He was, nonetheless, angry. Iris could not get out of bed when he wanted her to, but since John arrived, she had not only gotten out of bed, she had gone for walks, and now she was capable of going to the country. He pictured her getting ready to go, the bed strapped to her back, looking like a demented house mover in a bathrobe, or a monstrous turtle dragging along its horribly mutated shell. He would never, he told himself, think of his wife in this way if he weren't so angry. It was too bad she decided she wanted to go up to the country house on a Wednesday. He had a meeting he could not miss. Next week. Definitely. The word *definitely* hung in the air like a figure freed from a piece of stained glass. A beautiful word, implying that, once again, one could plan on things in advance.

In her room, which she left now for short walks, Iris felt Evelyn circling her as if she were an animal in a clearing and her daughter was in the forest, hunting her. What would the child get up to in her first fit of sexual fury? Nothing obvious. Deviousness was bred into her bones.

"Mother, what would you do if Daddy died?" Evelyn asked before dinner, looking at Iris as if her mother ought to be the first course.

"I don't know," Iris said.

"Would life be worth living?"

"Probably not."

"But you'd go on living because of us?" asked Evelyn.

"Of course."

"I know you're jealous," Evelyn said. "Because he kissed me."

"I am not jealous," said Iris. "Jealousy has nothing to do with it." Although, of course, it did.

"You just want me to be happy," Evelyn said sarcastically.

"Don't mock the truth," said her mother.

"If I slept with him?" said Evelyn. "After all, he's dying."

"Evelyn, if you sleep with anyone, *you're* going to be the one worried about dying."

She watched her daughter's face, rapt, her eyes intent on something visible to herself only.

"Playing with other people is wrong," Iris said. "Testing other people is wrong. People don't like to be tested, and they usually fail the test. Their failure is your failure. Worse."

Evelyn insisted she wasn't playing with anyone, or testing them either. Although, looked at in a certain way, her mother could be said to be testing them by staying in bed.

"No," Iris said, "I'm not testing anyone. My strength failed. You can't understand that."

The curiosity in her daughter's eyes turned to fear. "You're strong," she said resentfully. "Aren't you?"

"Yes," said her mother. "Do you want to go to the country house next week?"

"The country house," said Evelyn. "Do you think there's still enough snow? Enough for the snowmobile?"

Her mother nodded.

The child—yes, she was a child again—sat staring out the window, her face transformed. "The sky's a beautiful color," she said. "Purple. Look, Mother."

"I'm well acquainted with every conceivable shade of lavender and purple you can see from that window," Iris said.

"Oh, well, you should always look," Evelyn said, word for word the same admonition given hundreds of times by her mother when, on long drives, Evelyn would sit in the back seat sulky with boredom and refuse to look out the window, unrepeatable splendors passing her by.

Old people are like that, Evelyn used to think when her mother told her to look out of the window. They don't know what's important. They sit in the front seats of cars and talk about the nature of light on barns or the pinkish-white color gray trees turn in the winter sunsets. They forget their bodies, useless to them. Only their eyes move easily. An incontinence of images, an incontinence of words about those images. Idiot that she had been! Her mother was young enough to be a rival. Her mother would not look at the remarkable violet light in which the pink trees swam. Who else could she tell about it? Her father? Only if he were in the right mood. If not, he'd say, "Don't bother me," and wouldn't lift his massive head, bent over a book. People fell in love so they could say to someone, Look at the pink trees swimming in the violet light.

"Look," she said to John on the landing, "at the color of the trees in the light. Pink and violet."

"Beautiful," he said, his eyes on Iris, who was watching him from her bedroom. Lately, she rarely closed her door. "Evelyn," he asked, "can I talk to you for a minute?" He saw Iris slide down against the pillows, smiling slightly.

Later that night, Evelyn came into Iris' room.

"Yes?" said her mother.

She looked at Evelyn, who was apparently too outraged to speak.

"It's because of you," Evelyn said at last. "If it weren't for you, he wouldn't give me up."

Iris said nothing.

"The first person I ever really loved, the *first* person, and you have to spoil it!"

"I'm sorry," said Iris.

"You're sorry for everything, but you do it anyway!"

"John has a mind of his own," Iris said.

"*You* could make him change it!"

"I couldn't and I wouldn't," Iris said.

"I'm going to talk to Daddy."

"If you talk to Daddy," said Iris, "and if you tell him John kissed you, he'll throw him out before you have a chance to take a deep breath. Is that what you want? The man's sick, Evelyn."

Evelyn watched her. "He loves me. Not you. He said I'm not at all like you were when you were my age."

"If you're trying to hurt me, you're doing a good job," Iris said, and was shocked by the spiteful glee this comment produced.

"I'm not trying to hurt you," her daughter said. "I can't help it if he loves me. He said he never really loved you. At least not as much as he loves me."

"That's enough," said Iris.

"It's the truth, that's all," said Evelyn.

"Fine," said Iris. "Terrific. Go to bed."

"I hope I didn't upset you," said Evelyn.

"If you had a fifteen-year-old daughter who'd fallen in love with a fifty-year-old man, you'd be upset too," Iris said.

"*That's* not what's bothering you, Ma," said Evelyn.

"Don't be so smart," said Iris. "Go to bed."

The child marched off down the hall like a queen greatly pleased by the number of enemy heads brought her on a platter.

Still later, John came in.

"Did I do a good job?" he asked Iris.

"Out!" she hissed. "Do you want to spoil everything?"

12

UPSTAIRS, MIKE WAS still typing. In bed, against her pillows, Iris wondered whether she had found John so irreplaceable because she placed such tremendous value on herself. She was sixteen. Only one key to open the locks of her body, such a unique body because it was hers, as he was, unique and priceless, because he had opened her. Magic words, open sesames, the rock door in the cliff face sliding back, the apple lodged in the princess' throat, the splinter of ice in the young girl's eye, the insanity of women, insisting they were the first heroines, there were no other stories like their stories, even though their own mothers had read them to sleep with those stories night after childhood night. Glorify what humiliates you, the body said; forget the other stories. None of this has ever happened before.

She sighed and lay down. As a child, she would stay up until her parents were asleep, then take her pillow, put it under her arm, clutch it to her side, and make her way down the long dark tunnel that was the apartment of her childhood, into her grandmother's room. Once in bed with her, she would lie awake, tracing the wrinkles in the pillow, as if, could she only see it, they were a map of the place she was to get to. Her grandmother, her long silver hair falling way below her waist, over her long red-flowered flannel nightgown: in the mornings when she raised her silver brush backed with angels and the morning sun struck it, the winter sun, she looked like a princess who had grown old in a tower and was picking up a magic scepter that would finally set her free. What sorrow, when the scepter returned from the beam of sun and became itself again, a brush, moving through her grandmother's long hair.

> I'm forever blowing bubbles,
> Pretty bubbles in the air,
> They rise so high, almost touch the sky,
> Then like a glass,
> They shatter and die.

Her eyes on her grandmother's face in the mirror as she sang that song.

Poor Evelyn.

Her grandmother gave Iris an ivory egg filled with light. She made gauzy, various motions with her hands, which led Iris to believe that this was one of the ivory things her grandfather had brought back with him from his trip to China, and before she could take the egg, her grandmother took a key out of her chintz apron pocket and locked it in a china cabinet. If her grandmother could only understand that this was her birthday, and consequently she should be given the key and allowed to play with the egg, because it was her birthday, even if it was the wrong month for it, but it was her birthday, and she should be allowed to play with the egg.

She was walking around the room in a long red nightgown, her silver hair flowing down her back, and she picked up a small jewelry box covered with shells and there was the key, wrapped in a little piece of paper which came from inside a fortune cookie and which read, THE BEACH OF THE SEASHELLS WITH ROSES INSIDE THEM IS BLACK, BLEACHED AND BARE. The cabinet was gone but the key opened a rose in the wallpaper and there was the egg! It glowed like a lightbulb and her hand hesitated. It might be too hot to touch.

In her hand, the egg was warm, and a little door in its surface opened when she slid a fingernail into a tiny hairline crack and inside was a tiny telephone, its receiver off the hook. She picked up the receiver and heard John talking to her.

She said something or other and wandered away. She was in the country house, in her bedroom with the secret panel behind which they put all their valuable things they left after the summer, when she remembered the egg and went back to get it. It was there, behind the wall. She spoke into the phone, and there was his voice, saying something. She apologized for having kept him on the phone for so long. He said he didn't mind, but she didn't believe him. There was such sorrow at the other end of the line. She tried to think what to say next. She couldn't think of anything and put the egg back and left the room. Then she was on the beach, a beach covered with seashells filled with tiny black paper roses, and there was the egg, and when she said hello, he was there.

She woke up crying, feeling as if a sentence had been passed upon her, a decree, saying she could never be separated from John nor he from her, and yet he was dying, and she was married and loved her husband, and life seemed incomprehensible and hopeless, and she hated the egg, which she could still see there in the dark room, smug and self-contained, holding all it needed and all it would ever need.

She picked up her notebook and wrote the dream down.

Something like good cheer had invaded the house. John and Nate were making plans to go to a rock concert. Evelyn wanted to know where her ski pants were and why Etheline always *hid* things from her. Etheline was beginning to shout back at the children.

"What you mean, *hid* it, man? You got a junk store in there. That Nate, he steal my cookies, but he keeps a clean room."

Evelyn went on whining about her ski pants, and finally Nate shouted, "All right, I'll help you! God, can't you find *anything?*"

"All she care about, man, is that ridiculous Justin, and he a head shorter than she is."

"He'll grow! He'll grow!" Evelyn said.

"Don't count on it," said Nate. *"Here* are your pants. In back of your bookcase."

"Forget the clothes and start up on your homework," Etheline said.

Iris looked at her windowsill and found the book her husband had brought to her in the hospital: *The Dancing Wu Li Masters.* She picked it up, tied the belt of her Chinese robe, and went to sit on the couch of the television room.

"Move over for your mother, you big hulk of worthlessness," Etheline ordered Nate.

"It's all right," said Iris. "I have enough room."

She began looking through the book for the section on wave-particle duality, the subject that had fascinated her before the diabetic woman was installed in her hospital room. She looked up and found the family standing around, staring down at her. They were so tall, they looked like trees.

"What?" she asked.

"Oh, nothing," said Nate, and they wandered off again. From the hall landing came the sound of laughter, like the promise of a better life.

"I don't understand it," Iris said to John. *"How* can something be a wave and a particle all at once?"

"There's no such thing as a wave-particle duality," he said.

She pointed to the page.

He said the problem lay in the way of measuring things. The confusion began there. The particle did not lead a double life.

"Look," he said, drawing on a piece of paper. "This is the double-slit experiment. You fire a photon gun, and the paths of the photons are charted, and no matter how you do it, how far apart you space the firings, you end up with a wave. No one knows why. The photon is a photon, but when you follow their paths, you get a wave."

She studied his diagram. "Suppose you fired the gun so that photons were released every twenty-four hours? Then it couldn't be the individual fields of the particles interacting with one another. What would happen then?"

"You'd get a wave. The wave is the chart of their paths, not a picture of them."

She said she didn't understand.

"No one does."

"Photons have a life span, don't they?" she asked after a while. "If they have a life span, maybe the chart shows life expectancies. Some photons must be about to stop existing when they're fired. Others must be new. Could that be why you get a wave?"

"No one knows."

"*No one?*"

"No one knows. It's convenient to talk about photons as if they were part of a wave because you can predict with a high degree of certainty where they'll be. They act like they're waves or parts of waves, but they aren't waves. They're *themselves*."

"It has to do," said Iris, "with their life expectancies. Has anyone thought of that?"

"It's not an uncommon thought."

"But it makes sense. There are actuarial charts for people. People come and go in waves. There are folk theories about it. When one person dies, another soul comes into the world to take his place, so the dying person would be the part of the wave hitting the shore and the newborn would be the particle further back. Everything obeys the same laws. I'm sure it has to do with life expectancies."

"No one knows."

"How can they not know? It's basic."

"It's because it's so basic they can't work it out."

"Will they?"

"What do you think?"

"Someone will." Not, she thought, in our lifetime. But she liked to think of him, that hero, who would come and explain why what she pictured as a round, glowing object, the smallest possible tadpole of light, constantly traveled through the world with its brothers, leaving a wave pattern in its wake.

"I think about particle theory a lot lately," she said, "and how molecules of water in the ocean aren't said to move, just up and down, not all the way forward to the shore, but the wave moves all the way forward, moving the molecules up and down, but it's the wave, not the molecules, that reaches the shore. I don't understand it anymore. I once did."

"If you tied a rope to a tree, and walked away holding the rope and stopped when the rope was still slack, and began shaking the rope up and down, would the rope get any closer to the tree? No, it wouldn't. But you'd see the rope traveling in a wave pattern. Do you understand?"

Yes, she said, she understood, but she thought it was terribly sad all the same.

"Why sad?"

"To be forever fixed in one place."

"The molecule has degrees of freedom. Who knows what it thinks about? Forward motion might distract it. There's something to be said," he said slowly, "for having a place."

"But it never reaches the shore," she said. And then she said, "At the end of things, everything reaches the shore at once."

"What do you mean?"

"At some point, everything stops being separate. At the end of the world. When the angels stand at the earth's four corners and blow their trumpets."

"It would be nice to think so," he said.

"Don't you?"

"Sometimes. Sometimes not."

Out-of-body experiences, thought Iris, seances to commune with the dead, experiments in ESP. He needs to believe in it. I need to believe in it. It's an idea, not a belief. Still, whatever the photons thought about their individual lives, they reached the shore as part of a wave. Not separate.

In the hall, Evelyn saw the two of them, their heads bent together over a book, and thought, She gets everything. She gets everyone. Even if she has to study physics to do it.

"They're *friends,* Evelyn," Nate whispered in her ear, passing by.

Evelyn followed her brother into his room.

"What are you doing in here?" he asked her. "This is my room, or haven't you noticed?"

"If Daddy died, she'd marry him tomorrow," Evelyn said.

"Sometimes, Evelyn, you're a real ass," said Nate.

"She would," Evelyn said.

"It would be one short marriage," said her brother.

Evelyn started to cry.

"What's the matter with you now?" he asked her.

"Nothing," said Evelyn, leaving and banging his door closed behind her.

"Stop that slamming!" Etheline shouted from the television room.

Mike came home and said he wouldn't be able to go to the country with them. He'd tried to find someone to go to the meeting in his place but there was no one else who could go. Another budget crisis.

"Oh, no!" cried Evelyn. If her father came, she'd have a chance to talk to John. She was used to adoring him from afar, but she'd like to adore him at closer range.

"Think of someone beside your ownself, man!" said Etheline. Mike interrupted them and asked John if he thought he could drive the three hundred miles to Vermont.

"But I don't want to go without you," Iris insisted.

"Go. The kids want to go. They've kept quiet about it all winter. John wants to go. You want to go."

"You're being a martyr."

"You know me," he said.

"Then come."

"Iris, you want to go. Go."

"Not without you!"

"Pretend you're going to give a lecture," he said, secretly gratified by how frantic she was becoming. "You've gone off without me before."

"I suppose," she said, thinking it over, "if he got tired, I could always drive."

"True," said Mike. "But I'd feel better if he drove. You're out of practice." I would also, he thought, feel better if she weren't so easily persuaded to leave me behind.

Why wasn't it becoming a question of trust? He was normally a jealous man. It was unreasonable of him, as he'd told Iris, to be angry because she had been unfaithful to him *before* he ever met her. Was that how he saw it? she asked. Yes, he said. It was. In their own pasts, they had been unfaithful to one another. Please, Iris said, you're confusing the issue. Not really, he said. Not at all. He accepted the fact of her past infidelity and knew she wouldn't repeat it. Because the past isn't repeatable? Iris asked him. Something like that, he said; also, the present is inviolable. For us.

Also Iris never makes the same mistake twice, he thought.

Iris thought he was being too reasonable and she would pay for this later.

They left Wednesday afternoon, John driving, Iris next to him in the front seat, the two children in the back, Nate in charge of a large map.

"You'll need the map," Mike had said. "She'll know if you make a wrong turn because she knows how every inch of the way looks, but she still doesn't know if you go over the George Washington Bridge or the Triboro."

The men exchanged looks of sympathy.

"Ma gets hysterical attacks of blindness when she sees a map or a form from the IRS," Nate said helpfully.

Iris woke up in front of the Vermont house, a Wendy's bag on her lap.

"We're here, Ma," Evelyn said. "Take the bag. You didn't wake up when we stopped, so we bought you some supper."

"Evelyn said you wouldn't be hungry," Nate said, glaring at his sister.

"Stop arguing and get out of the car," Iris said.

She sat in the car while the other three climbed out, let themselves into the house, went down into the basement to turn on the water and the electricity. In the brilliant moonlight, the white frame house shone, its square eyes reproachful: *How could you have left me alone?*

Inside, it was cold, damp, the smell of unused rooms. Nate was bringing in the trash bags in which they packed their clothes, and the food box: an old carton, always the same carton they filled with food in cold weather so that they could come straight to the house without stopping at the supermarket. Had anyone turned up the heat?

"I turned it up," Evelyn said, her tone clearly implying that she did everything that needed doing in the world.

This was going to be some weekend, Iris thought. She was, she realized, more uneasy at being alone with her daughter than she was with John.

Nate was coming in through the door to the shed, his hair barely showing over a pile of logs in his arms.

"I'll start the fire," Iris said, but John said if she didn't mind, he'd like to do it. Oh, yes, she remembered: the wood stove in his Wisconsin lake house.

He and Nate went out to the woodshed and came back loaded down with more logs. John was expounding on the difference between hard and soft wood, and why soft wood ignited more easily. Nate, who knew all about wood, was listening politely as if he'd never heard any of this before.

She watched, uneasy. Anyone observing them from outside would mistake John for her husband. It seemed, at that moment, as if Mike had disappeared and been replaced by this man who was now so busy getting the house in order for them.

The house, the house! She walked through the first-floor rooms, the kitchen, the double parlors, opened the door to Evelyn's bedroom, and turned looking from the room in which she stood toward the kitchen. The place now wore an air of surprise and hostility as if she had caught it in the act, as if the chairs and tables were unprepared for these guests, these strangers. She sat down on the purple couch and silently apologized to the house for her truancy. It was possible for things as well as people to feel abandoned.

They had started a fire in the stove, a cast-iron stove that had once heated a New York City subway station in 1930. She had no idea how it had found its way up here. The flames burned brilliant molten gold behind the isinglass windows in the stove door, and the heat was melting down the stiffness of the unwelcoming house, its furniture and its walls. She went to the window and looked out. A full moon lit the drifts of snow in which the house seemed to float. Huge slabs of snow, some like oversized beams of wood, had been deposited by the snowplow that cleared the road and meadow in front of their house.

"We picked the *best* time," said Nate, coming up beside her. "It started snowing right after New Haven. It's supposed to snow tomorrow. Do you smell something?"

"What?"

"A funny smell."

"It's just the dampness," she said.

She was worn out by the exhilaration of being here. She had never expected to see the house again.

John walked in with another armful of logs and, halfway across the room, dropped them. They hit the floor like thunder. Evelyn and Nate jumped out of their way as they rolled heavily across the floor, and then they all stared at John, who was staring at his arm. Under the thick flannel of his shirt sleeve, the muscles of his arm were jumping, twitching from shoulder to wrist.

"Sit down," Iris said, getting up and steering him to the seat she had just vacated.

"I dropped them," John said.

"That's enough wood," said Iris.

Nate was collecting the logs and stacking them. Evelyn said she and her brother had decided to sleep in the rooms over the shed because they wouldn't bother anyone with their records and tapes there. John could stay in one of their rooms. Their rooms were warmer. From now on, Iris saw, they would conspire to keep an eye on John, to keep him out of danger.

Iris said John would sleep in Evelyn's room. You needed experience to navigate the steps, she said. She didn't know what made her wax them last summer. Downstairs, she thought, was the place for John. *Her* room was upstairs.

"Wise decision, Ma," said Evelyn.

The children disappeared into their rooms. Time passed. Outside, the snow glowed in the moonlight. Safer here, thought Iris, in winter, which preserves things, a longer season, more time in it.

"You should go to bed," John said. "You don't have to stay up and watch me."

"You'll call if you need help?"

"I don't need any help."

"If he needs help, he can call me," said Evelyn, opening the door to the staircase that led to the shed rooms.

"I thought you were going to bed," Iris said.

"I thought *you* were going to bed," said her daughter.

"Why don't we just stay up all night and watch each other?" Iris asked.

"Ma's getting better," Evelyn said. "She's her old sarcastic self."

"*Are* you going to bed?" asked Iris.

"I have to go to the bathroom," Evelyn said. "*If* you don't mind."

Iris went upstairs. From below, she heard John and her daughter, talking. She fell asleep listening to their voices, unable to hear their words.

She awoke in the middle of the night and thought she was at home, and then the light coming in the windows, the stars she could see through them, told her where she was. She got up and started downstairs to the bathroom and almost screamed when she caught sight of John, sitting in a chair, reading.

"Oh," she said. "You. What are you reading?" She watched him, nervous. Alone together.

He held up a book, her first novel, *The Statue Garden*.

"Well?" she asked, sitting down opposite him.

"Why did you write it?" he asked her.

"I don't know. It arrived."

"Like the Holy Ghost and the Virgin Mary?"

"I was looking over my life," she said. "I didn't have any other."

"I'm in it," he said. "The way you wrote about me. If that was all you saw, what did it mean? What was it *for?*"

"I was still angry," she said. "You'd left me. Haven't you ever read it before?"

"I read it before. When it came out. Fifteen years ago."

"If it annoyed you so much," Iris said, "why did you come back?" When guilty, she became defensive.

"All that about my sister and her affairs," he said, ignoring her question. "Did you have to write about that?"

She said she thought she did. At the time.

"There are *three* pages in here about me," he said. "That's all."

"It's a hard problem," she said. "The morality of writing about other people's lives."

He was angry because she had devoted so little space to him, as if he had taken up little space in her life.

Small spaces can swallow everything.

"You realize," he said, "that after this you're going to have to write about me?"

She asked him what he meant.

"Think about it," he said. "Think about the photon and the wave."

"John," she said. "Go to bed."

He smiled the smile of the totally victorious.

"You will. You'll have to write about me, and you'll write about me *my* way."

She regarded him narrowly.

"I'm in my right mind and you won't have any choice about it," he said.

At three o'clock, Mike put down his book on William Wycherly, looked at his watch, listened to the silence in the house, and

went into Iris' study. Someone had forgotten to replace the
quilted pillowcase she used to cover her word processor and he
started to cover the machine with it when he saw the small box
of disks she kept on the chair next to her desk. On an impulse
he picked it up. It felt full. He opened the box and began to look
through them: CPM, Wordstar, Poems I, Poems II, and then an
unlabeled disk. He reached in back of the machine and switched
it on and, feeling like a thief who has broken into a sealed house,
called up the directory. One listing only: NOTES. That was not
like his wife; she was meticulous in her listing of things. She never
threw anything out, no book, no sheet of paper, no letter. *You
never know when you'll need it again.* Deliberately, he typed NOTES
and called up the file.

A poem appeared, "Saying Goodbye to the Earth." He read
the first stanzas:

> 1.
>
> When the wind starts up
> High in the trees,
> When the first white flakes
> Fall through the trees
>
> I begin again.
> Looking for you.
>
> Who knows why the wind
> Has so many voices?
> Invisible things will make themselves heard,
> One way or another.
> 2.
> Today the voice of the wind is furious.
> It is tired of looking.
> It roars through the long
> Gray throats of the steeples.
> It seizes the oaks

As if it would choke them.
Thick-skinned trees,
Who have watched forever,
Tell me your secrets!

It howls on to another garden.
What has it learned?
I know it has seen you.
   3.
Today the sky is clear.
The branches freeze in place
As if forever.

The wind has retreated
To its clear castle of air.

I tried today
To believe in death.
Mine, not yours.

When the sun set, salmon-colored,
The moon was already rising.
   4.
I burned today with a fever.
All day.
Of what use are doctors?
These are seasonal fires.

As the winter empties itself of color,
As the birds leave,
As the sun pales to a thumbprint of ice,
The heart rebels.

It ignites.

It is your blood burning in me.
Will you be consumed? This time?
Mere ash on the wind?

Next door, the neighbor feeds his bonfire
While, around him, leaves fall.
From above, from high, secret places.
    5.
Today I heard your voice, high and excellent.
I should have felt fear.

The cornerstones of buildings must sound like that,
The deep sorrowful tenor of stones
The tall tower rests on.

As my life has rested on you.

Tell me.
Is there any joy in it?
Any joy in bearing all this weight,
Sinking, year by year,
Deeper into the earth?
    6.
I went back to the park today.
The bandstand was ice white,
The gazebo silent.

The ghosts of the bandsmen drifted over.
When I looked up, I saw a halo,
Black and circling the sun.

Are you gone now?
Where will you go?
Mourning, you said, can be as eternal as life.
Your smile was triumphant.
I did not believe you.

One of Iris' poems. Or was it? It was almost exactly like a
poem she would write, but she would never use such a title. All
her poems, some of which she kept hidden for years after she
wrote them, had one-word titles. He read on—it was a very long

poem; apparently there was to be one section for each month of the year—and gradually he concluded that Iris had not written it.

He scrolled the text up the screen. Something about a Chinese poet in the country observing the same rituals as his friend in the city. Something about a happy midwestern childhood. Oh, no, it was not Iris writing on this disk. It was John. He remembered Iris saying John had no verbal ability whatsoever. But this poem read like one of her recent ones. The last had won a prize just before she went into the hospital, mortifying her. "It wasn't ready to go out," she said. "I sent it to the editor to get an opinion."

He had spent considerable time studying parodies and imitations. They were only effective when the parodist understood the work he parodied: when he *became,* with some distortions, the writer he parodied. Mike scrolled back to the poem. This was not imitation. It was osmosis. What the hell was going on here? What the hell was going on up there in the country? He'd lived with Iris for nearly eighteen years and read every word she wrote, everything except her first novel—he didn't want to read about her first love, that was something, wasn't it?—he hadn't read the book, and now he had the man in the house, or the man had his wife in another house, and *he* couldn't possibly write a poem so much like one of hers. They were all up there in Vermont, sound asleep, the wood stove going, and in the morning Nate would start up the snowmobile and they would zip all over the place, Iris holding onto John's back.

Of course, Evelyn was crazy about John and would watch her mother like a hawk.

He called up the computer's main menu. To erase a file: E. Name of file to be erased? NOTES. He hit the return key and the file was gone. Gone completely. So much for "Saying Goodbye to the Earth." So much for John's insinuating his life into theirs.

Suddenly sleepy, he went to bed, pulled Iris' pillow over to him, and immediately fell asleep.

She awoke in a room flooded with brilliant white light. The room was bridal. She was the only one in the bed. She picked up the phone and called Mike's number but no one answered. He must have gone to work. She looked at her watch. Eleven o'clock. Either they'd been uncharacteristically silent or she'd been exhausted. Outside, she heard the unmistakable roar of the snowmobile engine. She went downstairs and looked out the window. There the three of them were, ready to go for a ride, right through the trees and into the creek, three perfectly reckless people. She opened the door and shouted for Evelyn. She and Nate came running toward the house. In their ski outfits, their faces flushed, they resembled overgrown snow-suited versions of their infant selves. "Look," she said, "you have to be careful with him. He's getting tired more easily and he doesn't like to admit it. You'll have to watch him."

They nodded solemnly. They understood their responsibility.

I raised two good kids, she thought.

"You show him *exactly* where the riverbank is, where the trench in the field is. You two be careful. Perfectly healthy people can get killed."

They would be careful, they would.

She watched John on the snowmobile, Evelyn's arms around his waist, Nate waiting for them to come back to have his turn. She knew exactly what Evelyn was feeling. She was not so happy to acknowledge her own emotion: jealousy.

She turned around, picked up a log, put it in the stove, and then scrambled two eggs. The house, the house, the ash-gray shadows of the trees on the snow, the brilliant blue shadows of the trees everywhere, the brilliant sky right above them, the sky above the mountain darkening to slate gray. Snow and more snow. They would be snowed in. The snow on the roof slid off and fell thunderously. She put on her snow pants and jacket, went out, and walked slowly away from the house: a short walk to the bench in front of the abandoned house on the other side of the narrow creek. Then she went back inside. *Now you'll write about me. You won't have any choice.*

She picked up a book. What was it? An autobiography of a pioneer woman in Utah. Good enough. It was warm in front of the stove and, still in her snow pants and jacket, she started to read. She was always cold.

She looked up and John was standing in front of her. "Come on, Iris," he said. "Just one ride."

"One ride?" she asked. The cold and the wind had reddened his cheeks, and he was standing outside her dormitory saying the same thing—"Come on, Iris, just one ride"—and behind him was the borrowed purple motorcycle. "Just around the block." She climbed up in back of him and they rode all the way to the sand dunes in Indiana, and coming back the machine broke down, and they stood on the edge of the highway, just past Gary, Indiana, watching the hellish red smoke rise in the air while Iris kicked stones and glared at his back and he tried to hail down a car. Eventually, a man in a blue pickup stopped for them, helped them load the bike in the back of the truck, and took them back to the university.

This feeling for him, it was all sentimentality. A gold light gilded everything over and done with simply because it was all unattainable. The Midas touch of the past, that was what it was. She got up and followed him to the door, thinking, No, that's wrong. There are also the tarnishing fingers of memory. They handle the past like a trophy for a race that's over and cannot be run again, darkening it to the dullness of iron or pewter, saying, Look, there was never any brightness to it. You imagined it all. Light and dark, the two properties of any object, the moon and its invisible dark side, the earth, which was more obvious, blunter, turning dark once a day, and for only so long. If you could slice your life in half like an apple or an orange, what would you find there? In the center of the apple, a star. In the center of an orange, a heart of light. In the center of her life, some small black seeds, of whom John was one. Into what would they grow? It was impossible to know. When you stopped wanting to know, that was death, not the stopping of the heart.

She got on the snowmobile and they took off, across the meadow, into the maze of woods, she never had the nerve to venture too far into the woods herself, and the wind and the cold were taking everything from her, her fevers, the patients in the hospital, none of it was fast enough to keep up with them, if they could keep going at this speed forever, frozen world, beautiful world, spaces like blank pages, their memories waking up like hibernating bears, dancing in the boundless, blue-white spaces.

"Why did we stop?" she asked.

"Can you drive this back?"

Through the trees, the impossible trees.

"Yes," she said.

She put her hand on his arm and could feel the muscles twitching wildly. She moved her leg forward, against his. The same thing.

"Can you hold on to me?" she asked.

"Yes."

She felt anger. Her final memories of him would be of weakness, helplessness. The anger turned to a firelike pity.

"Out," she told the children, who were eating potato chips in front of the stove. "Go to Gretchen's. Amuse yourselves."

Evelyn stared at her, frightened and resentful.

"For how long?" Nate asked.

"Until dinnertime," said his mother.

"Come on, Nate," said Evelyn. "They want to be alone."

"Oh, shut up," said Nate, throwing his snowsuit at her.

"I don't know what to say," Iris told John. "What do you want me to say?"

"It's what I've been waiting for," he said. "I thought you'd accepted it."

"Never. I never accept anything."

They sat quietly.

"No heavenly music as you go up the stairs?" she asked.

His laugh was bitter.

"Do you want to read?" she asked. He had that book in his lap, *The Unbearable Lightness of Being.*

His eyes, as he looked at her, were puzzled.

"*Can* you read?" she asked him.

"Not well. Muscles control the eye."

"Do you want me to read to you? That book about eternal return?"

He nodded, a slight, almost imperceptible motion of his head.

"He calls it a mad myth," she said, scanning the page. "No one returns. Events don't return. He doesn't believe in eternal return. *I* believe in it. It's not a myth. It's a law. Everything comes back. Everything *forces* its way back. People believe in the law of eternal return. Not in tombstones or dead bodies."

"Sleeping people," said John. "Dreaming people believe in eternal return."

"All tombstones do," said Iris, "is mark the day a given person stopped being visible to you when your eyes were open."

It was true. What you could not call up when awake—a beloved profile, gold light on warm brown hair—those things returned in sleep. The lost person returned to someone whose perspective, altered by time and experience, had different vanishing points, and the lost person silhouetted himself against different horizons, new contexts, and temporarily erased them all. The

214

past was always growing larger and the present existed only to feed it. When the past returns, it demands to be accepted and understood. Unaccepted, denied, it stops you, paralyzed in the present, while the future, which seemed so close, a huge sun on the horizon, sinks beneath the surface of the earth. When the past returns, it arrives like a conquering army.

"I want to talk to you," he said, "about my will."

"Just give it to me and I'll give it to my cousin," Iris said. "He's a lawyer. He'll take care of it."

"I want to leave my money to you."

"You know you can't do that! Mike would never stand for it."

"Then I'll leave it to Evelyn."

"You can't do that either. It wouldn't be fair."

"Because of Nate?"

"Of *course* because of Nate."

"Then I'll leave it to both of them."

"No. Don't. Find a charity." She didn't want to think about wills.

"It has to be left to a person," he said. "You can't stop me." Something else she couldn't stop him from doing.

"*Please* don't do it."

"They can always give it away if they don't want it."

"Let's change the subject," she said. "I'll read you the book."

"Forget that book," he said. "You're never going to be able to read that book."

"I wish you'd stop doing this," she said desperately. "It's like talking to a crystal ball."

"Oh, well," he said.

The children were back and the snow was falling heavily. Iris wanted to get out of the house, away from the book she had now been told she'd never read, away from discussions of wills, away from the telephone that did not ring and whose silence told her that Mike was at home and angry.

"Let's go out to eat," she said.

"Can we go to the Country Kitchen?" asked Evelyn.

When Evelyn was younger, she had loved that restaurant because it had four bathrooms, and during any visit there she inspected every one of them.

"What about a movie?" asked Nate.

"I don't know about that," said Iris. "We'll see."

"What *is* that smell?" Nate demanded.

"Just put on your coat," Iris said.

"I smell it too, Iris," John said.

"She can't smell anything," said Evelyn. "Her nose is always stuffed. She has a deviated septum."

"Mother!" said Nate. "It's coming from that drawer!"

Iris pulled open the door in which they stored clothespins and plastic bags. The smell became overpowering. She saw shredded bits of plastic, a chewed wooden clothespin, and a half-eaten cake of Ivory soap. A mouse's nest. "Give me the gloves," she told Evelyn. With the pink rubber gloves, she began picking up one thing after another, dropping them into the large black plastic trash bag Nate held open for her. Then she stopped. There it was, its fur plush and thick, its body emaciated, its tiny cheeks sunken. She stood still, staring at it for at least a minute, and then picked up the white plastic bag the dead mouse rested on and dropped the mouse and the white bag into the trash.

"Rest in peace, little mouse," she said softly.

"Come on, Ma," said Nate. "It's only a mouse."

"Tell that to your sister," Iris said. Evelyn was crying. Poor, poor mouse. It had eaten some of the poison they put out and had gone back to its nest, expecting to fall asleep and feel better.

Iris feels the same pity for me she feels for that mouse, thought John. And then he thought that her pity was not like other people's pity, condescending and self-congratulatory. No, she becomes the things she pities. She can't keep intact the membrane separating her from the rest of the world. No stimulus barrier. Freud called it that, a stimulus barrier. So that was what had happened in the hospital. She had allowed too many dying people in. And now she was taking him in. But he was good for her, he told himself.

She used to sit with him in his Chicago lab on the first floor, reading by a red light, and eventually she would play with one of the white rats in the cage. When she took it out, it nuzzled into her hair and slept on her shoulder. When she started to put the animal back, it began hanging upside down, twisting its head toward her, its small red eyes imploring and intelligent. It hung upside down until she couldn't stand it and took it out again. Eventually, she smuggled the rat out of the lab under the hood of her corduroy coat. The animal fell in love with her. She fell in love with him. Oephelius. He sat on her book while she read and contemplatively chewed the erasers from her pencils. He licked her cheek.

People who were horrified to hear she had a pet rat fell in love with the animal when they saw him with Iris. He followed her like a faithful dog wherever she went. When they went away for weekends, Oephelius took his revenge by chewing through electric wires, showing a distinct preference for the wires to her sewing machine and record player. For a while, all the machines in their apartment looked as if they had tried to slit their wrists.

"I have to punish him," she said. "*How* do you punish something that weighs four ounces?"

She hit on a solution, picking Oephelius up by his naked tail and dangling him in the air while she scolded him. The rat was entirely capable of twisting himself around and biting her on the wrist, but such an idea never entered its mind. He would twist his head back and watch Iris out of his sad red eyes.

The animal, she decided, was lonely. They were out of the

apartment too many hours at a time. At the main lab, she found a rat that opened its cage and every morning was found standing on top of it. She brought that one home. Oephelius and Daisy. They were happy. One sat on each of her shoulders. They knocked over glasses of beer, when she and John forgot and left them on the floor, and drank as much as they could get before Iris caught them and yanked them into the air by their tails.

Oephelius grew a tumor and John removed it. When Oephelius came out of the anesthetic, he began to run blindly, listing crazily to one side. She pursued him, picked him up, stunned by his instinct for survival, which made him run from the spot that, in his stuporous state, he perceived as dangerous. When the anesthetic wore off, he slept in her cupped hands. Eventually, he was crippled by arthritis and dragged himself along by his front paws, following Iris down the long apartment hall. When he died, Iris missed an exam for the first and only time.

Eventually, Daisy succumbed to an infected uterus, and Iris took her to the vet and to pay the man forged a check with John's signature. By the time Daisy died, John was in London, studying, and opened an envelope from Iris and inside found a black-bordered card: *R.I.P. Daisy Rat.* He would have called her in the United States, but the phone call would have been too expensive. Now he regretted it. She was right. He had been cheap.

There were also times when he suspected her of loving the rats more than she loved him.

She would come into the main lab, look at all the white rats in their cages, and say, These are the Jesus Christs of the world. Poisoned, cut, crucified, starved, so we can live. They have spirits too. She thought of animals as people in fur suits. Good people whom humans, if they were fortunate, would come to resemble when they had evolved sufficiently.

"All right," Iris said. "Put the bag out in the woodshed until we go to the dump."

"Iris," said John, "it's not an omen."

She looked at him, speechless.

"Ma," said Nate, "after dinner, let's go to the movies."

"What's at the movies?" she asked him.

"Something violent and exciting," said Evelyn. *The Road Warrior.*

"Let's go," said Iris. "I'll drive. I love to drive up here."

The children shrugged their shoulders and put on their coats. They knew their mother hated driving in the country, the sudden curves in the road, the unexpected amoeba shapes of black ice, the mysterious fields swelling up into darker blue mountains, teasing the eye and the car from the narrow road.

Iris put her coat on, trying not to look at John's arm, covered in flannel, probably with fabric his mother or sister had stitched into a shirt for him, carefully preserved all these years, and the muscles of the arm under the fabric, just that afternoon, twitching. Lately, she rated movies according to their ability to blot out thought. *The Road Warrior* was a four-star movie. She wondered how many hours she had spent in movie theaters, in the dark, watching invented lives, how many months she and John had spent in them: documentary films, films at International House, the films at the local movie houses. They must have seen three every week for seven years.

"That was very good behavior," Iris said when they came back to the house. "No fighting in the back seat, no fighting in the restaurant. Excellent behavior."

"Ma!" said Evelyn. "We're grown up!"

Why didn't Mike call? When she went upstairs, she would call him.

"All right, everyone," she said. "Start the fire, go to the bathroom, go to bed. I'm going to bed."

"Remember *Wild Strawberries?*" John asked her. "*Citizen Kane?*"

"Go to bed," she said.

She undressed and put on her long red nightgown and sat in her white wicker rocker, the lights off in her room. The hall light slanted in, painting a gold lane across their varnished floor. She had left the light on so that if John got up in the middle of the night he'd have no trouble finding his way to the bathroom. The rest of them could find their way around in the dark like bats. Her door was open so that if he began coughing she could hear him. All the same precautions she'd taken when the children were small.

She loved the dark. She loved the dark but there was always someone for whom the light had to be kept on.

When they'd bought the house, the upper rooms hadn't been touched in almost one hundred years. The wallpaper had peeled in thick patches from the walls, and the plaster collapsed into the lathing. Spiderwebs were everywhere. Mice regarded the house as their own. When Mike had knocked down the walls, he found skeletons of cats who had squeezed into them and could not get free and, in the corner of their bedroom, a little pair of black leather shoes placed carefully on top of a diary from the year 1881. *Hot and misty. No rain. Paid Mr. Osmond twenty-five cents. Received 2 yards of cloth off Mrs. Empson. Cows turned out for the first time since fall. Paid one dollar, Dr. Lewis,* and glued to the back cover of the diary, a photograph of a fat little girl, no more than two, wearing a ruffled white dress trimmed with handmade lace, a strange ossified toy bear sitting in her lap. Both bear and child looked straight into the camera.

Their house was two hundred years old. It had its own history, and now they were part of it. She and her husband had a history of their own, and yet she lingered in the corners of her past as if it were still going on.

As the light from a candle sputters, brightens, sputters again, and goes out, the sounds in the rest of the house were receding and dying down.

She got up and dialed Mike's number: busy. He had taken the phone off the hook. She would call him at the office in the morning.

It had been a long time since she was the last one awake in a house.

She got up and looked out the windows, the drifts of snow, wave on wave, white crests casting their bluish shadows. She thought about the time it takes starlight to cross space, and how old the light is when it finally arrives here to be seen. She thought about how long it would take images from this planet to travel back to one of the stars. By now, she thought, everyone knows all about this, everyone knows that the starlight illuminating this night is ancient, has been traveling for years from its point of origin.

It was John who first taught her these things. At times, she thought she had been half blind before she met him. The stars. Was that Orion? The Big Dipper? She could no longer find them but she knew they were there.

She sighed, tiptoed out of her room, took her bearskin coat from the storage closet across the landing, and sneaked down the steps, holding tight to the banister, avoiding the third step from the top, which creaked. At the bottom of the steps she listened, heard nothing but the regular breathing of the house and its inhabitants, put on her coat, slid out the front door, and carried her boots out onto the porch, where she put them on. All the other houses were lightless, white outlines shimmering in the moonlight. She crossed the meadow in front of the house, across the plowed space, and climbed into the drifts. It was slow going. The snow was crusty and she sank in up to her knees, but it wasn't far. She wanted to see the creek. Moving black glass, cold ebonies, strange white shapes of snow, the sound of subterranean water running. She found the rock she sat on in summer, sat down on it, faced the house, and looked up at the stars. Orion, where was it?

She felt warm and anchored in the coat. It weighed almost as much as she did. The house was two hundred years old and stood in the cleared, huge meadow dreaming its own dream of time. They had owned the house for seven years. From the perspective of the house, they were as temporary as mayflies. They *were* mayflies, arriving when heat quickened the rooms, flying about, then disappearing as if they had died or fallen back into an interminable sleep.

From here, the house cast a shadow whose shape was unlike the one she was accustomed to seeing from her bedroom window. From there, the house was an ash-gray shape on the snow, its chimney and its peaked roofs sketched on the snow like a child's drawing of a house, strange block shapes all at odd angles. In the spring and summer, she never stood at the window looking at that shadow.

She looked at the expanse of snow separating her from the house and thought of the snow-covered meadow as a map of the past. The past led to the present, the present to the future. In her path, there was an impediment. If she were separated from her house by a frozen lake, and came to a place where the ice was too thin, she could not go on. She would never reach the house.

The moon went behind a cloud and the snow reminded her of a desert, blank and empty, trackless, too dangerous to cross. That man asleep in her daughter's room was her desert. He always had been. Their time together was the thin ice on the lake. Deserts, thin ice. Did such contrary images go together? They did. They had gone from day to day, from extreme to extreme. *What* had they done to so injure each other? What had he done to her? Animals loved her. They followed her home. Children loved her. Her parents and her husband loved her. Everyone she had ever wanted to love her had loved her. But he had refused. More than refused—he had taken such vindictive pleasure in it, repeating again and again that he *could* not love her, implying that no one ever would. She awoke every day expecting to hear the same thing from everyone else. It would only be a matter of time before they looked at her as he had and said, *I don't love you, I can't love you, I've stopped.* In the hospital, she'd found that nightmare landscape again, but it was not an isolated patch of ice. It was the whole world.

In sleep, he said, everything came back, could be found again. She had been sleeping in order to find him, to allow him to come back.

Before they came up here, he told her he *had* loved her. Why should ancient things matter so much? An old planet, turning its dark side to the light, sending down different images, new images, down here, where she lived, deep beneath the past. Swords of light, cutting her loose. Such guilt while she was in the hospital, for having failed everyone, and yet it was an old guilt, felt first for John, whom she had not understood, whom she failed when she could not please him.

Oh, it was cold. Time to go back to the house.

She closed the door gently behind her, pushing it slowly backward until the latch clicked into place. She put her coat on a chair and went through the hall and into the woodshed where the dead mouse rested in its trash bag. She opened the bag carefully and looked at the mouse, stiff and cold. Such an enormous nest, so much work. She was sure it was a female. She was not familiar with the dead and the dying. Everything conspired to hide the end of things. She folded the mouse back into her shredded plastic bag and tied the trash bag shut. Illiterate it was, the mouse, and insignificant, but what set it going was the same spark that set her going, and the rest of the world. She should take time out to mourn the mouse, for whom they had set out poison, who had died to calm their nerves. She who honked the car horn at pigeons, who swerved to avoid cats, who mourned for rosebushes when they stopped blooming, how was she going to watch someone die in her own house?

She went back in and sat down on the purple couch in the living room, which adjoined John's bedroom. When her son had been an infant and ran high temperatures, she became so frightened she could sleep only if she got in bed with him. Thank God Mike was not here where he might be able to read her thoughts.

In high school, she had a brief friendship with a neighborhood girl from the Catholic school who took her to her grandmother's funeral. There was the old woman in a shiny black coffin, thin, almost weightless, floating on quilted satin, tallow yellow, a grotesque oversized doll from some unknown wax museum soon destined to be returned to the same museum from which it had come. Impossible to believe the woman had ever been alive, impossible to understand the bizarre sobbing of the people there, the exaggerated contortions of their faces. If she could have begun to believe then that all things withered and died, that they did so because it was in their nature, not because someone had willed it or made a mistake.

A book was at the other end of the couch, and she bent over to get it. Her first collection of poems. Terrible poems. She slid down the couch, closer to the lamp. The first poem, written eighteen years ago, before she had anything more serious than a cold.

SLAB

Now I am embalmed
And laid on my slab,
The room is shut up.

Wrapped in these thin strips,
A spoiled fish, I do not divide.
I am a long loaf no one will touch,

Seven days unclean,
And now the cats find me.
They claw at my door

And in the cold
I am waiting.

Blood, I say,
Cover me like locusts
Until I am black land.

Cover me like leeches
Until I am shining.

One at rest on my thigh,
Pressing,
One on each leg,

Another along my neck,
Claws flexing
Where she knows my eyes are.

The sun is a disgusting thing.
It is the black planet I want,
The leech planet,
Wasp planet,
Ash place,

Gold bones bending back to spring
Wherever it is I am going,

The dark side,
In this massing and massing of cats.

"Iris?" John asked, sitting down next to her. "I thought it was Evelyn."

Not again, thought Iris.

"Sorry," he said. Automatic, that defensiveness.

He leaned over to see what she'd been reading.

"Death isn't like that," he said. "Maybe at the end when the dying's almost over and you know it will finally stop. The stopping is beautiful."

She said nothing.

"When Celia was in the hospital, they gave her something radioactive to drink. They brought it in a huge thermos, a big lead canister. The technician who came in with it was dressed in something like a space suit to protect himself from the radiation. She was in a room at the end of a long hall and there was a big red circle on her door. No one would go in there. The nurses used to stand outside arguing about who had to come in to give her a shot. I learned to do it myself. I used to sit there day and night watching her. Her doctor was the only other person who would sit near her without one of those suits on. Even my wife dressed up in one of them, because if she married again she'd want more children. So when Celia looked at her, at her mother, she saw this monster from outer space.

"It's painful and ugly, and the worst thing about it is how the pain and the ugliness and the isolation take away your memory and your individuality, everything that made you a person. By the time you die, you're not a person. You don't think glorious thoughts about being devoured by cats. Maybe right after the diagnosis you do. Not later."

"You won't die that way," she said.

"No. Because I won't go to a hospital. What I've got isn't painful. I'll probably catch some bug or other and burn up."

"Burn up?"

"Fire is nice and clean," he said.

"Go to sleep," she said. "You're not dying so fast."

"You promised me," he said. "No hospital."

The silence grew stiff around them. She was uncomfortably aware of his presence, and the silence, the strangeness of having him here, in this house. It was familiar, that tension, that need to touch him and be touched by him. It was also forbidden.

He watched her as if he knew what she was thinking. In the soft light, she looked as she had looked over twenty years ago. She had a husband, she had children, but this house was not associated with them, not in his mind. He had no reason to be living in her house in the city. He had been allowed in because of his illness and the strength of her attachment to him, but there he had been one thread in a strongly woven web, the last thread, far from the center. Here, he had no established place. He was in a strange house in the country, and the children had disappeared as if they had never existed. Outside, the snow had erased the rest of the world. That's how it had been before, that's how she had wanted it, only the two of them alive in the world. She'd had no patience with his friends or his thesis adviser. They were only obstacles, irrelevant presences like talking statues. Until he became frightened by the risk of such a life, he'd wanted that life as much as she did. He had never admitted it before.

"Iris," he said, "I don't want to go to bed alone."

"Are you afraid of the dark?" she asked, laughing. She was horrified by her laugh, high and nervous.

"I'm not afraid of the dark."

She made an odd gesture with her hands, lifting them as if she were holding yarn, then bringing them back together as if in prayer.

"What do you want, then?"

"Would you consider coming to bed with me?"

There was no explanation for what happened. It was so quiet, it was so strange, the house no longer seemed like the house she knew.

"Lock the door," she said.

He lay down on the bed and she lay down beside him. He loosened her robe and put his hand on her breast. Cold. He traced the outline of her nipple with his forefinger. It was erect.

"I can't do this," she said.

"I don't want to sleep alone," he said.

"Turn over," she said, "and I'll hug you."

He laughed. His laugh was bitter.

"Turn over," she said again. "You'll fall asleep. You always did."

He turned on his side, facing the wall.

"Don't you want to sleep with me?" he asked.

"You know I do."

"Then why?"

"I can't."

"Because of Mike?"

"Because of Mike. Because it's not right. It's not really what you want."

"No?"

"No."

"It is what I want," he said.

"Oh, you don't. It would destroy me. You're tired of that."

"You were unfaithful to me," he said. "Once."

"Only because I didn't know what to do to get your attention. You were still there, but really, you'd already left."

"You loved him. Leonard."

"I loved him for *six years* before I slept with him."

"Then why did you sleep with him?"

"Did you give me any choice?"

"It was *my* fault?" he asked.

"It's the middle of the night," she said. "Just go to sleep."

"When did you first start loving him?"

"Oh, for God's sake," Iris said. "The first day he and I had a class together. About two weeks after I met you. If you hadn't been around, I'd be unhappily married to him now."

"You loved us both for six years?"

"Seven," said Iris.

"You loved him as much as you loved me?"

"He was a dream person," Iris said. "You always love people you dream up best. It was a dream. People aren't responsible for their dreams."

"They're more responsible for their dreams than for anything else," said John.

"Oh, no," said Iris, "that's not true." Were they now going to have a discussion of responsibility?

"Did you see him after I left?" John asked.

"Yes. It was a disaster."

"Why?"

"He expected to find a single woman. I was still part of a couple. You left but I wasn't separated. I had a phantom lover."

"I thought *he* was your phantom lover. When you were with me."

"You're going to stay up all night talking, aren't you?" she asked.

Some snow slid from the roof and hit the ground.

"I'll keep quiet," he said.

She put her arm around him and listened to the sound of his breathing until it slowed and became rhythmical. She had never felt such excitement. When she was sure he was asleep, she went to her own bed. The sheets were cold and she fell asleep, alone with her own wild will and desire.

13

WHEN SHE AWOKE in the morning, she thought she had dreamed their conversation, dreamed about getting into bed with him, and then she remembered her book of poems. When she went down, it was still open on the couch.

In the afternoon, they all drove up to Union Hill. They competed to see who could count the most ranges. Evelyn claimed she could see fifteen.

"Come *on*," said Nate, "no one's ever seen more than fourteen."

"I can see fifteen," she said stubbornly. "The one that looks like a shark's tooth is in New Hampshire," she told John.

The houses, the barns, the occasional horses standing in cleared places might have been standing there for two hundred years. The natives called this area the happy valley. It stopped time.

"When do we have to go back?" Nate asked.

"We should leave by three," Iris said.

"We *always* have to leave by three," said Evelyn.

"It still takes over five hours to get home," Iris said.

"We used to come up here and fly kites," Evelyn said.

"I remember," said her mother.

"You weren't in your room last night," Evelyn said. "Where were you?"

Iris avoided John's eyes. "Outside," she said. "Sitting on my rock."

"I *told* you those were her footprints," Nate said, exasperated.

"Outside? In the middle of the night?" asked Evelyn.

"Teenagers haven't cornered the market on stupidity," Iris said.

Evelyn stared from her mother to John. They didn't *look* guilty. "Can we go for a walk?" she asked. Sulky.

"You go ahead," Iris said. "We'll stay in the car where it's warm."

"I'm not allowed out on my own?" John asked her.

"I'll stay right here," Evelyn said. "I have something I want to show him."

"I'll go for a walk with Nate," Iris said.

"When we get back, can we have one more ride on the snowmobile?" Nate asked.

"*One*," said his mother.

In the right-hand lane, Iris drove back to the city.

She hasn't changed, thought John. She gets in one lane and stays in it until she reaches where she's going. He was sorry to see New Haven appearing on the horizon, its black smoke tangling with purple streamers of light. It would get dirtier and dirtier as they got back to New York. Past New Haven, the clouds resembled mountain ranges, mountains banded with broad silver rims, a grand illusion, those mountain clouds, making it possible to pretend it was possible to take the mountains back with you. In places, the setting sun broke through, leaving patches of radiance, meadows, whole towns. A whole world up above the surface of their own. Then the sun turned a brilliant rose, and the mountain peaks of clouds were rose-tinted also and fantastical in their colors, a fairy-tale world not permitted to mere people. The red sun shone behind the serrated mountains rimmed by trees; a familiar color, that red, the color of Iris' study.

He looked around him and thought of telling Iris and the children how what he saw appeared to him, but he was not used to saying what he felt. It was better if no one knew he had feelings. It had been a family pastime, ridiculing feelings. Had he gone into science to keep them all from following him and making comments? The talent was there, but the motive, where had that come from?

"The ineluctable modality of the visible," he said aloud.

Iris' eyes flickered over to him, startled. When had he started reading James Joyce?

"While you were sleeping, I was reading," he said. Now *she* would ridicule him.

She drove steadily, saying nothing.

"What does it mean?" he asked.

"I don't know," she said. "I never knew what it meant."

"Because you'd never look anything up in a dictionary," he said.

"I still don't."

"You're always telling us to use a dictionary," Nate said.

"Quiet," Iris said. "I'm driving."

"*We* distract her, but *he* doesn't," Evelyn said in a stage whisper.

Iris ignored her.

"Um," said Iris. "You might try *The Good Soldier.*"

"I read it last week. It's not the saddest story ever told," he said.

"No, but it's a true one," she said.

"Is it?"

"Look at us."

"John," Nate asked, "what was Mother like when she was young?"

"She was very smart. Also very pretty. She was a lot of fun."

"She still is a lot of fun when she isn't sick," Nate said.

Iris smiled at the road ahead. Nate always rushed to her defense. At three, in the playgrounds, he'd stand in front of strangers and order them off park benches. "That's my *mother's* seat." Lately, he shouted at her, told her she was stupid, didn't she know that *all* the boys in school wore sweatpants; he didn't *care* if she thought his looked like pajamas. Soon he'd have a girlfriend and he would be as bad at first love as she had been.

"And she was very kind, the kindest person I've ever met."

Please, thought Iris, let him stop this funeral oration.

"Also," said John, "for one entire winter in Chicago, the coldest one in fifteen years, she wore Bermuda shorts and knee socks and sneakers."

Now they were delighted and eager for more details. She would never get Nate out of his sweatpants now.

"She couldn't get up on time in the morning because she stayed up all night reading, so I used to call her at the dorm to wake her up. And she was too fat and couldn't stay on a diet, so every morning I would leave a Chinese cookie in her mailbox and she ate that for breakfast, but she didn't get any thinner."

"How about that, Ma?" said Nate. "Up all night reading!"

"When you're old enough to go away to school," Iris said, "you can stay up all night too."

"And you loved her very much?" asked Evelyn. The colors of excitement and resentment mixed in her voice like the blues and violets of the evening sky.

Iris inhaled and forgot to exhale.

"Yes, I did," he said, "very much. I didn't know it at the time."

"How can you not know something like that?" asked Evelyn.

"There's a lot we don't know," said John.

"But whether or not you love someone!" protested Evelyn.

"Find out for yourself," Iris said. She was upset. She wanted the subject changed.

"A lot of other people knew they were in love with her," John said.

"Did she love them?" asked Evelyn.

"Some of them." Hints of resentment, memories they had unearthed but not buried again.

Iris waited. Evelyn always took everything too far.

"Was she . . . " Evelyn began. "Was she faithful?"

What was he going to say now? Tell the whole truth in the tradition of his family? Bring up Leonard, with whom she had spent weekends during the end of that terrible year in Boston?

"Of course she was," said John.

Iris didn't dare look at him. "Almost home," Iris said. "Evelyn, shut up."

The front door opened as they pulled into the driveway.

"Have a good time?" asked Mike.

"Wonderful," said Iris. "They didn't ask to stop at every bathroom on the road."

"No one broke anything?" Mike asked.

"No, everyone's in one piece," said Iris.

She could feel Evelyn's eyes on her, she could hear the heavy logs thundering across the kitchen floor, rolling toward the stove and the table.

"Everyone was just fine," Iris said. "Can we talk later?"

"We can talk *now,*" he said.

She followed him into the bedroom and he locked the door as they used to when the children were younger. She looked at the locked door and smiled.

"It's not funny," Mike said. "I feel like I'm committing adultery with my own wife. Is this ever going to end?"

She sighed and rested her head against his shoulder.

"Thank God you're back," he said.

"Yes," Iris said.

* * *

234

Later, she went up to Mike's study and told him about the logs.

"I'm sorry, Iris," he said, "but I'm having trouble feeling sorry for that man."

"Why?"

"You know why."

"Because you're jealous?"

"Wouldn't you be?"

"Yes. In your place, I'd be jealous."

"You would be," he said, "raving."

"Why aren't you raving?"

"I am," he said, "quietly."

"I don't want to fight," she said.

"I do," said Mike. "Later."

When she went into her study, John was sitting at her desk. "Here," he said, handing her a folder. "I wrote more of that poem. Two more sections. Seven and eight."

She took the folder and began reading.

7.

There was a party of revelers.
In this weather!
Picnic baskets, bottles of wine.

At first, I thought it a float,
And waited for the next,
The inexplicable parade.

It was a boat,
Moving fast, as on black water.
Smooth as glass, but deep.

No one trailed his hand in the water.

Were you there?
Did you see me?
Trapped here? On dry land?

8.
Today,
A bird took my eyes up through the sky.
I saw the earth, soft and muzzy,
Bandaged in clouds.
The sun unwound them.

If you wait long enough,
These things happen.

I saw all the people,
Tiny but perfectly clear.

On one side of the world
They hung upside down
Their hair rested flat on their heads.

I had forgotten gravity.
I had forgotten how long it would take.
And then I could see into the earth
And its honeycombs.

I began searching,
Continent by continent.

I forgot my own life.
In the end, I was thrown back to earth,
Under the wild branches,
In the cold wind.

From the branches,
A cold eye watched me.

The wind said: *Take up your life.*
Of course, I pretended.

As if my arms were full of cordwood or laundry,
I went in.
Life or no life.

"What do you think?" John asked.

"I don't know," Iris said. " 'Saying Goodbye to the Earth.' It's about you, isn't it?"

"Or you," he said. "It doesn't make any difference."

"Ma," Evelyn said, materializing as Iris was brushing her hair, "should I call Dr. Chipwitz? I mean, is it legal to let someone *die* in your own house?"

Such a cold-blooded child she sometimes seemed. She used to say she wished everyone on the highway would crash so there would be more room for them.

Iris put down her silver cupid-covered brush. Tarnished. She would have to polish it.

"God, Evelyn," she said. "I don't know. I think I'll go and see Dr. Chipwitz."

"Are you here for a checkup or what?" the doctor asked her. "Put your chart down. You're not supposed to read it."

Iris waited until he took her blood pressure and then asked about John. Was it or wasn't it legal to let him die in the house? If it wasn't legal, she couldn't let him stay, not because she was afraid of getting into trouble but because she didn't want to cause the family problems.

"Legally," said the doctor, "he's in the clear. So are you."

"Why?"

"Because he went to a lawyer and drew up a paper saying he had full knowledge of his condition and as a Christian Scientist he refused hospitalization on religious grounds. By the time anyone got through arguing that legally, it would be a fait accompli."

How she envied doctors their knowledge of Latin, their rituals, slowly acquired, which distanced them from the horrors of the body.

"But he's not a Christian Scientist," Iris said.

"No?"

"No."

"How can anyone possibly prove that?"

"Then it's all right?" asked Iris.

"If it's all right with you. Remember what happened when the diabetic woman arrived in your room?"

"Nothing can be done?"

"Heroic measures: respirators, huge doses of antibiotics, stimulants, breathing tubes, I.V.'s. Plenty can be done."

"Nothing that will do any real good?"

"I told you. It's a mixed diagnosis. ALS, possible multiple sclerosis, idiopathic degenerative disorder. Take your pick. They're all terminal. Any signs that things are getting worse?"

"He drops things. He has trouble reading. His muscles twitch."

"A month," said Dr. Chipwitz. "Two months at the most. How's your temperature?"

"I'm fine. Still no energy, but otherwise fine."

"Same old song," said the doctor.

"Don't worry about it, Evelyn," she told her daughter, who met her at the door. Didn't the children lock themselves in their rooms anymore? "It's all perfectly legal."

"Well, it *ought* to be legal for someone to die," Evelyn said.

14

9.
Lately, I see less and less what is here.
As if it were caught in the tree's bare branches,
I saw the sun.

Happy to be consumed,
People walked its flaming yellow rim.
In the end, they resembled cloves,
Burned and blackened,
Little trees.

An orange sun, yellow-rimmed,
Covered with crosses.
Like a Christmas orange.

Today, your scent is everywhere.

"Mother sleeping?" Mike asked.
"No," said Nate. "She's up."

No,
She's up.

What a beautiful two lines, thought Mike. What a lovely couplet, two lines like doves trilling the message, *Good news*. That pleasant thought was immediately followed by anger. If she was up now, couldn't she have been up sooner? What had cured her? The passage of time creeping through the house in its cut velvet slippers. Surely not the arrival of that man. If not him, who? It was him.

Still, he had his wife back, at least at night. No more lying on the edge of the bed as if on the edge of a knife blade. A passionate woman, thank God, slightly disordered though, no longer gluing herself to his back at night claiming he was hotter than a furnace. She who had always been cold now suffered from sudden heatings up, the soles of her feet, the palms of her hands, hot to the touch. Her hand stroking his hair as he fell asleep, a hot hand.

During the day, she was not his. She watched over John as over an unhatched egg. For two weeks, that man had gone out every morning and come back with odd treats for everyone: bagels, lox, various cakes, all of it strange to John, who had grown up in Nebraska. Not to Mike. Bagels were pieces of years gone by, miraculously preserved.

Now Iris drove John to the store and waited until he was finished. Weakening. What had he done, letting John stay here? There were days when he expected to turn on the faucet and see blood instead of water. Iris' illness, now John's, was bringing back memories of his mother's death.

When Iris was sick, he used to come home from the hospital, go to his room, and cry. How would he raise the children alone? How would he manage? How could he live alone? He still suffered from sudden attacks of fear during which he asked himself what he would do without her. He was still afraid to admit she was well, as if such an admission would run time backward like a film, and Iris would scurry, making silly, frantic,

Buster Keaton-like motions, until she was back in her hospital
room.

When he told Iris he thought having John around was bad for
the children, she said it was the best thing that could happen to
them. Those two shining beings. "We know the score," Nate said
when Mike tried to talk to him about being careful. John was
weak. John was dying.

"We *know*, Dad," said Evelyn. "I'm taking him to a rock
concert," said Nate, as if that justified everything.

Ten in the morning. Iris would soon be back from the store.
With John. In the mornings, John read in her study chair and she
lay on the fainting couch. In the afternoons, they traded places.
At night, Iris, John, and the children sat on the long yellow couch
in the television room and watched movies on the VCR. When
Mike came home from work or down from his office and saw
them, they looked as if they were listening to a sermon in a
synagogue.

"No," said Dr. Chipwitz. "Don't worry about it. It's not
contagious."

"You're not going to see *Iron Maiden,*" Iris told Nate, "and
that's final. Don't argue with me about it."

"Can we ever watch anything but *The Natural?*" Evelyn
asked. "I'm sick of it. I don't like baseball."

"Keep quiet," Iris said. "Nate and John like it."

"Iris," John said, "there's a Bruce Springsteen concert. I could
take him to that."

"You're going to go with Nate to a Springsteen concert?" Iris
asked. "Do you know what that means? It's the same music he's
been blasting through the house for the last two weeks."

John said he'd never gone to a rock concert, but he'd studied
a map and it shouldn't be hard to get to the Brendan Byrne
Stadium.

"The what?" asked Iris.

"It's in the *Meadowlands,* Ma," said Nate.

Of course. New Jersey, home of Bruce Springsteen. How could she have forgotten?

"You put John up to this," she said to Nate.

"I want to go," John said.

Iris said the concerts were dangerous, people got hurt, she'd have to ask about to see if this one was safe, and her son told her she lived in the Middle Ages and *he* was the only person in the eighth grade who hadn't been to a rock concert.

"And if you have trouble with the driving?" she asked John later. He promised he would stop and call her and wait in the car for them, for hours, for however long it took, and no, he wouldn't be stupid enough to get out and walk around in deserted areas.

"Let me go, Iris," he said finally.

She said people really did get hurt. Three years ago, some kids were trampled to death.

"I did some research," John said. "The audiences are more respectful of Springsteen. Not respectable, respectful. We'll get good seats."

"Did Nate tell you how bad the sound is? They amplify the music so Martians can hear it. You hate it when sound distorts."

"It's only one day," he said.

It was decided. Iris called a friend, who got two fifth-row tickets. Nate locked himself in his room and sang along with his Springsteen tapes. Everyone else in the house shouted, "Turn that down!"

"I wanted to go to the Ritz," Evelyn said, "and you wouldn't let me."

Iris reminded her that the Ritz was a *club,* served alcohol, and since she was only fifteen, it didn't matter what she, her mother, said; the *club* wouldn't let her in.

"I could get a phony ID," said Evelyn. "I *look* sixteen."

"That's it," said Iris. "Not one more word about rock music." Saturday was far away. Something might happen. Springsteen might come down with food poisoning.

Saturday arrived as predicted, and Springsteen was in perfect health. Iris watched John and Nate drive off in their silver car, crusted with dirty ice from the country roads. "Why wash it over and over again?" Mike asked. "It's like doing dishes. This way no one wants to steal it."

"Or ride in it," Iris said.

The stadium was surrounded by a chain-link fence and it was a long walk from the car to the gate. When they got to it, guards frisked them.

"Boy!" said Nate. "What do they think we've got?"

After they walked from the chain-link fence to the stadium entrance, guards looked them over again.

"A lot of security here," John said uneasily.

"It's to protect the *performer*," Nate said. "Ma's crazy on the subject."

"She's just worried about you," said John.

"She worries too much," said Nate, staring about him as if this were his last day on earth and he wanted to remember every minute of it. John wanted to know why, if they had numbered tickets, everyone was pushing everyone else. Nate shrugged his shoulders. He appeared to be under the impression that he had stumbled into heaven and was going to be the first person to bring back reliable descriptions of the angels.

"Hey, man!" Nate said. "Look at that guy!"

"Who?" asked John.

"The row behind us on the left. Don't let him know you're looking."

The person in question was naked from the waist up except

for the tattoos that covered his upper body and both arms. His head was shaved except for a strip of dyed hair in the middle. It stood up like the brush John used to clean snow from his windshield. It was also the same color. His chest was crisscrossed by thick black leather bracelets whose two-inch spikes radiated out from their bands like rays of sun in old drawings.

"Cool!" said Nate, who seemed to have acquired a new vocabulary John had never heard in the house. "I wish I had a camera!"

There were people with pink and green hair. Two rows in front of them, a girl with hair dyed orange and black was leaning forward. She was wearing green makeup.

"Look at her," John said.

"Oh, wow!" said Nate.

"Does Springsteen dress like these people?" John asked him.

"Like a regular person," Nate answered distractedly, looking around. His eyes edited out the mass of people wearing blue jeans and flannel shirts, settling on the boys, some of them his own age, who had long hair teased up into twelve-inch black spikes, safety pins in their ears, dark sunglasses; girls with orange and pink hair that rose straight up from their scalps as if electrified, black girls with hair teased into wild manes; a man with cheeks painted with black lightning bolts and wearing a belt that fastened with real handcuffs; a blond girl dressed like everyone else in his classes except for her belt, which was covered with huge spikes. This was where he was meant to be.

To John, the people here looked crazy. The sweet smell of pot was beginning to thicken the air, which was already making his eyes burn. In the row ahead of them a sixteen-year-old boy stood up, turned around, bowed to the row in back of him, then to the people on his right and left, and proceeded to put his hand down the front of his pants as if about to yank out his penis and display it to the interested crowd, but instead pulled out one can of beer, then another and another, until he had taken out ten cans.

"How," Nate asked, "did he *walk* with all that in his pants?" He looked at John. "You know the worst thing that ever happened to me? I wanted to go to this Stones concert and Ma said I could go with some friends from the block, and I couldn't get a ticket. I just couldn't get one. And Eric got one and he got drunk and passed out and slept through the whole performance. That was the *worst* thing that ever happened to me."

"When does it start?" John asked. The smoke, the smell of beer, the spikes, all of it was making him edgy. The boy was his responsibility. He could see why Iris had worried.

"They never come *right away,*" Nate said.

Naturally not. Royalty took its own time.

"Could I go and get a T-shirt?" Nate asked. "I brought money. For souvenirs."

"I don't know," he said. He was too tired to fight back through the crowd, and looking around him at the people whose hands were raised in black gloves and spiked bracelets, he doubted if they could get back to their seats without trouble.

"Go ahead," he said finally.

He sank into a dream of his own. He and Iris were sitting in the balcony of Mandel Hall waiting for Alfred Deller to sing English ballads. She'd never seen anyone sing live before and sat up straight, her hands folded in her lap. When it was over, she asked if they could come back again the next night. He'd seen the Deller records, dusty, on the bottom shelf of the hall bookcase. When he left, he had given her everything. At the time, she said she deserved it. Spoils of war. And then she gave most of it away. Or so he had thought.

When he got back from this concert, he'd have to ask her to take him through the house. There were rooms he hadn't seen yet: their dining room, their library, rooms whose sliding doors were kept shut in winter to keep the heating bill down. The house, Iris explained, was built when the oven was expected to heat the first floor, which had no heat registers of its own. What heat it had came up the stairway from the basement. He'd like to see the rooms, but it wasn't right to go into them without permission.

He knew what Mike's study looked like because Mike left his door open. He'd gone into Iris' study because she'd given him permission. He was a relic, burdened down by principles, a survivor of a quiet childhood where leather was used for belts and shoes and saddling horses. People with skulls and crossbones on their black leather jackets, staring empty-eyed sockets—the first time he'd seen a skull was when he went to see *Hamlet,* and that skull was made of papier-mâché. Music had been the church choir singing, remarkable liquid beauty filling the gray stone buildings, pouring from the same throats that, during the week, made screaming sounds at their children, cried, and called their offspring in for dinner before dark. Transformation in church, transporting. What was this mob? How could ecstasy come out of this? Was this a world worth living in?

"I got *three* T-shirts," Nate said, sliding into the seat next to him, "and *four* programs. For Eric and Matthew and Harold. I promised them."

He asked how much the T-shirts were.

"Only twelve dollars." Nate removed his backpack and put everything inside it, one black shirt, one red, one chartreuse. Hideous. Streams of beer were pouring down the floor from the rows behind, wetting his shoes. "We're going to stick to the floor like postage stamps," Nate said, ecstatic.

John's eyes must have closed because the thunderous roar in the stadium made him jump. The band was running onto the stage. A huge black man with a saxophone ("That's Clarence!" Nate shouted in his ear) and a small man with a headband walked up to the microphone.

"That's *him!*" Nate said.

John looked behind him. Some people had climbed up on their

seats. Others had moved out into the aisles and hoisted their girlfriends onto their shoulders. Before the first number began, fights were breaking out. Someone had looked the wrong way at someone else's girl. In his day, that would be an occasion for hurt feelings, not assault.

The sound was deafening, the acoustics poor. He withdrew into a kind of trance, occasionally punctuated by phrases from the stage—*mansions of glory and suicide machines, this is your hometown, your hometown, baby we were born to run, son, take a good look around, I hope I don't sit around dreaming about it, but I probably will, glory days, in the darkness, our wedding house shone, born in the USA, born in the USA, I guess there's just a meanness in this world*—energy, that was what the performance was about, the man up there holding the microphone as if he were about to chew on it, flying around like an accelerated particle, this must be what it felt like to be in a cyclotron; the man kept raising his fist in the air, some kind of gesture of defiance and victory, and the crowd raised their fists too; he was dissolving as he sat there, becoming part of the overheated mass of people, drunk from the vapors and the smoke, misty-eyed, thinking, my hometown, his hometown which he had thought so wonderful, why did he take a job so far from it, perhaps he never wanted to go back. Family reunions, the way they looked at you, all the things they said without saying anything, every expression telling you how you'd disappointed them, that whatever you'd done was not what they'd wanted you to do; it would have been better never to return at all.

The mausoleum hovered in front of him, almost tangible, a ghost image between his eyes and the stage, his family eating dinner in it, downstairs, but this time they didn't ask him to come in. They didn't want him because he didn't want them. He was free to go where he pleased and he'd come here. The dream had changed. He looked around and saw the stadium had gone dark and was filled with stars; no, not stars, but flames. The audience was holding up cigarette lighters like lit candles. They glowed in the dark. This was wonderful, this was prehistoric. Civilization was gone. They were thrown back, a tribe around a fire, a reduction but a simplification too. He hoped they would never turn the lights on.

What was Springsteen singing now? Something about turning out the lights, over and over again. Turn out the lights, turn out the lights. He looked at his watch. Two hours. Where did time go?

"Down in front!" said a loud voice behind them, and a hand shot forward and knocked Nate on the side of the head.

"It's OK," Nate said. "No problem." He strained forward to see the stage.

"I said *down in front,*" the voice said again, and the hand came forward, and John saw the bracelet with its long spikes and he twisted around, grabbed the arm, and yanked the boy to whom it belonged forward so hard that his body hit the back of his seat. The other boys with whom he had come jumped up. The first of them tried climbing over the back of John's seat. Someone said something about what an old man like him was doing with a young kid; other things, too, he couldn't hear. Someone was pouring a bottle of liquor over Nate, who had gotten up and started hitting back while John still had his grip on the first boy. He didn't want to let that arm with the spikes loose, and the next thing he knew, the boy had his other arm free and slammed John's arm against the back of his chair. An impossible pain shot through his arm and up into his shoulder and neck, then up the side of his head. His arm wouldn't move, and he grabbed the boy again with his left arm, but he couldn't see Nate. Where was he? And then he saw him, lying in the seat next to him, his head rising up from the armrest of the chair, a gash above his eye deep and already discoloring, swollen, and he thought, How am I going to explain this to Iris? when the security guards descended on them and someone was asking him, Are you all right, fella? And he said No, something happened to my arm, and the boy's head was hurt. Can you walk, fella? they were asking Nate, who said, Sure, stood up, and fell. Dizzy, he said to John. Sorry.

"One's got a broken arm, one's got a broken head, out of the way, folks," the guards said, pushing everyone back: *Out of the way. Now!*

Two of the guards picked Nate up and carried him out. The songs were going on without them. Someone was holding on to John's good arm, steering him out of the stadium. No one in the audience was paying any particular attention to them. When they reached the lobby, the guards called someone over, was he a doctor or what, and the man looked at John and Nate and said, It's the hospital for these guys.

John was cold and nauseated by the pain. Nate's eye was swollen shut, already discolored.

"What about the car?" John asked.

A blackness lit by candle flames opened up and took him in.

"Iris," John said into the telephone. "Don't get frightened. We're fine. We had a little trouble, but we're fine. We're in the hospital." He held the telephone away from his ear. "Iris," he said. "Iris. We're *fine*. They're going to put a cast on my arm and they've got Nate fixed up. Some kind of fight. I don't know. He has two stitches. No. It's already done, don't worry. At the worst it's a slight concussion. It is *not* a fractured skull. They already did a scan. They're very efficient." He gave her the name and address of the hospital and directions. She didn't want him to call Nate to the phone. She'd talk to her son when she got there.

"Don't scold him, Iris," he said.

She hung up.

* * *

She found them both in the same room. John's arm was in a cast, supported by a sling around his neck. A thick gauze bandage covered Nate's forehead.

"Terrific," Iris said to Nate. "Suppose you tell me what happened?"

"Oh, Ma, it was *wonderful*. You should have seen the *people*. They *frisked* us before they let us in. When I went to the bathroom, there were people throwing up all over the place."

Apparently, the concert had realized his wildest dreams.

"There was beer all over the floor, and broken beer bottles, and the floor was sticky, wasn't it, John?"

John nodded.

"And you should have seen the people. There was someone there with *green* makeup all over her face. And in the ambulance? There was all this equipment. It was the best."

"And the music?" Iris asked.

"Oh, that was OK," Nate said. "We were up so close we could see everything, but it was so loud you couldn't hear too well."

"And how are you?" she asked John.

"It doesn't hurt," he said, looking at his arm.

"What an expensive way to commit suicide," Iris said.

"And *Ma,*" said Nate, "they told us Bruce Springsteen's going to autograph our programs."

"Marvelous," said Iris.

"He's a great guy," Nate said dreamily.

Iris looked at John, who raised his eyebrows.

Several hours later, Mike arrived.

"Thanks," he said to John, "for taking care of the kid."

"I tried," said John.

"I wasn't being sarcastic," Mike told him.

"I should have done better."

"How?" asked Mike. "Did you have a machine gun?"

John looked at Iris. *Before I was sick, I would have done better.*

"It wasn't your fault," Iris said.

"He was great, Ma," Nate said. "He grabbed this kid's arm, and you should have seen the spikes on that kid's bracelet. He could have gotten killed."

"Spikes?" asked Iris.

John shook his head.

"Like *knives*," Nate said.

No, Iris told Mike, she wasn't leaving the two of them alone in the hospital. Everything that went wrong went wrong at night. She was staying. If he had to get back to work, he ought to go. No, he didn't have to come and pick them up tomorrow. She'd drive them back, slowly.

Mike left, thinking, One way or another, that man winds up alone with my wife at night. Nate was in the room with them, but still.

"Ma," Nate said before he fell asleep, "I'm going to remember this all my life. *All my life.* Nothing better's ever going to happen to me."

"And you," she whispered to John after her son fell asleep. "What did you think?"

"I had a mystical experience," he said. "We ought to go to one. I mean you and Mike and I ought to go."

"Oh, please," Iris said.

Once back in his study, Mike called Ed, a friend of theirs who had known Iris before he met her, and who had once been a good friend of John's.

"John went to a rock-and-roll concert?" Ed said. "He wouldn't let Iris play Beatles records."

"That's not the point," Mike said.

"The point is," said Ed, "she married you."

"Maybe she's sorry," Mike said.

"She never would have married him. Never," said Ed.

"She told me he left her."

"Look," said Ed, "he met her in September and took her to meet his family that Thanksgiving. If she'd wanted to marry him, she could have married him a hundred times. She always knew she wouldn't marry him."

"Then why did she stay with him so long?"

"She was infatuated. He was strong, at least she thought so. *I* thought so. He seemed so sure of himself. You know your wife. She spent her time rescuing lost dogs. Boy, did *he* need rescuing!"

"If he was so strong, he didn't need rescuing," said Mike.

"You're smarter than we were," Ed said. "*You* wouldn't have fallen in love with him. A strong person who still needed rescuing, you can see how that would appeal to Iris. At least when she was young and thought she wasn't strong enough to get through a day by herself."

"She's not so strong now," Mike said.

"It's not the same," Ed said. "She *is* strong now. Everyone's entitled to a collapse."

"If *he* left," Mike asked, "why did he leave?"

"Because he knew the score. He knew when she said she didn't want children. She had a pet rat, *two* pet rats, a stray cat, an abandoned dog, everything but a gopher. A very maternal woman, your wife."

"Not with me, she isn't," Mike said.

"For God's sake, Mike, that's the whole point. She wanted a husband. She didn't want someone to mother."

"Her feelings for him are maternal?"

"Not exactly. Whatever they are, she still wouldn't want to marry him. She's happy with you."

"How do you *know?*" Mike asked.

"I know," Ed said. His voice was bitter.

"How are things with you and Lenore?" Mike asked him.

"She drinks too much," he said, "and other things. Don't worry about Iris."

Mike hung up the phone thinking, Everyone who has memories is a bigamist. Why should his wife be an exception?

No, Dr. Chipwitz said, the broken arm has nothing to do with the increased weakness. The disease was progressing. If John started to run a fever, she should call him and he'd come over. They could give him antibiotics to control an infection. There were a few other things he could do, but nothing important. How was the arm healing? Not that it mattered, but as it healed, his spirits would rise.

Iris said John's spirits were fine. She didn't understand it.

"It's a phase," the doctor said. "Next he'll get angry. Then he'll resign himself and turn silent."

"I don't think so," said Iris. "I think he was angry and resigned himself before he came here."

"We'll see," said the doctor.

15

10.
There are pictures, hundreds of them.
Children long dead,
Protecting their favorite dolls.

An old woman, translucent-eyed.
See how the light shines through me already.

A girl churning butter in an empty world.
Time has scoured it.

The best parlor, a family portrait of sorts,
The organ, the fringed lamp.

The man, hands on his hips, in front of his house.
His wife in her best chair
Carried out into the light
On the still-muddy grass.
We built this.

The wedding couple
Safe in their cake-white skins.
The Bible school class
Safe in their black gowns,

A bible over each womb.
The gymnastics class
Proud in their white shirts and tights,
Their dark shorts,
Against a painted backdrop of stone and tree.
Eternal world.

The town, the valley,
Seen from above.
Nothing can harm us.

A daguerreotype with your face.
So you have lived before.
The border of tarnish, greenish-blue,
Moving in.
Like algae on a pool.

If you have lived before,
You can live again.
See how little I learn?

The tight blossoms of the magnolia were cracking out of their egg-crate shells and showing stripes of pink. Crocuses came up in the backyard, and chartreuse puffs floated on the branches of the elms and swayed in the breeze. Outside her bedroom window, the doves burbled to one another like water bubbling up from hidden places. The dead gray cardboard vine was playing Lazarus and resurrecting long green wires that sprouted tightly curled leaves. *We can die and return again,* said the vine. Small red leaves slowly uncurled themselves on the rosebushes. Little shoots emerged from the red nodules at the joints of their branches. The yard had been raked and the grass was turning from beige to green. A leaf blew by at an astonishing speed and turned into a bird whose name she didn't know, but recognized from previous years. In the country, barn swallows would be laying eggs in the two nests they'd built on both sides of the kitchen door. In the suburbs and the country, people entered their houses through garage and side doors.

John gave her the tenth section of his poem, "Saying Goodbye to the Earth," and she wondered if he'd finish. He intended to write thirteen sections, apparently a baker's dozen of months. He wanted to look at the dining room and library and she was astonished. Why hadn't he gone into them himself? It was time to open the rooms. The sun was heating up the house and soon it would be too hot. She liked the cold weather.

"The dining room," she said, opening the heavy walnut doors. He walked in and leaned against the wall. There it was, the dining room set she had bought at the Maxwell Street market from a vendor who had it in the back of his truck: fifteen dollars including delivery, and then she had borrowed money from her grandmother to have it refinished. What had she told the poor woman she needed the money for? A kidney infection.

It was magnificent. He didn't remember the sideboard and asked her about it. Oh, she'd found that at a Catholic Salvage after he left. Amazing, wasn't it, to find a matching piece? The ceiling was covered by a rose window from a church. Stained glass windows leaned against the three windows of the dining room. The dining room table was covered by a sheet of glass and in the middle of it was a computer. Zones of time collide here, he thought, thinking of the rock concert, the beam of blue-white light on the singer. Antique dolls in elaborate costumes sat on top of the china cabinet.

Iris followed his eyes. "I dress them myself," she said.

He said he didn't know she could sew and she said when you wanted something enough and didn't have enough money, you could learn to do anything.

"You could never follow a pattern," he said.

She said she didn't use patterns. She copied from pictures.

It was a beautiful room, he thought, but oppressive, another century resting upon the one they lived in. How could she stand the weight of so much time?

They went into the library. Dark paneled walls, leaded glass bookcases, more stained glass, heavy maroon velvet curtains, carved furniture, a strange carved tower of some kind. Oh, yes, from the font of a church.

"It doesn't depress you?" he asked. "It's all from a dead time."

"I love it," she said. "It's anchoring. There are no dead times. I used to come into the library when I came home and sit there in my coat and look at the windows and think, I'm in my own world."

"Do you need to be in your own world?"

"Very much. These are," she said, gesturing around her, "safe rooms, safe things. They all have voices. They tell stories. It's my version of a rock concert, sitting here, listening to all of them. They take me in."

"They're not alive."

"But they are. Sit here long enough. You'll see."

"I won't. *Live* things don't seem alive to me."

"You're improving," she said.

"A little late."

"Still," she said.

16

11.
Today, I looked in the china closet.
I saw my heart.
In each chamber, a beaked thing,
Trying to get out.

There was no wind.
I heard your voice.
Stop them.
It is not allowed.

I watched until one broke through,
Ugly feathered thing.
Yet it will fly.

I felt no pain.
I left the glass door locked.
The heart was where it belonged.
In there. Gathering dust.

A week later he began to cough and ran a fever. Dr. Chipwitz
came to the house, listened to his chest, told him he'd be fine in

a few days, and talked to Iris in the hall. His lungs were filling with liquid. A diuretic would dry him out. All salt should be eliminated from his diet and they were to give him the pills he was prescribing. What were they? Penicillin. No, he wasn't stalling. He couldn't stall. They could only make things easier. When she asked if she should take John's temperature, Dr. Chipwitz asked her what would be the point.

It was dreamlike, Mike thought, a nightmare. Now Iris sat in a wicker chair in John's room and, until he fell asleep, read to him. If he wanted to talk to Iris, if the children wanted to talk to her, they had to signal to her and she would come into the hall. She was gone again, Mike thought, swallowed up by another room in the house. She and John had switched places.

"Iris," Mike said, "this is going to be too much for you."

"If it's too much for me," she said, "I'll let you know."

"At least let Evelyn stay with him."

"She does. Last night, she had a fit and accused me of depriving her of her last opportunity to be with John. She said I was selfish to keep him to myself when I knew how she felt about him, and she'd never forgive me."

"How she feels about him?" asked Mike.

"Isn't it obvious?" Iris asked. "She's fallen in love with him."

"You know, Iris," Mike said, "once he's dead, I never want to hear his name again."

"Tell that to Evelyn, not me," Iris said.

"This must seem awfully romantic to a fifteen-year-old. A hospital would be the right place for him."

"No hospital," she said. "He saved me."

Saved her from what? Mike wanted to know. From what he'd read in her journals, John was the cause of her trouble. He hadn't taken care of her when *she* was sick in Chicago. Iris told him that whenever she tried to explain why she felt so guilty about falling ill herself. Now this eternal vigil at John's bedside. When he, her *husband,* got sick, she became furious, anything he said started an argument, and she refused to leave him in peace. She seemed to believe she could argue him back to health. Mike knew she was frightened whenever anything happened to him. Still, he wouldn't mind the sort of attention this man, whom time ought to have made a stranger, was getting.

Iris sat in the room watching John sleep and thought, The emotions come back. She looked out the window and thought she was like a tree that had stood all winter with bare arms and now the birds returned and flew right into her arms, into all her empty places until she was no longer only a nerve pattern set against an iced-over sky, but a thing, half rooted, half feathered, and she remembered again how birds sang most loudly when the light began dying. She remembered sitting in old classrooms in which everything stopped until the singing stopped because no one could hear himself over them. The birds started again when the sun came back. Did they believe, in their small brains, that they made the sun rise and set? Humans had such necessary delusions. What counts, she thought, looking out the window, is that the birds are back.

If she were an apple tree going through her seasons, she would have reached that time when almost all her leaves were gone and some small gold apples hung from her branches like gold balls in the green-gold light of the day's end, and the birds, in the days before winter, dove at them and ate them, ate them fermented and then whirled in ecstatic and eccentric circles in that green-gold light which had just come and which promised a storm.

This was the man her parents hadn't wanted her to marry and whom she had been so determined to marry. She thought of Emily Lee, her son's tutor in English, whom she used to see in the mornings, always early in the morning, before the school buses arrived, while she sat in the car in order to see her daughter safely cross the street, and Emily Lee would cross the street right after Evelyn. She had no idea Iris was watching her. She was a very attractive woman in her mid-thirties and unmarried, the sort of woman every mother wants her child to have for a teacher, because Emily Lee had no children of her own and so adopted other people's.

As Emily Lee looked up at the huge square brick edifice, waiting for the light to change, her expression would become that of the child who did not fit in, who dreaded school but knew he must go anyway, and who crossed the street toward the building as if he were voluntarily sentencing himself to a term in prison. Iris knew that in that moment Emily Lee was wondering if she would spend the rest of her days in that school surrounded by creatures who were never more than ten years old, if she had come as far as this to end where she began, in the classrooms of the same public school she had once attended.

If it had not been for John, if in the beginning he had not accepted her ambitions and encouraged her, if he hadn't made her believe the world was a great and marvelous place, she might have given up and come back hopeless, here, to Brooklyn, where she now lived after so many years in other places, taken up high school teaching, and someone else would be watching her as she had watched Emily Lee. Mike believed she owed John nothing. Sooner or later, he said, her character would have forced her into the kind of life she now led.

Life was intolerably strange and prevented all judgments. The same man who had just forced her out of bed had also driven her to an overdose of sleeping pills. He had awakened her passions and in the end had stripped her of her womanhood. She had carried on a long affair with someone else, justifying her behavior because he refused to protest it. Instead, he cooperated with her in it, asking her when she wanted to be picked up when the weekends were over, and she had never forgiven him for his own infidelity—one night spent with the girl who lived in the apartment across the hall from them, a girl who slept with everyone in Hyde Park.

Now they were together in this room. She listened for the sound of labored breathing, set her alarm watch so that his doses of penicillin would be administered on time, attempted to keep her daughter away—Evelyn, who wanted to have soul-searching conversations with a dying man, convinced that what she said to him would enable him to die happily—and tried to believe that one day the room would be empty, it would once more be the guest room, and that would mean John had died.

Meanwhile, although *he* was dying, her own life flashed before her eyes. She remembered skating up and down the asphalt streets of Brooklyn. She remembered coming home with scraped, bleeding knees, washing them in the locked bathroom, sitting on the edge of the chipped enamel tub examining the scratches, sure they were maps of some other place she could find if only she could decipher the red lines crisscrossing her arms and legs. She remembered the day she got engaged to Mike, the two of them buying her engagement ring. She remembered how self-conscious she had been the first day she wore it. The dazed state, the dopey happiness caused by that ring lasted for months. She contemplated the ring for hours, looked at its prongs and worried about them: they might lose their hold on the diamond. The person who had done that seemed so young. Where was the ring now? In the cinnamon canister. Eventually, the prongs did become loose, the diamond fell out in her lap, and she taped the diamond to the ring and put it away to have it repaired. That was seven years ago. Every time she suggested taking it out and having it repaired, Mike said he really ought to get her a larger stone. The original one, he said, was about the size of a grain of salt. But she didn't want a larger stone, she wanted the same ring, and so she left it in the canister.

She remembered Evelyn's birth and her strange choking cry, her constant fears for the child's life, and how long it took Evelyn to finish drinking her formula, so long that Iris, who fed her on a cot in the dark red library of their old apartment, would fall asleep, Evelyn on top of her. She remembered the rock songs Nate wrote, which he insisted she not only type up but Xerox, and his endless rehearsals with children on the block. He was eight then.

After several days in the room, she began to relive her stay in the hospital. She remembered the man in the room next to hers, the one who was always asking her for ice because the ice made it easier for him to breathe, and how she was told not to give it to him, while in the hallway, the nurses loudly argued with him about when he could next have more ice. She remembered the resident telling her not to get too friendly with him because he wasn't going to last long. One night, she awoke to the loud sound of machinery. In the hall, some kind of pump was going on and off while the doctors and nurses shouted at one another and the sick man.

"Let's get this tube down your throat, damn you!"

She could hear the man struggling, the doctors cursing, the nurses making suggestions, asking what exactly it was the doctors wanted.

In the morning the bed was empty, and when Iris asked where he was, one nurse told her he'd gone home. Another said he'd gone to Intensive Care. She waited until the intern came and asked, "Did you hear what happened last night?" and he said, "I never thought he'd go down the tubes so fast."

Dead.

So many people she asked about. Gone home, the nurses said. *Gone Home,* said the tombstones in Vermont. So much she had tried to forget. Yet forgetting could poison.

She had always dwelled on how hopelessly different John was

263

from her, and yet they were the same. They both believed more strongly in the dry trackless spaces than in the green lands they saw all around them, and so they had left one another, and so, in the hospital, she had given in and allowed the world to be taken away. In the end, they both retreated to an empty place, safe simply because it was empty. His family's invasions, her family's silences.

"Do you remember taking those pills?" John asked her, startling her. He had been watching her while she stared at the wall, thinking. "Did you ever want to do that again?"

"Oh," she said, "when I get discouraged, I have trouble believing there's any point to things."

"But something like the pills. Did you ever think about that?"

"No," she said. "Life caught me in its sticky, sticky web."

"You were lucky."

He began to talk about his unfulfilled ambitions, his first wife's unfulfilled ambitions, his sister's, his mother's, his father's.

"*You* always knew what you wanted," he said. "That's why I was interested in you."

"I didn't know. I was only sixteen when I met you. I thought I wanted to be a nurse."

"Everyone knew that when you found out what you wanted, you'd get it," he said. "I was jealous. I tried to stop you."

"You never tried to stop me!"

"Remember the night you were up late doing a term paper? And next door there was a party and you wouldn't come? It was the last paper you had to write for a course, and when you passed that course, you were going to start your thesis. I'd just failed part of my orals. I went off alone because I was angry. That's why I went off with her."

"You went off with Miss Easy Crotch because you thought *I* knew what I wanted? I thought you did it because you didn't like me. My body. You were always talking about my body."

264

"It had nothing to do with your body. You were so attached to life. Every time I looked at you I knew I wasn't."

"You were jealous of me?"

"How *couldn't* you have known?"

The light poured in through the windows, warming the polished wood.

"I'm jealous of you now," he said.

"Well, of course. I'm healthier."

"Not that. What you've done here. It's an ark."

She said she was a terrible mother, she had no patience at all, she wasn't a good wife, she refused to cook because when she did she gained weight. She still didn't know how to clean a house properly and if Etheline ever left they'd be condemned by the Board of Health, and he stopped her, saying she was superstitious and trying to explain away her good fortune.

She said it *was* good fortune that she'd found Mike, nothing more than that, no one else could put up with her.

"No," he said, "it's not true. Everyone could always put up with you. *You* couldn't put up with people. When you were sixteen, you thought I was wonderful. When you were twenty-one, you didn't think so. You were fed up with me when you started sleeping with Leonard."

She said nothing because it was true. She had been twenty, young, she didn't know how to end anything, she had promised to stay with him forever, and she hadn't known that there were some promises that couldn't be kept and should never be made.

"Yes," she said. "It's true."

"That's why it was never clear who left whom," he said. She asked him what he meant. "After the pills, after you got out of the hospital," he said, "I wanted to stay. You called my parents and *demanded* they tell me to get out. Don't you remember?"

"Not really."

"You did, though."

265

She was capable of terrible things. At twenty, she could not admit to that. He was telling the truth.

"I don't remember," she said. That was true too. Memory was a wonderful editor of the text. "Are we free of each other?" she asked. "Now?"

"No," he said. "Now we'll never be free of one another. But now you won't want to be. I wish," he said slowly, "someone would remember me."

"I will."

"You'll be the only one."

"Eventually, everyone's forgotten," Iris said.

"Write about me," he said.

"I can't. I've never been able to write about people close to me. I've never written about Mike or Nate or Evelyn."

"Try."

"I can't."

"You will," he said, his lips curving into that strange smile she'd seen before. "One summer when I was twelve," he said, "my mother sent me to stay with her sister in San Diego. There was nothing to do, and after school, I didn't know anyone, and I used to go to the zoo and walk through the canyons, at least I remember them as canyons, and from one end to the other, you could hear the big cats, the pumas and the leopards and the lions, roaring to one another, answering one another while the sun was setting. I remember that so well. Even the colors of the sky, the peach streaks in the pale blue, those palm trees. Big dead gods with long beards."

"You sound like me," Iris said.

"We were always alike."

"Ma!" Nate shouted, bursting in. "Guess what? We just got a big envelope from Bruce Springsteen. We got his autograph and he signed programs for us! He wrote a note and said he was sorry we got hurt! It came by *messenger!*"

"That's wonderful," Iris said.

"Oh, wait until Eric hears about this!" he said. He peered anxiously at John. "Do you want yours now?" he asked him.

"You can keep mine," John said.

"Are you *sure?*" Nate asked.

John nodded and the child flew down the hall and thundered down the front steps. "He said I can keep his too!" they heard him telling someone, probably his friend Harold, who seemed to live in their house.

"Aren't you late for school?" Etheline was asking Nate.

"It's a half day, man," Nate said.

"Don't be fresh!" Iris called out.

"When I was a kid," John said, "I would have been whipped if I called my mother 'Ma.' It wasn't considered respectful."

He was interrupted by a fit of coughing. Her alarm watch went off and she picked up a sheet of paper from the end table near her chair. One diuretic and one penicillin.

"I made arrangements," he said when he stopped coughing.

"Arrangements?"

"I went to a funeral home and the director and a lawyer drew up a contract. It's not your concern. I like the idea of ashes. I used to watch them fly out of the chimney in the lake house. There's life in them even after they burn up."

Were they right? Was she going to prove incapable of living through this? Her throat was tight.

"And what do you want done with the ashes?"

"Anything."

"If you could choose *anything* at all, any place at all to have them scattered, where would you choose?"

They used to play this game long ago. If you could have anything you wanted, if you could do whatever you wanted, what would you do? His answer was always the same. *One thing is as good as another.* It appalled her.

"I'd choose Cornwall. On the coast. I was happiest there."

"With your second wife?"

"With the one who told everyone I tried to drown her on her honeymoon. My second wife and I went on a canoe trip for our honeymoon."

"Oh," said Iris, who understood immediately. On her first trip to his lake house, he'd taken her out in his sailboat and persuaded her that if she got into the water and held onto a rope, the boat would pull her through the water and she would love it. It was so much fun. The wake buffeted her brutally. She couldn't get her head above water, and when she began choking, she let go and started swimming in the middle of the lake while the boat disappeared, headed to the opposite shore. It took him some time to notice her, treading water a quarter of a mile from shore.

"She couldn't swim," said John.

Iris nodded.

"And we went over rapids and the canoe turned over. Why are you smiling?"

She shook her head, grinning.

"Do you remember my first wife?" he asked her. "You met her once. On the street in Boston."

"I remember her," said Iris. The woman had rushed up to her, told her she recognized her from pictures John had shown her, asked her how she liked living in New York, told her she had once wanted to go there herself, but now she was afraid of violence and she didn't like driving, she didn't understand it, such things had never frightened her before. And Iris had thought, It's starting again. He's bought a car she can't drive and she's becoming dependent on him and frightened. It's what he does. It's what he wants a woman to be: completely dependent. And then he becomes tired of the burden.

When he tried to pour himself a glass of water and found the pitcher empty, she got up, went out, and filled it.

268

"The concert," he said when she came back. "I wish you'd seen it."

Iris said she heard Nate asking him about it and *he* didn't seem to have seen it himself. He couldn't remember Bruce Springsteen walking out into the audience, he didn't remember the blond girls who climbed up on stage to kiss him, he didn't remember a group of Vietnam veterans waving some kind of giant pennant when Springsteen sang "Born in the USA." Where had he been?

"In a dream, a mob-induced dream," he said. His skin had dissolved and he was part of that enormous overheated smelly mass of people. He had been there with spikes on his wrist and a girlfriend dressed in black leather with long straight black hair. And he had had a hallucination.

"A hallucination?"

"I saw," he said, "the mausoleum, but they wouldn't let me in. It was like a church, except that inside prayers were answered right away. It wasn't the same. It was changed. It was a good place." He watched her face. He said he knew what she was thinking: the change had taken place too late. But he said it wasn't too late. Now he knew he *could* be attached to life. Why was that something? Because if you had to die, knowing that even if there was another life, knowing that even if you got to come back, you'd come back incapable of doing anything but listening to your own heartbeat, then you'd feel damned. But now he was not damned.

Once, she remembered, he'd been religious. He took those words seriously: damned, saved, answered prayers. On Sunday mornings in Chicago, before anyone else was up he'd sneak out of their apartment and go to Bond Chapel. They never spoke of it. She was Jewish. The chapel was something that might come between them. On weekends, they would sit inside it when there were no services and talk. They sat in Rockefeller Chapel and listened to the organist practice.

"Saved," she said softly.

"Both of us. We are."

She shook her head. She wasn't sure about herself. Mike still drove the children to school every morning. He knew she wasn't ready to take back the responsibilities of daily life. She needed time and Mike was giving it to her, but would it do any good?

"You'll be fine," John said. "You'll see."

"And you?"

"I'm *here*. I have a place."

"When you die," she said softly, "it will finally be over."

"Nothing's ever over," he said. "Just changed. It's already changed."

"I don't want you to die," she said.

"I wouldn't mind sticking around either."

"Ma!" Evelyn shouted. "The phone! Dr. Chipwitz!"

"Iris," he said, "you wouldn't do anything stupid? Like leave a bottle of tranquilizers near his bed?"

No, she wouldn't. She couldn't let anything die. It was her besetting sin. She fed ancient rosebushes expensive plant food so they could produce their summer's one feeble blossom. She once had a cat who developed a tumor and she asked the veterinarian what his chances were. Three percent. Three percent was not nothing. She took him home and in the end had to have him put to sleep. At the time, she swore she would never do such a thing again. Was she, she asked Dr. Chipwitz, doing the same thing again?

No, the doctor said. Soon the medicines would lose their effect and it would be over quickly. The fever was putting too great a strain on the heart.

She went back in and began reading aloud.

"You're reading *Ulysses?*" Mike asked, amazed. "You hate *Ulysses.*"

"I don't have time to read *Remembrance of Things Past,*" she said.

"You want to hear a Bruce Springsteen tape?" Nate asked John from the doorway. "I have a new one. *Darkness at the Edge of Town.*" He sat on the floor and turned on his tape recorder. Iris fled, her hands over her ears.

"Do you like this?" Evelyn asked later, coming in, wearing a pink backless dress. "Do you think it's too old for me? You do *too?* Wait a minute. I'll be right back. I'll show you the other one." She disappeared and came back in a white lace dress. John said that was better. Evelyn told her mother she'd take over the reading. She needed the practice. Her voice teacher said she read in a monotone. Of course, her mother also read in a monotone, but she didn't have to pass a class. Iris thought back to her first reading, reading so fast that someone later said he couldn't tell the last line of one poem from the title of the next. All she wanted to do was get off the stage. "You always had your own ways of getting attention," John said.

"I wore a shocking-pink dress and black lace stockings," she said, shaking her head. "A minidress."

"Mother," said Evelyn, "are you going to let me read?"

"Be my guest," said Iris, going out.

And so it went on.

"The children are taking this very well," Mike said. Iris said there were times she thought they were older than she was, and when Mike said she was doing a good job, she started to cry.

Dr. Chipwitz had a portable oxygen tank delivered and instructed them in its use. *You won't need it long.*

"I was dreaming," John said. "I was in the lake and you were in the boat and you came back to get me, but I was still in the water."

That was the last thing he said.

During the next hour, his breathing grew increasingly tortured. Iris fastened the oxygen mask carefully, covering his mouth and nose. Little by little, she thought, he is sinking. Little by little, I am burying him under things: blankets, masks. She felt his forehead. It was so hot and dry her hand pulled back of its own accord. She stared down at him, horrified.

"I *cannot* accept your death," she said aloud, softly, but he didn't appear to hear her.

What she could not accept was about to happen.

Should she take his temperature? There was no point. She could not give him any higher doses of antibiotics. If she called the doctor and reported a fever of what must be 106 he would feel it his responsibility to send an ambulance and take John to the hospital. She had promised.

Still, there had to be something she could do. The will to live was said to be indomitable. She pulled her chair up to the bed, put one hand gently on his burning forehead, and began reading aloud from *Ulysses*. "You want to know how the book ends, don't you?" she asked the comatose man. "You can't die before you know the ending." He was competitive. Perhaps he would rise to the challenge. Perhaps wherever he had gone, deep into the house of his body, he could still hear her voice, hear the words she was reading.

She read until her throat was hoarse, stopping to ask him questions.

"What do you think will happen next?" Or "Don't you think this is pretentious? Do only women think so or do men think so too? A friend of mine called this book a party to which women were not invited." No answer, just the same labored breathing, turning to high-pitched agonized gasps, the same burning forehead. Her throat began to hurt and she shut the book and began stroking his forehead. How well she remembered the terrain above his eyebrows, the hills above each eye, the valley in between. She'd always thought of those swellings under the skin, not as part of his bone structure, but as visible evidence of his superior brain. Oh, how she had loved him. How she loved him now. He knew things about her she had forgotten herself. If spirits could move from one person to another, and she believed they could, then she too was lying in that bed. She too was dying.

"John," she said, her tone conversational, "please wake up."

He didn't move. His chest rose and fell, testifying to the continuing effort of the body to preserve itself.

"Oh, please," Iris said softly. Please commute the laws of this world, just this once, the same prayer every husband, every wife, every mother, every father, every child, must say over the dying body of the person they love.

Was it her imagination, or was he breathing less regularly? He was. Each breath was rougher, the air taken into the lungs in shorter gasps. His color was not good; the blood flush was gone. While she watched, he was going to die. She looked down at the cover of *Ulysses,* and when she looked up, his chest had stopped rising and falling.

She got up quietly and locked the door to his room and sat down in the chair next to the bed, leaning over so that his head rested on her breast. That was not enough. She got up and lay down next to him as if she could prevent the warmth from leaving his body or persuade it to come back. She had never known there could be such a silence in the world, such an emptiness, as if she had just discovered the horizon was made of glass and, in front of her eyes, a huge wind or a hand punched through it, leaving a hole, and through the hole she saw an emptiness which could stop the heart.

She began crying. She cried lying next to him all afternoon before she got up and called anyone.

There are procedures to deal with a death, and they clicked

into operation. Evelyn told her mother she and John had gone to a lawyer's together and the lawyer would call them as soon as he was notified of his client's death so that he could read them the will. There were, the lawyer said, no difficulties.

"But," said Iris, "there are his *clothes!*"

"We'll give them to charity," Evelyn said. "They're good clothes."

"Not yet," said Iris.

Mike said it had to be done and the children agreed with him.

"His shaving things, his books, a draft of a scientific paper, his wallet, what are we going to do with them?" Iris asked.

"We'll put the paper in a safe-deposit box," Mike said, "or send it to the chairman of his department and throw the rest of it away."

"Not yet," Iris said.

She decided to take a nap, and while she was sleeping, Evelyn packed the clothes into boxes and carried them out to the car, and Mike drove everything to Goodwill Industries. When Iris heard that, the crying began again. Her crying was frightening. She lay on her bed, doubled up as if by cramps, holding her stomach, sobbing, harsh sobs that could not be stopped and that the doctor told the family ought not to be stopped. Etheline, who thought crying made people ill, was given time off. Mike sent Evelyn to her friend's and Nate to his.

While she cried, she looked out the window and saw herself wandering the Midway with John. She remembered a friend's deliberately exposing the radiation badges at the Fermi Institute as a joke and coming to the lab the next day and finding the doors nailed shut, heavy wooden planks hammered in a cross over them, and government signs in red ink nailed to them. She remembered first meeting Mike, her wedding, the friend she stopped talking to suddenly and never spoke to again, and it all ran together, it all became one thing, the man in the hospital who did not want the tube in his throat, the weeks in the house staring at the trees, the massed crosses transformed now by the heavy green flesh of the new leaves, the concert, her dreams: everything flowed together. The desert places were not gone, but she had traveled most of the way across them.

The crying stopped as suddenly as it had begun. She felt contaminated by what had happened, dangerous to others. Evelyn snapped at her constantly. "I don't know what you're carrying on about," Evelyn said. "You're not the only one who cared about him." She told Mike she wanted to go away for a while.

"Go away! Again?"

She said she wanted to go for two weeks, maybe three. Maybe less. She might be back sooner than she thought. But she had to go.

Where? Where was she going?

"Cornwall."

"You hated Cornwall!"

"I never came to terms with it," Iris said.

"I don't care whether you came to terms with it or not!" Mike shouted. "You're not going anywhere! If you pack a suitcase, take everything you've got. You go out that front door and you're not coming back."

Iris said if he'd been reasonable for so long, he could be reasonable for a little longer.

"I wasn't reasonable!" he shouted. "I was crazy! He takes Nate to a concert and almost gets him killed! Evelyn says her life will never be the same now that he's gone! He takes you off to the country, and all of you look pretty strange when you get home. First I have to take care of you and the children, and then I have to take care of you and the children *and* a dying man. When does it end, Iris? When does it end?"

She said she was sorry, she hadn't *made* herself sick.

"I wouldn't put it past you," he said.

275

"You think I *made* myself sick?"

"Don't you?"

"Yes!" she said. "But it had nothing to do with you."

"It's convenient for you to think so," he said.

"It had *nothing* to do with you."

"Is that supposed to make me feel better?" he asked her. "That all this had nothing to do with me? *I* might as well have been dead for the last few months. You don't care about me. You don't care whether I'm dead or alive!"

"Oh, stop," said Iris, starting to cry.

"You never like to hear the truth."

"It isn't the truth," she said, crying.

"The truth is, he meant more to you than I did."

"Then why did you let him in?"

"*I* didn't let him in. *You* let him in. *You* started talking to him. You wouldn't talk to me. *You* let him in."

"You're twisting things; you are!" she said, crying.

"*Didn't* you let him in?" he asked her. "Didn't you?"

"*Twenty-four years ago!*" she said. "Not this time."

"I can't talk to a crazy person," he said.

"Leave me alone," she said.

"You're the one who wants to leave me," he said.

"I don't want to leave you. I want to go away for a few days. It's not the same thing."

"You'll pardon me if I can't tell the difference anymore," he said coldly.

"Oh, stop," she said. "Let me go to Cornwall. When I come back, it will all be over, all of it, the fever, everything."

"Whatever *everything* is," he said. "*Why* do you have to go?"

"I don't know," she said miserably. "It doesn't even seem like my decision."

"We all would like a vacation," he said. "Why not? It's only money. It's only my time. You go to Cornwall and I'll take care of the children and go to work! Why not? Just don't come back!"

In her room, Evelyn was crying. Iris pointed at their daughter's door.

"Let her hear!" Mike shouted. "Let her find out what a selfish bitch her mother is! It took me long enough to find out! That's all I'm good for, is taking care of you and letting you do whatever the hell you want. You know I'll do whatever you want and you take advantage. You always take advantage! You don't care! Your father was right! You don't have a brain in your head, and you don't care about me! You never did!"

"I've *always* cared about you!" Iris said, shocked. "You know I have. Why are you doing this?"

"Why am I doing this? Why am I doing this *to you?* Everything happens to *you*. Why are *you* doing this to *me?* You want to go to Cornwall? Go. *I'm* leaving!"

He went into their bedroom, pulled a suitcase from the top shelf of their closet, and began throwing clothes on the bed.

"All right," said Iris. "I won't go."

He continued hurling shirts onto the bed, then his socks.

"*I won't go!*" Iris shouted.

"A little late for that, isn't it?" Mike said. "I can read the writing on the wall. You wanted him, you can have him. Now you want to go off and live with his memory? Go ahead. Just do it without me around. There are other women in the world."

"What other women?"

"Other women. One in particular."

"Who?"

"*I* don't advertise my infatuations," he said, slamming his suitcase closed.

Iris went into the television room and sat on the couch. Had he met someone else? It was entirely possible. She had been gone for so long. She heard Mike stamp down the front steps and the front door slam. "He'll come back, Ma," said Nate, sitting down next to her. "He always gets over it."

"He's always a little crazy after you've been sick," Evelyn said, materializing on her other side. "You're not *that* selfish. Not as selfish as he says."

"Shut up, Evelyn," Nate said.

"Do you want to watch television?" Evelyn asked her. "Nate, see if anything's on.

"What will we do if he doesn't come back?" Evelyn asked after a while.

"Don't you ever shut up?" Nate asked his sister.

They sat in the room, staring at the television set, listening for the sound of a key in the lock. At nine o'clock, Iris said she was going to bed. She should never have told John how happily she was married; it had brought them all bad luck. She tried to imagine life without Mike and began shaking as if she were sitting in an icy wind. He might never come back. He had been angelic while she was ill, almost saintly. But there were no saints on this earth. Perhaps she had worn him out.

When he came back, she was underneath a mound of blankets.

"Iris," he said. "I'm sorry."

"Where were you?"

"Playing billiards."

"All this time?"

"All this time."

"Do you want a divorce?" she asked him.

"No, I don't want a divorce," he said. "I want you to go to Cornwall."

"I don't want to go."

"You're going."

"Do you want to get rid of me? Are you tired of me?"

"I'm not tired of you. I'm not even angry."

"You just said you weren't coming back. Just a few hours ago."

"You know I don't stay angry for long," he said, surprised. "Don't tell me you took me seriously?"

"Of course I did. You knew I would."

"Well, I wasn't serious. I'm never serious when I threaten. Were you really worried?"

"Not worried. Only suicidal. Sit down," she said, patting the bed. "Please. Did you tell the children you're back?"

"They're listening at the door."

"How do you know?"

"Evelyn," he said, "Nate, go back to your rooms." They heard their footsteps going down the hall. "Where will you stay?" he asked his wife. "You could call Diane. She usually doesn't use her cottage until July. You were happy there four years ago. We all were."

"Do you still love me?" Iris asked him.

"Yes. Do you still love me?"

"You know I do," she said.

"Then lock the door," he said. She got up and locked it.

Etheline helped her pack and reserved a space in the corner of the suitcase, just as Iris had asked. Into that space, Iris put the square metal canister of ashes. "Do you think it will go through Customs?" Iris asked her.

"The dead can go anywhere, man," said Etheline.

PART THREE

Outside

17

12.
There was a woman
Who believed, she said, in her own death.

Forty stories above a flat land,
She executed her will.
A God's-eye view.

Her face living on in her children.
Speaking of her.
Years pass.
Speaking of her.

Then the awful silence.
Then the sound of the wind.

Some facts will not be facts.
They change in the light,
They decorate themselves.
Not words only,
But world seeds.

I do not believe her.

She landed in London and took the first train to Penzance, a local train that took eight hours. She was wide awake even after the plane trip. At the train station in Penzance, she rented a small blue Austin and sat in the front seat, staring out over the pale gray ocean, listening to the cry of the gulls, before she started driving to Morvah and the cottage in which she and her family had stayed four years ago. She took the long way so that she could see the stacked buildings of Penzance rising up above the oceanfront. She had forgotten how narrow the roads were, in places no wider than her own driveway, the hedges nine feet tall, the countryside only visible through the bars of the farmer's gates where there were breaks in the impenetrable hedgerows.

Nothing changed in Cornwall. The granite walls, built up stone on stone, separated field from field, each field oddly shaped, some triangular, some oblong, not like the geometric fields of New England, the same buildings, the same moors, the same sea, the same trees, barely surviving, twisted like badly crippled bodies, appearing to bend forward from the waist, shaped by the gales and winds that poured over the moors from the north. At home, when she thought of Cornwall, she forgot about the absence of trees. These small tortured beings seemed not trees but spirits.

The cottage was cold and damp. She let herself in and found the coal scuttle, went outside and filled it, came back in and started up the Arga. The water was on. The house had been swept. Diane must have called the local artist who looked after the house. Whenever Diane left the cottage, she left it in disorder.

All right, Iris, she said to herself. You don't really know why you're here. Morvah, landscape of dreams. She looked around her and shuddered.

Every morning, she would pin up her hair, cover it with a kerchief to keep it from the wild fingers of the wind, and walk through the dun-colored meadows to the edge of the honey-brown jagged cliff, sit on a stone fence, and stare out at the sea. Every morning she took a large brown envelope with her, and every afternoon she returned with it unopened. Around six, she would drive into Penzance, buy fish and chips, return to the cottage, and carry the oil-stained package back through the fields to the cliff edge, where she ate slowly.

She cleaned Diane's cottage, which did not need cleaning, washed her own clothes by hand, and hung them out. She felt like the last person left alive in the world. The two other vacation cottages to the right of hers were empty, and the farmers, whose houses and buildings she could see from her second-story bedroom, would leave her alone until she introduced herself to them once more.

It was still cold in Morvah and powerful gales were ripping from the north over the moors. Cottage roofs were in danger of sliding off. Mists rolled in and pressed against the panes of the house. She peeled onions and carrots, pickled beets, ate odd things at odd times, set things to cook on the Arga, and went out into the fields again. All the walking was bringing her strength back. The walk to the edge of the cliffs, which had taken her an hour when she arrived, now took her twenty minutes.

Once or twice, she went down to the Zennor pub, where the conversation seemed to be about the town's effort to preserve itself against the forces of modernization, or about the drought, which would soon pose a danger to crops and livestock. The third topic was a local woman's attempt to seduce an architect who had come down from London to recover from a nervous breakdown.

She said little but found herself drawn to an old man whose head was so bare and so round it resembled a large, smooth ball oddly decorated with strange growths, his two protruding ears. His face was deeply carved by time and a life spent in the sun, and she listened to him as he explained why he could only paint outdoors. Eventually he began to tell her about the time of his great fame, when he toured the world exhibiting his paintings. "I'm all but forgotten now," he said, "but I go on."

"Why?" Iris asked.

"I don't know what else to do," he said.

He asked her if she would like to come down to his studio and look at his paintings and she said she would. He gave her directions to Newlyn. She carefully wrote down the directions but later put off going.

"I remember you from your last visit to Cornwall," he said. "Do you remember me?"

"No," she said. "I was in a daze the whole time."

"It's Cornwall," he said. "All the electricity in the air and the ground and the radon gas in the houses. It's not a normal place, you know. There are forces here. It takes the mind and the body time to find an equilibrium. I've been here for forty years, but if I go away for too long, I feel it again."

"Is it true, about the radon gas?" she asked.

He assured her it was. In modernized houses, with double-glazed windows, it accumulated in dangerous levels.

The cottage she was staying in, she told him, had double-glazed windows.

"Oh, that explains it," said the old painter. "Open them."

At the end of the first week, she looked around her and thought she was wrong to have come. The view from her window was so beautiful that it was impossible to stay inside and so she went out, and when she did, the land grabbed hold of her and she stopped thinking. What she needed to do was think.

From the granite house, field upon field sloped down to the cliffs, which did not come into view until after a walk of a mile and a half. To get to them, she sometimes climbed the granite stone walls, opened cow gates, and found herself in the middle of herds of cows, animals she had never seen closely before. She was shocked to find them ambling toward her like great mobile buildings, shocked to enter a field and find a herd of thirsty cows entering through an opening on the other side of the field.

The cows surrounded her. Frightened, she climbed the granite wall and began talking to them, trying to persuade them to go home. But they seemed fascinated by the sound of her voice and came closer and closer until they formed a semicircle in front of her. The more she talked, shouted, and pointed, the more she told them to go home, the closer they came. They were all curious, they all wanted to lick her sneakers or her slacks, as if they'd never seen people before. Probably the people they did see never climbed up on stone walls to talk to them as if they were a proper audience assembled for a lecture.

She found herself surrounded by a punishing beauty. There was nothing flat, and every attempted walk brought home the truth of how gracelessly she was aging, and how fast, and how ill she must have been. She should have gone, she thought, to Nebraska, where there were no walls to worry about but the thickening walls of her heart.

She asked herself what was the point of coming in the first place? To scatter ashes? Ashes could be scattered anywhere. To fulfill a dying wish? But the person was dead. At times, she didn't believe she was here but that she was only dreaming, and that once again she was dreaming John's dream, not her own.

She thought she had found a hill she could safely climb, but a farm woman she met on a walk through the fields cautioned her against it. They'd just found a man who'd been lost for over two years two hundred feet down the shaft of an abandoned tin mine. The local people, the woman said, believed he tripped, hit his head, fell down, and tumbled into the shaft. The hills were wild and rough, bracken-covered, gorse-covered, impossible to get through and full of hungry mouths.

There was something about the way the land ended, right in

front of her eyes, the sea tilting like a vast plate, sometimes up, sometimes down, some kind of reversal of all perspective, so that the sky often seemed beneath the last field, several hundred feet below it, and the sea and the sky indistinguishable so that sometimes the sea seemed to hover above everything, all of it reversing what the mind expected; this upending of everything was terrifying, catching her off guard, convincing her that the world had already come to an end and she'd failed to notice.

At night, the sun set late, and when it did, it polished part of the wide sea to the color of scoured aluminum, while the rest of the sea was still sky blue. When it set, the sun was so large it seemed on a collision course with the nubby meadows, and before the eye could accustom itself to the sight of a sun so large and close it sank suddenly, without warning. If she didn't keep her eyes wide open, she missed everything.

Just then, two horses, one black, one white, were grazing in the third field down from the house. The landscape here confounded the animate and the inanimate. There were times when she was afraid of sitting still too long lest she find she'd been turned to stone. When she looked out at some of the sheep-size stones, she wondered if they knew what had happened to them, or if it would take many hundreds of centuries before they realized once and for all that they could not get up and run.

Because of the drought, she decided not to wash her hair more than once a week. At home, in Vermont, she washed her hair in the creek in front of her house whether or not there was a drought. But here she faced an entire ocean she could not reach, and so her hair went unwashed until the appointed day.

There didn't seem to be many insects, but the old artist had told her there were one or two poisonous snakes and she should wear boots when she went for long walks in the fields. The only birds she'd seen were shades of black and white. On her walks, she sometimes saw some white-and-black-striped birds. When she saw them from her window, they flew along the hedges instead of across the fields. There was no shortcut she could find that didn't end in trouble.

She was sitting in what she would call an empty house. Diane did not believe in furniture. It was all white stucco walls and huge windows, as if the house were inviting the view outside in. There were window seats built into all the deeply set windows, comfortable didactic-looking things instructing her to look outward, not inward. She wondered about the people who lived in the house before Diane, why they wanted shelves instead of drawers, how they felt about living in a house that, after a time, came to seem like a sun-bleached skull with square sockets, each of which constantly called the inhabitants to look out through them.

After the first week, she went to Hayle to rent a television, but it was cheaper to buy a used one, and it sat sacrilegiously in the almost empty living room. In the beginning, Iris was ashamed to watch it in a house that clearly expected her to spend her time looking out its huge square windows, that must have been cut at great cost, labor, and danger in the gray, four-foot-thick granite walls. This, thought Iris, is the landscape of mortality, a place where hills were marked with what looked like gravestones, granite stakes warning the living of the long thin mine shafts, the empty graves waiting below.

Finally, she went to the old artist's house. He didn't want to take her in to see his paintings. All his new ones, he said, were in his studio. Instead, he took her to look at the shelf like openings in the granite walls behind the house. He said he'd always assumed people used the shelves to store food, although that was foolish, because the animals would have gotten to it if it was left out there. What they really were, he said, were burial places. People were buried right in the walls bounding their property.

Iris thought of the square metal canister on a shelf in her borrowed cottage and felt, for the first time, that she had come to the right place. She said that many of the rocks near the cottage looked like skulls. "Oh, yes," he said. "It's a strange place, isn't it? Nothing like it in America." She said she was going into Penzance for fish and chips. Would he like to come? He said he would. He often forgot to eat these days. He didn't imagine it boded well, outgrowing a need for food. "If you're still here next week," he said, "I'd like you to see my paintings."

Later, she drove him back to his house, then returned to the cottage. People said a woman who once lived in the cottage had been driven mad by the wind. Iris couldn't understand that. A wind that sounded like a human voice, however wild or mad, would be something in a place so silent and indifferent to human beings. At any minute, the land, which sloped up so acutely from the sea, might decide to rear up like the back of a huge gray animal and throw everything human into the water.

She had a muddled dream. She was going to a house in Brooklyn where she had lived as a child. There she had loved the cold and in the winter liked to stand on the porch that opened out from her bedroom, wearing only her nightgown, her feet bare, until she felt as if she herself had turned into the weather. Then she would go back inside, jump into her bed, and fall asleep before she was aware of having once more become warm.

But she could not find that house because it turned into the house in Cornwall, that house on the edge of the world, at the rim of the boundless water, whose cloud formations appeared to be great masses of land but would clear off on sunny days, and the land would turn out to be nothing but water, endless water, so that there was always confusion about what was solid and what was not.

In the house, her husband was in a bedroom and was ill and was to go somewhere for treatment, but he had not yet come, although he was there. There was a woman in the house who Iris learned was dying. She was lying on the bed with her back to

Iris, lying on her side, wearing nothing. Her skin was very white, like marble in winter light, and she had a long pale scar on her back. Her husband was refusing to take care of himself and Iris was furious, determining to leave him, to take all the money from their bank account and go.

Then everything disappeared but the woman. When she died, her body was cremated somewhere on the premises, and Iris was inside, but she could see the house as if she were outside. It was a tall rectangle made of gray granite blocks. Its windows were deeply set. Medieval saints were buried in deep sockets in rock walls resembling those windows.

Then the smoke, which was the woman's body and spirit, began pouring out the windows and doors, a pure white smoke which was also like a living fog or mist, lit from within by a brilliant white light or sunlight. She had always thought of mists as living things, the spirits of people who had gone. Iris stood there, on a porch which was the porch of her house in Brooklyn, the house where she was born, watching the smoke pour out of the house like smoke pouring out of the openings of a skull, which the Cornwall house was also, a great skull in which she was now living, and she was greatly relieved that the woman's spirit had been freed, and now it could travel, and the woman had not really died, or if she had, she had not been annihilated and now she would travel through the world forever, and this made Iris very happy.

Iris awoke and thought that in Morvah, which was so near the cliffs and sea, the mists surrounded the house as if they were trying to get in. In her dream, the mists were pouring out from inside the house.

The confusion of perspectives, of what is up and what is down, the muted colors of the land, gray, green, and tan, and the brilliant oranges of the sunsets, the huge size of the setting sun which seemed close enough to touch, the path of light on the sea toward it, confusion between the solid and the not, the nights so bright as if the sun had really set into the earth itself, the fields, the scratch bushes, the pocked silver moonscapes of cow dung turned silver, filled with flies that lived in its craters, the dung the texture of cardboard, crackling like silver paper under one's shoes as if to say that here dung could turn into precious stuff, as if the whole world and one's expectations of it were being rewoven, the cows with their painted white numbers on their rear flanks, their sad and menacing faces, the sea seeming to form a full circle as if the limiting horizons had been erased, the other farmhouses, their shapes, odd, like ruins that seem ancient but are often newly built, the hills filled with holes, at the same time spilling forth animals and flowers in a crazy profusion, the bleak look of the land as if it were a cold place, and the palms which grew there, and all things tropical, the sense of vast hidden life, so that after a storm snails would be out shining in the sun, armies of them, the house at the top of the highest hill overlooking everything as if it were not a house but a living being, the sun striking the rectangular windows of the houses until they poured forth a radiant light like the eyes of gods: there was something so utterly strange about the land here, something that so success-fully eradicated the boundaries between the living and the dead, that she often felt as if she were violating the boundaries of sacred ground, and was consequently in great danger; and then that sense of danger faded and a sense of merging with everything took her over, and this too was terrifying, but in the end it was something to which she surrendered, glad to surrender, and again and again, the same thought: Perhaps this is the crossing-over place, one of the crossing-over places. And finally there was no doubt about it: Creation was still going on here, God had not yet decided on the nature of spaces and perspectives he wanted, everything was still in flux. This *was* the crossing-over point. She had come to the right place.

Then there was her hunger for going out in the winds and feeling her flesh scoured down and away until she shone in the wind, against the granite, as if filled with a strange light, as if filled with memories not her own, but transmitted through the skull she had become, a skull through which the mists of the spirit could pour outward and upward, a spirit which until then had been trapped, confined in claustrophic rooms, as if she had become a house for a spirit that had been freed from its body but had not found rest, and was inhabiting her until it was finished with this world.

She thought about the dream. The man who was ill became a woman and died and poured from the windows, while in life it had been the other way around. She was the one who had been ill and recovered while John had died. It was his spirit in woman's form which turned into the beautiful white mist, pouring out the windows. Here it was possible for a man and a woman to blend together, to be neither male nor female but both.

She decided it was time to go down to the cliffs and open the envelope.

As she expected, there was a copy of John's will, leaving his estate to her children. There was a note thanking her family for taking him in and asking her to read what was in the long white envelope when she was sure she had recovered. She sat still, looking at the distant waves breaking into white foam far from the shore, and opened the white envelope. Inside was the poem, "Saying Goodbye to the Earth." She had read sections of the poem before, but now when she first began to read it, she thought it was something she had written, put away, and forgotten. That often happened. And then she realized it was the poem John had been writing just before he died. She hadn't thought he finished it. As she read, the earth beneath her seemed insubstantial. The poem seemed to be both about them and the place she was now observing. Then it must be true, she

293

thought. Our skins are only permeable membranes. Our spirits can move in and out of one another. What I wanted when I was younger, I am being given now when I no longer want it and have stopped asking for it.

She read it through again, "Saying Goodbye to the Earth," and the wind blew a moist film against her cheeks and hands, dampening and softening the paper. She found the last section, the last month, a thirteenth month for his last year, the month she was living out now.

13.
I know what you want.
Peace. A place to hide.
To be lost in.

To join the voices that have gone.
To become part of the high,
Sad sound of the wind.

Indistinguishable.
Anonymity.

The house has become a skull full of rooms.
My hands are chalky.
Chalk dust whitens my hair.

Of course, there are others.
Like cloud faces, they blow by,
Real and alive,
Pinked with blood,
They blow by, reaching for me.

This is how it will be,
My skeleton arms, my fingers,
Combing the air.

You will not forgive me these betrayals,
This constancy of purpose.

This falling out of darkness
Into darkness, looking for you.

If there was no such thing as reincarnation, there was a twining
of souls in life, and while one lived, so did the other.

She looked down over the meadows and saw a remarkable
thing. Three meadows below her, a round, smooth bald head,
scalded red by the sun, was emerging from the earth. As she
watched, it was followed by shoulders and continued to grow
until it was a figure of a man visible from the waist up. He
continued to pull free of the earth until he became an old man,
making his way toward her with the aid of a gnarled walking
stick, part of the harvest of the windfall from the landscape's
tortured trees.

She had seen people appear this way before. The way the fields
sloped down to the cliffs, gently and then steeply, the way the
cliff walk wound through them, kept people from sight until
they appeared, apparently head first. The people she saw emerge
this way, on their way along the cliff walk from Saint Ives to
Morvah, were ancient, and their great age, in such contrast to
their evident physical strength, convinced her they were created
by the landscape itself, spirit creatures, tortured trees made mobile, turned human.

This spirit, as it approached her, was one she recognized. The
old artist waved his stick at her and made his way toward her
until he stood in front of her rock. "On my way to Zennor,"
he said. She asked him if he'd like a cup of tea, but he said no,
the fellow who had given him a lift to Morvah expected him at
the pub in Zennor by noon. But if she'd stop by tomorrow
afternoon, he'd show her his paintings and take her to see the
oldest landlord in Cornwall.

"The oldest landlord?" Iris asked.

"The oldest pub owner," he said. The last time the oldest pub owner in Cornwall was scheduled to meet the Queen he died of fright. He didn't know if any more royals intended to make an assault on this one.

The next day was gray and rainy and the mists had moved in. At two, Iris got in her car and drove to Newlyn and the old artist's studio, a stone cottage that resembled his own house and all the stone cottages in Cornwall. She brought jars of pickled beets and tuna fish sandwiches and stopped at the local store for six bottles of ale.

He took her straight to the rooms in which he'd hung his latest paintings. They were all circles within circles, their shapes sometimes distorted, different colored. His breakthrough, he said, came when he added the broken line. Each of the circles was penetrated by a line of varying thickness and color, but all broken, like unset bones, each entering the circle from a different place and angle, each penetrating more or less deeply.

She looked at them a long time and asked him if they were meant to represent his picture of eternity. He said you could see whatever you wanted in them. They were only forms to him, forms that evoked feelings.

"And the broken line?" Iris asked.

"Is it broken?" he asked her.

She stared at the paintings, her temper rising. All artists were steeped in pretension. Of course it was a broken line. What else could it be? And then she thought of sticks in water, entirely whole, but broken by the refractive properties of the water.

She had always conceived of eternity as a ring, each event, past, present, and future, fixed on a point along the ring. From each point, it was possible to see every other point, time past, present, and future, all visible at once, the definition of eternity, but each instant, each event, each life, sealed off from every other instant and life. She looked at her wedding ring. There it was: eternity.

She told him what her picture of eternity was, and he said everyone had his own picture.

"Is yours different?"

"Yes," he said. "Look." He pointed at his walls. Circles within circles within circles.

"I like your pictures better," she said. In his pictures, nothing was excluded, nothing was separate. Everything was contained within everything else. Except for the stick.

"It's not a stick," he said. "It's a line. You're not capable of abstraction."

"All too capable," said Iris.

"Well," he said as they sat on the floor and ate their tuna fish sandwiches and drank their ale straight from the bottle, "they must mean something to me or I'd give them up, wouldn't I? They're also," he said, considering his paintings, "landscapes of Cornwall. Of course, no one sees that but me."

Before they left for the pub, he gave her a small painting, no more than four by six inches, and said, Things tended to go in circles, didn't they? Someday he might be famous again and she'd be glad to have it. One never knew.

She asked for tissue paper to wrap it in and carried the envelope out to her car.

"No," he said. "I'll drive. You'd never find it. I could make it sound asleep. I *have* made it sound asleep."

Iris thought she knew every inch of the ground between St. Ives and Penzance, but he took her by a route that wound through narrow roads past churches and buildings she had never seen before. They pulled up in front of what looked like an ordinary granite house, the upper story dark, the ground floor ablaze.

"Here we are," he said. "You're going to meet some *real* Cornish, not exhausted specimens from London who come down here to go on the dole."

Inside, behind the bar, was the most ancient man she'd ever seen. His head bobbed and nodded and what he said was incomprehensible since he had no teeth and seemed, when he became audible, to speak some unknown dialect. Invisible life-support systems must be keeping him alive.

"This here's a lady from America," said the old artist, who began introducing her to everyone.

She found herself surrounded by cheerful farmers who began to ask her if she found them quaint. Everyone who came to Cornwall told them how quaint it was and how quaint they were, while they did not find themselves quaint at all.

No, she said, she didn't think they were quaint. They were just like people she knew in Vermont. Farmers, she concluded silently, were the same everywhere.

Everyone, it turned out, had a relative in America, and one plump woman with red cheeks, who might have stepped out of one of Iris' children's books, said she had been born in Detroit. They began asking questions about America, what she thought of England, wasn't London a dirty, terrible place, there weren't too many Cornish in Cornwall any more, hadn't she seen the signs sprayed on the big rocks: FREE CORNWALL. The woman born in Detroit laughed. "If we told you who did it, you'd never tell?" she asked. Iris said she wouldn't.

They were curious about her and what she thought. Her old shyness returned when she found herself backed up against a wall surrounded by fifteen strangers, all smiling and talking at her. This is how an animal feels when a human chooses to befriend it, she thought. I'll never walk up to a frightened cat again and impose myself on it.

The old painter came up to her. "Feeling right at home, are you?" he asked. His smile was kind but also ironic.

"Well, *give* her some real Cornish pasty," said the woman born in Detroit, whereupon a plate was produced and thrust at her. She ate the pasty under the eyes of thirty people. It was delicious.

"It's the most delicious thing I've ever eaten," Iris said.

The crowd smiled with satisfaction.

"All grease and no meat when you buy them in the stores," said one of the women.

"Come try my wife's," said one of the men.

"Time for this lady to get home," said the old artist, who had decided to rescue her. "She hasn't been well."

She left among sighs of sympathy.

"How did you know I hadn't been well?" she asked when they were back in the car.

"I assumed," he said. "To come all this way alone."

"Oh, well," said Iris.

"Ready to go back yet?"

"Almost. Where was that place?"

"Never mind," he said. "You'd never find it."

Of course not, thought Iris. It doesn't exist.

When she got back to her car, she felt great relief, as if she'd been returned from an unknown place to the actual world. She thanked him again for his painting, kissed him on the cheek, and said goodbye. His skin was cold, as if his blood was too thin to warm it.

18

THE NEXT DAY was cold and clear and Iris put on her heavy jacket and started on the cliff walk down to Seal Island. Four years ago, during the summer she and her family had spent in Cornwall, they had made two trips to Seal Island, exhausted themselves, terrified themselves when they looked down and saw how steep the drop was from the cliffs to the sea and how narrow the path, listened in horror to the small stones as they rolled over the edge and fell, seemingly endlessly, downward.

"Look how beautiful the view is!" Diane kept exclaiming, but they were afraid to take their eyes from the narrow pathway.

When they reached Seal Island, they found barnacle-covered rocks too slippery to walk on, water with strong currents, and no seals. They swore they would never go to Seal Island again, accused Diane of trying to kill them, and when they got back to their cottage, collapsed on the floor and looked blankly at one another.

She was going there now. She packed a canteen, two chocolate bars, and the little canister of ashes into a backpack. The path down the cliffs was even narrower than she remembered, but this time she was alone and felt less fear. She hung on to a vine growing out from the brown cliff face and looked out over the silver-quilted sea. It was a beautiful view.

The rocks of Seal Island were just as she remembered them. She sat down on one, ate a bar of chocolate and drank some water, and, when she caught her breath, began taking off her clothes. No one else would come down here in this weather. She folded her clothes neatly and walked into the water, hugging her breasts. They had always been large and now they hung down, their nipples pointing toward her toes, like two blind seals. She slipped and grabbed onto a jutting rock, steadying herself, got up, and went on until the water was deep enough to float in. Here the water was grayish. Farther out it was jade green. Her skin was dead white, rough with goose bumps, and the top of her head felt numb. There was a jagged rock not too far from shore and she swam out to it and, when she reached it, held onto it and felt the current lift and drop her body. It would be warmer in the water than out.

Then she saw the seals. There were two of them far beyond her rock, watching her out of their polished black eyes. Their little heads were sleek and their whiskers startled white against their furry faces. A giant hand seemed to have stuck them down in the water. Were they really there? Suddenly, the two of them flipped over backward and swam closer to her. How intelligent they looked! One was golden brown. She had visited the seal sanctuary in the little town of Gweek and she had not seen a seal that color. How had it gotten here? The second seal was gray and black.

The golden-brown seal seemed to be watching her, the other seal's eyes focused on something behind her. As she watched them, she felt fear, as if she were watching spirits, not animals. They were not seals at all. They were souls, hers and John's, alive in the unsegmented little bodies she was watching and being watched by. They regarded her with patient, unsurprised eyes. If she listened, she would hear what they were thinking, what they were trying to tell her.

Suddenly the two of them flipped over backward and then

301

swam closer to her. She clucked at them and they swam farther out until she could barely see them. Then they changed their minds and came closer in. She let go of the rocks and did a backward somersault in the water and they followed suit, flipping themselves over again. Then she held on to the rock and watched them.

There was a chill wind on her face, and although she did not feel cold, she decided she would soon have to return to the shore. She wanted to swim farther out, to reach the seals, but the currents were treacherous. *Come with us,* said the seals. "Come with *me,*" said the gray and black seal, speaking with John's voice. She let go of the rock and began swimming out after them. It would be glorious to go with them. If she followed them, she would find what she had been looking for. Eternity. Immutable, immutable life.

She let the strong currents pull her away from the rocks and out to sea and began to swim slowly after them. But her muscles rebelled against her intention, stiffening in the cold water. She looked back at the shore, and her eyes, which had been the seals' eyes, became her own again, and she saw how far she was from land and turned back. Just as she reached the rock near the shore, she turned and looked behind her and saw that the seals had followed her in. They were now almost close enough to touch. *Come with us,* they said. Little souls in wonderful shapes, whose heads were not separate from the rest of their bodies. She imagined their bodies and brains so thoroughly fused they could experience no confusion, no misery, happiness only. Her soul and John's soul.

She pulled herself up on the rock, an aging mermaid, and looked at them. "Go in peace, little seals," she said, and as if that was the answer they had been waiting for, they flipped over once more, swam out to sea, and disappeared. Everything that should be over was over.

She let the chill wind dry her body and then put on her

underpants and jeans. When her hair was damp, she put on her brassiere, sweater, and jacket. She carried her shoes in her hand as she waded back to the shore and the foot of the cliff path. Now she was cold and shivering uncontrollably. Halfway up the path she was warm again, took off her jacket, and tied it around her neck. She patted her hair. It was almost dry.

Ahead of her was a broader than usual place on the path. She took off her backpack and took out the little canister of ashes, unscrewed the cover, which she had loosened before she left, and tossed the ashes into the wind, which had come up again, hard. The wind was pouring down over the moors, past the cliffs and out to the green sea. It blew the ashes away from her, a tiny cloud of gray bees swarming, smoke from a small chimney, and then the wind shifted suddenly and the last of the ashes blew back into her face and her hair. She thought her face would be smudged as it often was after she touched her cheek with her hands when she finished building a fire in the wood stove, but her face felt clean.

Her fear of heights was gone and she continued climbing slowly, watching the white gravelly path, counting as she breathed in and out. It was a very long and steep climb back. It was always longer going up than coming down. By the time she got back to the cottage, her hair was dry but completely wild. She looked as if she were inhabited by the same spirit that possessed the wild, gnarled trees she now saw on the moors. When she looked up, she saw a woman from the farm beneath her cottage.

"Hello," she said to her. "I look a dreadful mess."

"Did you go *swimming?*" the woman asked her. "Where?"

"Seal Island," Iris said.

"Seal Island!" said the woman. "In this weather!"

"Well," said Iris, embarrassed, "I was bored."

"Oh, yes, if you're not used to it," she said. "Did you see any seals?"

"No," she said.

"They've moved off to Newlyn, or so everyone says," said the woman.

Iris apologized for not having come to say hello. "It's depressing," she said, "how fit the English are. I see really ancient people, they must be eighty, on the footpath coming over from St. Ives."

"Those are the ones who are still *alive*," said the woman. "Come have some tea."

That night, Iris called the airport, made reservations for the next night, and then drove into St. Ives. It was too early for tourists, and the car park near the shore was empty. She walked down the steep street to the beach shops and bought shell necklaces, little stone pastel boxes, exquisitely detailed sea anemones carved on their lids, several huge shells that she arranged to have shipped, some odd dolls, and many pictures of Bruce Springsteen as well as pirated tapes of a concert he'd given in London.

"You're a fan of Springsteen, then?" the man asked her.

"My son likes him," Iris said.

"Everyone does, it seems," the man said, wrapping the parcel. "A lot of noise, so it seems to me."

She bought two bags of potato chips, took her packages, and sat on the damp gray sand, throwing chips to the gulls. The last time she'd been here, small boys had been throwing rocks at the birds. Now it was peaceful. She looked out over the water, hoping to see the seals, but knew they would not come back. Spirits never offered invitations more than once.

Oh, he was right, she thought. He's won. I'll write about him. I'll think about him. There's no escaping him now.

"You'll freeze out here," said the storekeeper, coming up in back of her with tea in a paper cup. She thanked him. "Odd to see an American this time of year," he said.

"Oh, well," she said. "I came to think."

"A good place for it, I'd say," he said, going back to his store.

It occurred to her, sitting there, that it had been almost a year since she'd spent any money. She went back to the store and asked the storekeeper if he sold any suitcases. He disappeared and came down with a large one, a brilliant red plastic. "It's the end of them from last summer," he said. She was happy to have it.

When she got back to the cottage, she called the operator and asked how to call the United States. How did she want to place the call? the operator asked her. "Collect," she said, and then wondered whether Mike would accept the call. He might not.

He accepted the call.

"Iris," he said, "don't call collect. Use Diane's account and pay her back. It's cheaper. Iris?"

"I thought you might not accept the charges," she said.

"Stop it, Iris."

"How's Evelyn?" she asked.

"*Evelyn* might not accept the charges," he said.

"I want to talk to her. How is she?"

"She goes out with Justin and comes home and cries about John. She takes after her mother."

"What's that supposed to mean?"

"Iris, calm down. You feel guilty and you take everything the wrong way. You have to get used to things again."

"I want to talk to Evelyn," she said.

"She's asleep. I'll get her."

She heard Mike put down the phone, heard him saying, "Take the phone. Evelyn, *take* the phone."

"Hello, Evelyn," said her mother.

"I don't want to talk to you," her daughter said.

"Oh?" said Iris.

"If you want to know," said Evelyn, "the only thing I want to tell you is to bring back some of his ashes. You took them *all*."

"They're not exactly the kind of thing you divide up," said Iris.

"Ma," said Evelyn, "I don't want to talk to you." But she didn't hang up.

"I'll bring back some ashes," she said. "Put your father back on the phone.

"She wants some ashes," Iris said.

"I heard."

"It's a good thing there's a coal stove here," she said. "Ashes are ashes."

"Look," he said. "Let me go up to my study and we'll talk. I'm standing in the hall."

Iris propped her feet up on the windowsill and leaned back in the chair. When he picked up the extension, she began to tell him what the weather was like there, about seeing the old artist again, did he remember him? "I went down to Seal Island," she said but didn't tell him about the seals.

"I miss you," he said.

"We've never been separated before," she said. "Except for the hospital."

They began talking about the children, about the house. The magnolia tree was no longer blooming but was leafing out, and the tulips were almost gone.

"When you come back," he said, "it will be the same. You'll start driving them to school, you'll start writing again, they'll complain you never have enough time for them, you'll wear your earplugs when their friends come over. In two weeks, you'll be a harried mother again. You'll be complaining about how much time I spend at work. I can't wait."

"The same old routine," she said, smiling.

"The same old routine," he said, "except we're going on a trip."

"To make up for my taking a holiday?" she asked.

"Iris, I'm not angry," he said. "We're going to Rochester. Tell me when you're coming back and I'll make reservations."

"*Rochester?*"

306

"Home of the Kodak collections."

"*Rochester?*"

"I've wanted to go for years."

"I'm coming home tomorrow," she said. She gave him the name of the airline, the flight number, and the arrival time. She said she was worried about coming back. Evelyn and Nate would be angry for years.

"Weeks," he said, "weeks. You'll argue with Evelyn for ten days straight and that will be the end of it. You'll tell her how much that man loved her, do something like give her his urn, and she'll forget about it."

"I doubt if she'll take the urn with her when she goes to college," Iris said.

"There you have it," said her husband.

"How are you, really?" she asked.

"Oh, you know me," he said. "I can be unhappy anywhere."

She said things would be different when she got back. She didn't know where he'd gotten the strength to put up with everything that happened.

"Everything?" he asked.

"John," she said.

"What should I have done?" he asked. "Pushed you under a train like Anna Karenina?"

"*I* would have pushed *you*," she said. "If your ex-fiancé had shown up at our house and asked to come in, it would have taken me three seconds to go straight out of my mind."

"That long?" he asked her.

"You must be worn out," she said.

"Exhausted," he said.

She told him not to stay up all night watching television.

"Good night, Beast," he said, finally. Her pet name, which he had not used since she came home from the hospital.

"Good night, Beast," she said. Beasts, as in beasts of the field.

The next morning, she got up early, closed up the cottage, and put the key back under the coal scuttle. She walked around the house, checking to see that all the windows were closed. They were. She had no excuse for lingering. Yellow and fuchsia flowers tumbled over the granite wall in front of the cottage.

She drove back to Penzance, turned in the car, and got on the train. A computer expert across the aisle explained to her that computers were very strict and rarely made errors, but people's errors were so complicated that the computer was always blamed. She smiled and listened. He lived, he said, in Mousehole and commuted to work in London. The trip passed quickly.

In London, she went straight to the airport. On the plane, she settled back in her seat, thinking, There are patterns everywhere. In Morvah, the wind is patterning the water into a diamond-stitched silver quilt; the trick is to live long enough to see them. In the last few months, nothing had really happened. Events had only undone themselves, unraveled. John had not died, he had not left her over twenty years ago, he had not disappointed her, he had written the poem she had in her pocketbook over twenty years ago when she was incapable of reading it. The tear in the fabric of the world through which she had been disappearing had been mended. The very nature of the past had changed, and the present was altered, and the future was certain.

Surprising world, she said to herself, take me back.

"Coffee?" the stewardess asked her, and she looked up, surprised and delighted, as if she'd been offered a ticket to heaven itself.

"Coffee," she said.

They took off straight into the sun, huge and gold, like a medal for dangers averted, and it was impossible, by looking at it, to tell if it was rising or setting. They were flying toward serrated white clouds that looked, from a certain angle, like the wings of angels.

Then she looked out the window, and as if she were dreaming

while she was awake, she saw the whole silver ocean rising up, wave on top of wave, building a tower of water, a great wall, higher and higher, each of the waves reaching the horizon, a silver mountain of water, layer on layer, at the edge of the world, all at the same time.